SPECIAL MESSAGE TO READERS

THE ULVERSCROFT FOUNDATION
(registered UK charity number 264873)
was established in 1972 to provide funds for
research, diagnosis and treatment of eye diseases.
Examples of major projects funded by
the Ulverscroft Foundation are:-

- The Children's Eye Unit at Moorfields Eye Hospital, London
- The Ulverscroft Children's Eye Unit at Great Ormond Street Hospital for Sick Children
- Funding research into eye diseases and treatment at the Department of Ophthalmology, University of Leicester
- The Ulverscroft Vision Research Group, Institute of Child Health
- Twin operating theatres at the Western Ophthalmic Hospital, London
- The Chair of Ophthalmology at the Royal Australian College of Ophthalmologists

You can help further the work of the Foundation
by making a donation or leaving a legacy.
Every contribution is gratefully received. If you
would like to help support the Foundation or
require further information, please contact:

THE ULVERSCROFT FOUNDATION
The Green, Bradgate Road, Anstey
Leicester LE7 7FU, England
Tel: (0116) 236 4325

website: www.foundation.ulverscroft.com

Libby Carpenter lives in Preston with her family. She completed a BA in English Literature and Language with the Open University in 2011. She was awarded a Northern Writers' New Fiction award, and was longlisted for the Yeovil Literary Prize and the Mslexia Women's Novel Award. Libby loves living in the north of England, and sets most of her stories in the area. She currently works as a bookkeeper. *99 Red Balloons* is her debut novel.

You can follow Libby on Twitter @LibbyCPT

99 RED BALLOONS

Eight-year-old Grace is last seen in a sweet shop. Her mother Emma is living a nightmare. But as her loved ones rally around her, cracks begin to emerge. What are the emails sent between her husband and her sister? Why does her mother take so long to join the search? And is there more to the disappearance of her daughter than meets the eye? Meanwhile, ageing widow Maggie Taylor sees a familiar face in the newspaper. A face that jolts her from the pain of her existence into a spiralling obsession with another girl — the first girl who disappeared . . .

ELISABETH CARPENTER

◆

99 RED
BALLOONS

Complete and Unabridged

CHARNWOOD
Leicester

First published in Great Britain in 2017 by
Avon
London

First Charnwood Edition
published 2018
by arrangement with
HarperCollins*Publishers*
London

The moral right of the author has been asserted

Copyright © 2017 by Libby Carpenter
All rights reserved

This novel is entirely a work of fiction. The names,
characters and incidents portrayed in it are the
work of the author's imagination. Any resemblance
to actual persons, living or dead, events or localities
is entirely coincidental.

*A catalogue record for this book is available
from the British Library.*

ISBN 978–1–4448–3674–5

Published by
F. A. Thorpe (Publishing)
Anstey, Leicestershire

Set by Words & Graphics Ltd.
Anstey, Leicestershire
Printed and bound in Great Britain by
T. J. International Ltd., Padstow, Cornwall

This book is printed on acid-free paper

For Dad

1

I squint at him. The sun's in my eyes and he looks like a shadow monster.

'I can't,' I tell him. 'I've got to get home. I'm only meant to be getting sweets from the paper shop, *then straight back.*'

He crouches in front of me. He's wearing a woolly hat, which is funny as it's really warm today.

'But your mum asked me to fetch you.' His eyes crinkle at the corners as he smiles.

I fold my arms. When I tilt my head, his face blocks out the sun.

'You might be lying,' I say. 'Mummy warned me about men with sweets and puppies.'

The man laughs, like Gramps does when he's Father Christmas.

'I know,' he says. 'What's she like? She's such a worrywart.'

He's right: she is. I drop my arms to my sides.

'Anyway,' he says, holding out both of his hands, 'I've no sweets and I've no puppies. My name's George — she's always talking about me, isn't she? She's waiting at the bus station, says she's got a surprise for you, for being a good girl at school.' He taps his nose. 'And we all know what you've been asking for.'

'Really?' I try not to jump up and down. 'They've got me a horse?'

He winks and puts his finger on his lips. I try

to wink too, but it turns into a messy blink. He holds out his hand, and I take it.

★　★　★

I'm allowed to sit on the front seat, but I'm not allowed to tell Mummy. On the radio, a song plays that I know: 'Ninety-Nine Red Balloons'. I'm warm inside because Mummy sings it a lot. She sings it in German sometimes: *Noin and noinsick* or something. It's an old one, but I like it.

'Are you feeling all right?'

He's looking at me as though I've got spots all over my face.

'I think so.'

Mummy's always worrying about me. When I had a bad cough in the middle of the night three weeks ago, she ran a hot bath and called the ambulance, but it was a *false alarm*.

He stops the car at a mini car park on the side of the road, just as the song is ending. Without his hat on, he looks older than he did before. He puts his hand on my forehead.

'You do feel a bit hot.'

As soon as he says it, I feel it. I'm burning up.

He turns to the back seat and grabs a plastic carrier bag. I can't read the supermarket's name, but I recognise the red and green. He gets out a flask and pours a drink.

'Here,' he says. 'Your mum gave me this in case you got car sick.'

After I've drunk it, I give the plastic cup-lid back to him. I'm really tired. There are things I

2

have to say to him, like, *Mummy's never mentioned anyone called George*, and, *I never get car sick*, but I can't because my mouth doesn't work any more. I try to smile at him. I wouldn't say those things to him anyway 'cos I don't want to hurt his feelings. Has he turned the radio off? Everything's quiet. I can't stop my eyelids from shutting.

2

Stephanie

Emma's running up and down the street. Angie, her next-door neighbour, is standing at her gate in her dressing gown.

'What's happening, Mum?' asks Jamie, sitting beside me in the passenger seat. 'Why's Aunt Emma outside shouting? I thought we were coming for tea.'

'I don't know, love. Wait in the car.'

I get out. Angie pulls her dressing gown tight around her middle, shivering, even though it's not that cold yet.

'She can't find Grace,' she says.

'What do you mean she can't find her? Where's she left her?'

'Nowhere. She hasn't come home from school yet.'

It's nearly half past four.

'Shit.'

I run after Emma, following her into the newsagent's a few doors down. She's showing Mr Anderson a picture of Grace on her phone, even though he already knows what she looks like. He shakes his head.

'I told you ten minutes ago,' he says gently. 'She came in, but she didn't buy anything. She came in with her friends, and then they went. I thought they all left together. Assumed she was with them.'

'Did you actually see her leave?' Emma rushes to the door to the back room of the shop. 'Could she have sneaked through here? Maybe she's hiding from someone. Grace!'

The door to the storeroom squeaks as it opens.

'I doubt it, but you're welcome to look.'

'Angie's calling the police,' I say.

Emma glances at me, seeing me for the first time. She grabs hold of my arm. It's dim inside. I pat my hand along the wall for the light switch, flicking it on. Boxes of sweets, crisps, toilet rolls are stacked up in rows — the back room smells sweet, like Nice biscuits.

'Grace! Grace, it's me, Mummy. I'm not cross. Come out, love. No one's angry at you for hiding.'

She moves every cardboard box away from the wall. Nothing. But then, Grace is not the type to play hide and seek, especially in a dark back room of a shop — she's too sensible to do anything like that. Emma stands in the middle of the room, both hands on her head.

'It's not been long,' I say. 'Perhaps she's gone to a friend's.'

She wrinkles her nose — it's her way of stopping tears falling from her eyes.

'She's usually home ages ago. I've phoned her friends — none of them have seen her.'

'Did she arrange something at school and you've forgotten?'

'I've driven to the school already — it's locked, there weren't any lights on.'

'Who was the last to see her?'

5

'Um.' She shakes her head, her eyes flick left and right. 'Angie's daughter, Hannah.'

I grab her by the hand. 'Thanks, Mr Anderson,' I call to him before leading her out of the shop.

We run past Emma's neighbours — they're all standing on their doorsteps now.

'Have you seen Grace?' I shout, but they just shake their heads. Bloody useless people, staring at us.

'It'll be getting dark soon,' says Emma, bending over to catch her breath. 'She's never home late, never. I need Mum here, can you ring her?'

'Of course.' I get my phone from my pocket. I dial Mum's landline — cursing her that she still doesn't have a mobile. There's no reply. I leave a message for her to get here, but don't tell her why — not over the phone. 'Someone must have seen Grace — she can't have just vanished off the street, not so close to home.'

It's not only her I'm trying to convince.

When we get to Emma's house, two police cars are parked either side of my car.

'Shit — Jamie.'

How could I have left him when Grace has disappeared? He might be thirteen, but you never know what kind of maniac is out there. I run over and open the passenger door; the window is open.

'Have you found Grace?' he says, his eyes wide.

'Not yet. Are you okay? Did anyone come to the car?'

He shakes his head.

The police are guiding Emma through her front door.

'Come on, Jamie.'

I offer my hand to help him out of the car like I used to when he was little, and he takes it.

★　★　★

Two detectives arrived ten minutes after I did. DI Lee Hines is sitting with a notepad resting on his knees. He's sweating in a long grey overcoat that's grubby around the cuffs; his tie is loose around his collar. DS Rachel Berry is standing near the living room door; she's wearing a trouser suit. She hasn't spoken yet, but she's looking at us as though we've done something wrong.

Emma's rocking forwards and backwards; her arms wrapped around herself. My hand is resting on hers, but I don't think she realises I'm here. Where the hell is Mum? She doesn't usually go out on a Monday evening. Grace has been missing for nearly an hour. I've tried to get through to her at least three times. I get out my phone and dial her number. Her machine answers, again. She must be on her way.

'Is there any chance Grace could have gone to meet a friend that you don't know?' asks Detective Hines. 'Does she talk to anyone online?'

He's perched on the edge of the armchair that Matt usually sits in. Instead, Matt's standing up with his hands going crazy — in his pockets, out of his pockets, through his hair. He looks out of the window, but the house lamps inside are too bright against the darkening sky outside. All I can see is the room reflected back at us.

The sound of the police helicopter gets louder as it flies over the house. Police officers traipse in and out, up and down the stairs. They open and shut cupboard doors, look under the stairs, in the bath, behind the shower curtain. Others are opening the upstairs hatch, pulling down the ladder. Their heavy footsteps are loud on the loft floorboards, even from down here.

Emma stops rocking.

'Chat online? Of course she doesn't. She's only eight. She wouldn't know how to do things like that.'

'Does she have a laptop? A computer in her bedroom?'

'No,' she says. 'She uses the family laptop for homework.'

Everyone turns to the machine on the desk in the corner of the room as though it might tell us where she is. The two detectives look at each other. I know what they're thinking: surely this kid will have gone onto chat sites, Facebook, Twitter. But Grace would rather talk to her friends face to face; she's too young for social media. The police don't know she's not the kind to want a mobile phone. I wish now that she were.

Matt walks over to the desk and turns his back on it.

'I don't know why you're asking questions like this. She's out *there*.' His eyes are wide as he points to the window. He's trembling; there are beads of sweat around his hairline. 'It's getting late, for fuck's sake, and we're just going over the same fucking things.'

I wince, and hope Jamie doesn't hear from the kitchen — that he's too distracted with his homework, but I doubt it — he's probably listening to every word. He'll be worried. Jamie and Grace are so close; he treats her like a little sister — they spend hours playing *Minecraft* together.

Emma's cry pierces the room. Her shoulders are shaking as she buries her face in her hands. I grab her closer to me and put my arms around her. Her hair is in my face and it blots my tears. Grace is their only child. I can't believe she's not here. She should be at home, having her tea with us, talking about school, doing her homework.

DI Hines shifts in his chair and glances at DS Berry.

'We have everyone we can spare looking for Grace.' He writes something in his notepad. 'Can we just go over it one more time?'

Matt runs his hands through his hair. He's done it so many times his hair's stringy with sweat. He looks up to the ceiling. If you didn't know him, you'd think him religious, looking for guidance, but he's not.

'She walks home from school,' says Emma, her voice barely audible. 'Sometimes with Hannah, sometimes with Amelia — there are three of them usually, but I've spoken to their mums. Amelia's said Grace and another friend decided to stop at the shop for sweets. She's usually home by quarter to four at the very latest.'

'So Amelia didn't wait for Grace?' says Hines, narrowing his eyes. 'She just walked away? Does Grace often walk to the shop on her own?'

'Grace is eight; she's not a baby. The school's only down the road. We've been through this three times,' says Matt. 'We're repeating ourselves.'

The detective scratches his forehead with his pen. Perhaps he's thinking that a few minutes ago Grace was too young for a computer, and now she's old enough to walk home by herself. It feels as though Emma and Matt will be judged on the decisions they made for her.

'Sometimes it's the tiny details that are the most important.'

'Why did we start letting her walk home from school?' Emma says to Matt. She turns to the detective, wiping her face with the sleeve of her cardigan. 'They only started coming back by themselves last week — she'd been begging me for ages to let her — they've only been in Year 4 for three weeks. We . . . the other mums and I . . . told them they had to stick together no matter what. Every day last week I waited across the street from the school gates, followed them until they got to the newsagent's. Then I'd run home so I could be there when she got back. I should've done that today — I thought they'd be fine, like they were last week.'

A thought runs through my mind that plants a heavy feeling in my stomach: what if someone else was watching Grace walk home today?

She went into the newsagent's and never came

out. How is that even possible? The image of Mr Anderson's face comes into my head. He might have owned the shop for a few years, but how well does anyone know him?

'Have you questioned Mr Anderson?' Everyone looks at me and my face burns. 'The newsagent, I mean.'

Hines gives a brief nod. Did he just roll his eyes?

'Yes, yes.'

He doesn't elaborate — they don't give much away. He makes me feel stupid — guilty even — just by looking at me.

'Is there anyone you can think of who might have taken her?' he says. 'A relative? Someone with a grudge?'

'No, of course not,' says Matt. 'This is real life, not some bloody soap opera. We're normal people. We don't go around making enemies.'

My ears tingle as he says it. No.

There is someone, I want to say. But it shouldn't be me saying that. Has Emma forgotten?

'Did she argue with you before she left this morning? About something mundane, trivial even?'

'Grace isn't like that,' says Matt. 'We don't argue in the morning.'

'What time did you leave for work today?'

'Just before eight.'

'Mrs Harper — Emma.'

She looks up.

'Did *you* and Grace argue before she left for school this morning?'

11

She frowns and shakes her head. She looks to the mantelpiece at the many photos of Grace. One of them is the obligatory school picture. By the time Jamie has left school I'll have twelve — one for every year. I can't breathe when I think that photo of Grace might be her last.

Hines writes in his notepad again and looks to me.

'So just to get everyone's name right. You're Stephanie Palmer — Grace's aunt?'

'Yes,' I say, too loud probably.

No one reacts. And why should they?

But it feels like a lie when I say it to a stranger.

My stomach is churning. I stand, swaying slightly, and squeeze past DS Berry in the doorway before rushing up the stairs. I get to the bathroom just in time to empty the contents of my stomach into the toilet.

3

Maggie

I don't feel old enough for a shopping trolley, but I am. The handles on carrier bags these days cut my hands; they're much too thin, too cheap. Monday means it's meat and potato pie for tea, which means calling into the butcher's, then the vegetable shop.

Everything aches, especially my knees. I'd spend all afternoon in the bath if I could, but I'm not sure I could get myself out of it. Besides, it's my routine that keeps me from staring at the walls, the television, the photographs.

It's raining — again. It's always raining. Wearing my long raincoat and ridiculous matching hat I could be anyone. It's like my invisible cloak.

'Are you all right, Maggie?'

The voice makes me jump. I wish I *were* invisible. I look up, lifting the wide brim of my hat.

'Oh, hello, Sandra. Didn't see you there.'

She's holding an enormous golfing umbrella that's emblazoned with *Benson & Hedges*. Do they even sell those any more? A fat drip of rain from it lands on my hand and splats onto the top of my trolley.

'I'm not surprised,' she says, 'with that thing you're wearing.' She regards my hat as though it

13

smells of rotten eggs. She shouldn't pull that expression; someone should tell her it makes her look even older. 'And you didn't hear me either. I've been shouting you for the past ten minutes.'

Sandra's a big fan of hyperbole. I don't reply; she doesn't notice.

'How are we this afternoon?' she says, her head tilted to the side. 'I said to my Peter, *I know I'll see Maggie this afternoon 'cos it's Monday. And every Monday she —* '

'Got to run, Sandra.' I pull the brim of my hat over my eyes and start walking. 'I've got an important appointment later.'

I need a new routine. If I bump into her again I might actually scream in the street — or jump in front of a moving car.

After a few minutes of walking, I've left Sandra behind. She's probably going to tell her Peter that I'm a miserable old crone, but I don't care.

The rain pauses.

I hear Sarah's voice.

I look up to see if the face matches the sound. From behind she has the same brown hair in a bob on her shoulders. I can't stop myself. I walk faster until it's a light jog. My shopping trolley trips over the cracks in the pavement. I haven't run for at least ten years and it shows. I slow to a walk before my knees give up, and I'm only a few feet away from her.

She laughs.

It's Sarah's laugh. I can't help myself, again.

'Sarah', I shout.

A passing bus splashes a puddle that misses me by inches.

I tap her right shoulder.

She stops in front of me. She turns round slowly and I know before I see her face that it's not her at all.

Her eyes meet mine; they're blue. Sarah's were brown.

'Sorry. Wrong person,' I say, before she says it for me, like others have before her. She looks at me kindly, whoever she is, and smiles. No doubt she sees me as the ridiculous old lady that I am.

'That's okay.'

She turns back round and crosses the road. Probably to get out of the path of the crazy woman. I might actually be crazy, I don't know. Of course that wasn't Sarah. It could never be Sarah, and I should know that by now. Sometimes I think I could die from this loneliness, but I carry on. It's torture. It's too hard being the only one left. Being happy seems such a faraway memory. Why did everyone leave me?

The rain starts again, which is a good job because I've reached the butcher's. The water disguises my tears. It'll never do to be crying in the street.

4

Stephanie

The detectives have gone. PC Nadia Sharma, the Family Liaison Officer, is opening and closing cupboards in the kitchen, too polite or too considerate to ask where the cups are.

My eyes feel red raw and twice their normal size. Emma's gripping my hand so hard it's numb, but it doesn't matter. Her eyes are glazed and fixed on the carpet. She hasn't spoken for nearly half an hour. I can't ask if she's okay, because I know she isn't. I can't ask her if she wants a drink because her mind won't care what her body needs. I release the hand she's holding and put my arm around her shoulders.

'They'll find her soon, Em,' I say. 'She'll walk back through the front door, you'll see.'

It's almost cruel to say it, but it feels like Grace will come home. Any minute now.

Where is she? She's eight, but she's not a street-smart eight. Perhaps she's had an accident, fallen somewhere and can't get up. She tries to be brave when she's hurt, especially if she's in front of Jamie. She fell off her bike last summer. Jamie helped her into the house, her knees and elbows grazed. I'd carried her up the stairs as Jamie watched from the hallway, biting his lip. As soon as we reached the bathroom, the tears rolled down her cheeks.

16

'Mum should be here in a minute,' I say. 'But with me and Jamie being here, there might not be enough room for us all to stay the night.'

'I want you here,' she says, her eyes still focused on the carpet. 'All of you.'

I reach into my bag and check my mobile. It's been almost an hour since I managed to get hold of Mum. She said she'd been in the bath when I'd called. I had to tell her about Grace, otherwise she might not have come.

'But I've already dressed for bed,' she said. 'She'll have gone to a friend's.' She sighed when I told her that none of Grace's friends had seen her since she went into the shop. 'I'll have to get some proper clothes on then and wait for a taxi. She'll probably be back by the time I get there. You girls were always home late from school.'

'But we weren't eight,' I said.

Mum only lives ten minutes away — traffic can't be that bad. I don't know how she stayed so calm. If it were my granddaughter, I'd run as fast as I could to get here.

Matt can't keep still. He sits in his chair for only a few seconds before going to the window.

'I shouldn't be here doing fuck all. I should be out looking for her.'

'I ought to know where she is.' Emma's voice makes me jump. 'I'm her mother, I should be able to sense it. I keep trying to picture where she is, but I can't.' She turns to face me. 'Why can't I picture it?'

The tears betray me and trickle down my face. 'I don't know.'

I wish I knew.

'She wanted French toast with Nutella for breakfast this morning,' she says. '*Don't be silly,* I said. *That's a weekend breakfast.* Coco Pops I gave her.' She starts rocking back and forth again. I'm rocking with her, my arm across her back. 'Shit. Why didn't I just make her the French toast? Fucking work. Rushing out of the door every morning to make it there on time. Why do I work? If I stayed at home, I would have made it for her. And then maybe she wouldn't have gone for sweets after school.'

Matt strides over and crouches at her feet.

'How can it be about that? How can she have vanished just because you work in a fucking office?'

He's almost shouting. He stands while fresh tears pour down Emma's face.

I wish he hadn't snapped at her, but then who am I to monitor his behaviour when their child has just disappeared?

'What is it?' he says, to himself rather than us. 'What are we missing? Perhaps she *has* met someone on the internet — maybe a friend from school told her which sites to go on.'

He looks around the room and walks towards the computer desk.

'Where's the laptop?' he says.

Emma doesn't move, just stares at the carpet.

'Did you see them take it?' he says to me.

I shake my head.

'The police always take things like that, don't they?' I say.

'How the hell should I know?'

18

Matt puts both hands on top of his head.
'Shit.'

★ ★ ★

Emma said she was going to the bathroom, but she's been upstairs for twenty minutes. I climb the stairs, but not so quietly that I startle her.

The bathroom door is open; she's not in there. There's a glow from underneath Grace's bedroom door. There's a sign on the door — one like Emma used to have on hers, only Grace's is purple and has her name written in silver. I gently push it open.

'It's only me, Em.'

She doesn't look up. She's sitting on the edge of Grace's bed. The quilt cover's laid diagonally across it, and her giraffe teddy bear is near the pillow — she's had it since she was a baby. Emma's switched on the fairy lights, which twinkle on the headboard. Loom band bracelets are piled on her bedpost, untouched for months as the phase was replaced by another. I kneel on the floor, not wanting to disturb anything. Under the window is her dressing table, covered with pens, three jewellery boxes, and two mugs that she decorated herself. Above her headboard is a photo collage of her friends from school, and pictures of Emma, Matt, Jamie and me stuck to the wall with Blu-tack. Alongside them are posters of Little Mix and One Direction. One of the boy band members' faces has been obliterated with a black marker.

Emma's holding one of Grace's books. She

lifts it up: *Everything You Need to Know About Horses.*

'We got it from the library two weeks ago,' she says. 'It's due back on Friday. She's decided she wants to be a vet. Last week she was going to be a hairdresser. Matt said he'd buy her a shop. At the time, I thought, *Don't be so silly, we can't buy her a whole hairdresser's.*' She places the book back on Grace's bedside table. 'When she gets back, I'll get her anything she wants — anything.'

Emma looks around the room. Her eyes rest on a little shoebox that Grace made into a bed when it was her turn to look after the school teddy bear a few years ago.

'I need to do Grace's washing,' says Emma. 'I'm so crap.' The white plastic laundry basket next to the desk is overflowing, the lid three feet away from it. 'But what if I do that and she never comes back? I won't be able to smell her any more.' A tear runs down her cheek. 'Where is she, Steph?'

I crawl to her and rest my head on her lap.

'I don't know.'

I try to picture Grace, like Emma tried before, but all I see is her cold and alone, the rain falling on her face as she lies in the dirt. It's not even raining outside.

On the day she was born it had been snowing. I held her in my arms and looked out of the hospital window; the car park and the treetops were covered in a snow blanket. I hadn't yet seen her open her eyes, but when I said, *We'll have to wrap you up warm when we take you home,*

20

little one, she gripped my finger a little tighter.

She didn't have a name for the first week. Emma and Matt hadn't wanted to know if she was a boy or a girl before the birth. They expected a boy, simply because Matt's family were mainly men. 'I must get her name right,' Emma said. Every day they tried a different one for her: Jessica, Natasha, Lily are the few I remember. When Emma said *Grace*, I knew it was the perfect name for her.

'You will stay here tonight, won't you?' says Emma, breaking the silence.

'Of course, but — '

'It's fine that Jamie's here. I need him here too. Will you both be all right in the spare room?'

'We'll be okay anywhere, don't worry about it.'

There's a growl of a diesel engine outside. We both jump to the window.

'Oh.'

We say it at the same time.

It's a black cab: Mum. She hasn't driven since 1996, or whenever she had *an experience with an HGV*. I can't remember her ever driving us anywhere before that though — it was always Dad.

Dad. What would he have been like in this nightmare? He'd have come straight over and taken control of everything. It's been four years since he died. Sometimes it feels a lifetime ago; at other times it seems like yesterday.

I rush downstairs and open the front door, waiting while Mum pays the driver.

'Where have you been?'

She rakes her fingers through her hair as she

21

walks through the door. Her face, usually impeccably made-up, is red with broken veins on her cheeks. Her eyes are surrounded by puffy skin.

'I had to get myself together. How's Emma bearing up? Is she okay? And Matt?'

I narrow my eyes at her. Get herself together? Is she really going to be like this now?

'Emma's been asking for you. I rang you ages ago.' I reach into my pocket for my phone. 'It was five to six when I finally managed to talk to you after God knows how many times I rang — you said you were on your way. It's gone seven o'clock.'

She frowns at me; her eyes are bloodshot.

'It's not the time to be pedantic, is it? I said I was sorry.'

No, she didn't.

Jesus. My heart nearly pounds out of my jumper. I can't think.

'Where is she?' she says.

For a moment I think she means Grace.

'Upstairs.'

★ ★ ★

In the kitchen, Jamie's sitting at the table, his face a hint of blue from the light of the laptop he takes with him everywhere.

'Bedtime soon, love.'

'It's only early.' He glances at me and nods. 'Okay.'

'Has there been anything on the internet about Grace?'

22

'Not yet.'

How long does a child have to be missing to make it onto the news?

My phone vibrates three times in my pocket. It might be Karl. He and I have only been seeing each other a month, but we've worked together for years. This is the first time I've thought about him since Grace went missing; should it be like that? I take out my mobile.

It's a message from Matt.

My heart flips. He's sitting in the other room — he's barely looked at me since I got here hours ago. I promised myself I wouldn't think about him in that way any more. Grace is missing. What kind of person would that make me?

My hands are almost shaking as I click to open the message. Jamie's standing at the doorway, waiting for me to show him to bed in a house where he seldom spends the night.

The message opens: *I forgot to delete the emails.*

5

Before I open my eyes I feel that I'm rocking. Where was I before? With George, the man wearing the woolly hat. We were in his car. 'Ninety-Nine Red Balloons' was on the radio.

I open my eyelids just a little bit, so I can look around without him noticing I'm awake. It worked last week when Mummy came into my bedroom at night to put a coin under my pillow. She couldn't tell that I waited up until she went to bed. I knew the tooth fairy wasn't real anyway, so I wasn't *that* sad.

I'm lying on an orange seat and there's a table near my head. I can see his legs under it. He's wearing the same trousers as before: grey with multi-coloured bits on them — like little dots of rainbow.

'Ah, you're awake, little one,' he says.

I must have opened my eyes properly by accident. I pretend to yawn and sit up.

'Where are we?'

'Change of plan. Your mum is planning an even bigger surprise. We're on the ferry.'

He looks around. I do too, but I can't see Mummy. There's hardly anyone here.

'Are you hungry?' he says. 'I picked you up a few things from the café.' He puts some food in front of me: a bread roll, Jacob's crackers, and a Mars Bar. I shouldn't eat the Mars Bar as I'll get *hyper*. I've never eaten a whole one before — not this size.

I look around again. It's the biggest café I've ever seen, but no one else is eating. I can see other people now, lying on the sofas under the tables like I was. They must be sleeping. I don't think there are any bedrooms on this boat. Through the windows is blackness — the only thing I can see is the moon.

'How did you get me here from the car? Did I sleepwalk?'

He laughs. 'Well aren't you a clever little thing — thinking about logistics.'

I don't like him calling me a *little thing*. My teacher, Mrs Wilson, says that people can't be *things*; only objects are *things*.

'I pushed you in this.'

He reaches behind the pillar next to him and pulls out a buggy. It has red and white stripes like the one in my gran's shed. My face feels hot. Everyone must think I'm a big baby. Mummy used to call me that when I couldn't walk all the way home from the shops *without whining*.

'But it doesn't matter,' he says, leaning closer. 'I've seen at least four big girls in buggies. It's night-time you see — how else are they meant to sleep?'

I shrug and swing my legs off the seat. I pull the Mars Bar closer. I slowly unwrap it, looking at George, wondering when he's going to stop me.

He doesn't.

He just shakes his head, smiles and goes back to reading the paper.

I take a bite of the chocolate bar and it's *delish*

— that's what Mummy says.
   There'll be no sleeping for me tonight.

6

Maggie

It's not Thursday, but I head to the newsagent's anyway. I used to get the job papers for Sarah on Thursdays. She never looked at them much, mind. I just thought they'd give her a little push back into the world. The habit of buying them has stuck with me. I always leaf through them, seeing what jobs she might have liked, and ones she would tut and roll her eyes at. 'As if, Mum,' she'd say on a happier day. Catering — that had always been her thing. She'd wanted to be a chef since she was eight years old. It never happened though.

Anyway, why do I think about these things? It's not even jobs day. At least I know I won't bump into Sandra today.

It's nearly the end of September; we only had a week of sun this year and that was in June. Now, it seems to be either raining, or just about to rain. It's as cold inside the paper shop as it is out. Mrs Sharples is standing behind the counter, clad in about three jumpers, a quilted body warmer and fingerless gloves. I'm surprised the magazines and newspapers don't blow away with that back door open. 'Keeps my blood pumping,' she says when people complain about the arctic temperature. She's the type who's grateful for waking up in the morning.

27

'Morning, Maggie.'

She's using that tone — what is it? I haven't heard it in a while.

Pity.

Something must have happened. I wonder if she comments on bad news pertinent to every customer or reserves that honour for me. I scan the array of front pages. There it is. The *Lincolnshire Gazette*. It's the only copy next to the many local papers bulging from the shelf. 'Have to give the people what they want,' Mrs Sharples usually says. It's only Mr Goodwin who reads the *Lincolnshire Gazette* — it's probably days old.

My head is telling me not to buy it — don't give her the satisfaction — save the paper for Mr Goodwin. But my hands betray me. Before I know it, they've reached for the copy. I tut at myself. Predictable as night and bloody day. Oh well. Mr Goodwin won't miss it — he doesn't know what year it is, never mind what week.

'Ah, you saw it then,' she says.

I try not to roll my eyes at her.

'What's that?'

I hold the paper with both hands and look at the front page. Why am I play-acting? Mother said I'd never work on the stage with my hammy expressions. Mrs Sharples knows I'm pretending. I'm hoping my ruddy cheeks hide the blushes.

'Oh yes,' I say, anyway.

'I do hope she'll be found.'

'Yes.'

Of course we hope she'll be bloody found, I

want to say, but I just fake a smile. As well as I can.

'Must be terribly difficult for you to read articles like that,' she says.

'It's difficult for anybody to read.'

'I mean . . . Oh, never mind.'

She probably thinks she's caught me on a bad day, though I'm hardly the laughing kind on the best of days. She gives me my change, her hands like little claws peeking from her fingerless gloves.

'Apparently, the grandmother grew up in Preston.'

I look up from my purse.

'Excuse me?'

'The grandmother . . . of the little girl in the paper. I suppose you shouldn't believe every-thing you read in the papers. Can't say I've heard the name. Preston's a big place after all.'

Her light laugh fades to a hum. She's always been one for stating the flaming obvious.

'Right you are, Mrs Sharples.'

I fold the paper and put it under my arm. I reach the threshold just as she shouts, 'I've told you, Maggie. You can call me Rose. We've known each other long — '

'Will do,' I shout back.

But I won't. Nosy old bat.

★ ★ ★

I lay the newspaper across the kitchen table, straightening out any creases. Ronnie used to like his paper ironing — fancied himself as one

29

of those posh types. I only did it for him on Sundays, and his birthday. 'It's not because I like it straight,' he'd say. 'It stops the ink running.'

'Get away with you,' I said.

I wish he were still here with me. I'd iron it every day.

Oh, stop it, you daft fool. I can hear his voice in my head. *You know you'd only iron it 'til the novelty of me being back wore off — two days, tops.*

I sit down at the table. I'm daft having these conversations with myself, but after forty-six years of marriage I usually knew what he was going to say before he did.

Grace. That's the little girl's name.

She's wearing her school uniform in the picture — it's on the front page. I can't make out the name of the school from the badge on her jumper, though I'm not sure if that's my eyes or the quality of the print.

She was last seen walking into a newsagent's.

Newsagent's.

I look up at the wall. How odd. I wonder if she was getting sweets, just like —

The phone rings.

'Hang on,' I shout.

I shuffle the chair back and rest my hands on the table to lever myself up. Damn legs.

'Wait a minute.'

I walk as fast as I can to the phone table in the living room. People can be so impatient these days. Some folk only let it ring five or six times before they give up. Never enough time for me.

'Hello?' I say. Ron always used to tease me

30

about my telephone voice. 'Hello?' I can't have been too late, there's no dial tone. 'Is anyone there?'

I listen as hard as I can. Is my hearing getting worse? There's traffic noise on the other end of the line. Are they calling from a mobile telephone or a big red box?

'Can you speak louder? I can't hear you.'

The click of the phone makes me jump. They've hung up, again. I replace the handset and wander back into the kitchen. Was that the fourth or fifth time this week?

What if it's *him?* I can't remember what he sounds like; I should remember his voice, shouldn't I? It's been too long. Every day I try not to think about how he broke my heart. I can't even look at his photograph any more without it bringing back awful memories.

Tap, tap, tap.

The window rattles.

I still my breathing. My heart's thumping.

I should get up and hide in the pantry, but I can't move.

The handle turns — the back door opens slowly.

'Morning, Mags.'

I breathe again.

'For goodness' sake, Jim. I wish you'd warn me before just waltzing in.'

He takes off his cap.

'That's what the taps are for — they're *warning* you I'm about to come through the door.' He pulls out a chair. 'Shall I whistle before I tap next time? A warning before the warning?'

'Don't be ridiculous.'

'Anyway, it's hardly the surprise of the century — I call round at least twice a week.'

I shake my head at him and flick the kettle on. He's been coming round to check on me ever since Ron died. They'd been friends since they started working together over fifty years ago.

'Though, Maggie, you looked as though you'd seen a ghost when I walked in.' He looks around the kitchen. 'I know you like to talk to yourself, but you haven't actually *seen* anything, have you?'

I grab a tea towel off the kitchen counter and throw it at him. He holds out his hand and the towel drops into it.

'You'd better watch yourself, Jim. One of these days it'll land where it's intended.'

'I doubt that,' he says, sinking slowly into the chair. 'Bloody hell. My back's getting worse. I can't get comfortable these days.'

'Watch your language.'

'I'd rub my back if my arms could reach. Don't suppose — '

'Not on your life!'

'Margaret,' he says soberly. 'If you'd care to let me finish. I don't suppose you've got a hot water bottle handy?'

I ignore him. I'm not in the mood for tomfoolery. I turn my back on him as I make the tea. Do I tell him about the phone calls? He'd only worry if I did. They're probably a wrong number anyway.

His ensuing silence must mean he's seen the newspaper. He's not even mentioned the leftover meat and potato pie on the kitchen counter. I can imagine what he's thinking. *Not again, Maggie.*

I wait for it.

I place the pot of tea in the middle of the table and fetch over two cups, saucers, and the sugar bowl. He still hasn't uttered a word.

'Come on then,' I say. 'Out with it.'

He grabs three sugar cubes from the bowl with the tongs and drops them into his cup. Each one chimes as it rings against the porcelain.

'I'm not saying a thing. Not after you got so upset last time.'

'I wasn't upset.'

'Call it what you will, I offended you. I won't be doing that again. Not on purpose at least.'

He turns the newspaper anti-clockwise. His eyes meet the little girl's.

'I hope they find her,' he says, words I've heard for the second time today. I bet the parents have heard it a thousand times — if they've even ventured out of the house yet.

Maybe I should contact them, let them know they're not alone — that I've felt like this, that I still feel like this? No. What comfort would that be? What hope would that offer if I still haven't got Zoe back? I've sent a card to the parents of every missing child I've seen in the newspapers over the last three decades, giving my full name and address just in case they ever researched other cases. A simple *Thinking of You* card is usually fine. I never heard back from any of them though; I suppose they might've thought I was some sort of crank.

'There's always hope at the beginning,' I say. 'And she's not been missing long.'

'It's the first twenty-four hours that are the most important, that's what they say, isn't it?'

'I suppose.'

'You know,' he says. 'I was thinking about what happened to our Vera. Remember I told you about her? She died in the Salford raids. She was only four years old.'

'I remember.'

'I didn't hear about it from my mother of course. It was only after Mother died that my aunt Patricia told me about Vera. Fancy my mother and father keeping that to themselves all those years — just having to move on and get on with your life after your child dies.'

'That's what people did then, Jim. That's what everyone did. It's how everyone managed to get up in the morning. Death was all around us.'

'It's all different now,' he says, looking down at the picture of the little girl.

'And rightly so.'

The police didn't even search the house when Zoe went missing — there certainly weren't any helicopters.

Jim jumps slightly as the phone rings, but I don't tease him about it.

'Shall I get that for you?' he says.

'No. Let's leave it. It'll be a wrong number.'

7

I'm so tired. I can hardly keep my eyes open — even after having a glass of Coca-Cola. We're back in George's car. Everyone else is sitting in their cars too, ready to drive off the ferry. I wanted to sit in the front seat again, but he said they're strict with things like this in Belgium. I've never been to Belgium so I didn't know that.

I don't dare ask about Mummy and Daddy again. 'I've told you, they're waiting for you,' he said. I think he might be lying. I have to stop thinking about them or else I'm going to start crying again. George doesn't like *histrionics*. I know that now.

I look out of my window. There's another girl, probably older than me. I wave at her, but she just stares at me. She says something, but I don't know how to lip-read. It's probably to her mum because *she* looks at me too. She doesn't smile either. She frowns and moves her head closer to the window. She looks at George and points.

'Do you know that lady, George?'

His hands are gripping the steering wheel tight, like he's scared we're going to fall into the sea. He turns round and looks where I'm looking.

'No.' He hardly moves his lips. 'For fuck's sake, kid, what have you been doing?'

The woman is still looking at him; she looks at me again.

'Smile and wave,' says George, through his teeth.

He says it in a way that makes me think I really have to do as he says. Tears are coming to my eyes, but I smile my biggest smile — the one my gran always likes — and then I wave.

Slowly, the woman's frown goes away and she smiles a small smile.

'Thank fuck for that,' says George.

I wish he'd stop saying naughty words.

The mummy looks at George. He rolls his eyes at her while smiling. She does the same. Adults can be copycats too.

A siren sounds; it makes me jump.

'Right, kid,' he says. 'Doors are opening now. Make sure that seat belt is visible.' He turns round again. 'And don't even think about looking at strangers again. There are some right nutters out there.'

It's what my daddy says all the time.

8

Stephanie

It's been forty-two hours. It feels like it's getting darker in the mornings since she's been gone, but I must be imagining it; the clocks don't go back for another month. Grace will be back before then. She has to be.

The only person who's slept longer than a few hours is Jamie and that's because I made him. Even then he woke up upset, asking if Grace was back. The last helicopter patrol was last night. The sound of the propellers reminded us that Grace is out there somewhere. The police have searched the newsagent's, playgrounds, car parks, her friends' houses, neighbours' houses, and places I didn't know existed in town. It's like she's just vanished.

Between us, Mum and I have managed to straighten the house and get it looking as though it hasn't been pulled apart. Unlike the initial search of the house, the police were more thorough yesterday. They tried, but didn't put everything back as it was. We ran Emma a bath so she didn't have to watch as we put things away.

People have been bringing round dishes of lasagne, sausage casseroles, pies, which cover almost every kitchen surface. We've only eaten the ones from the next-door neighbours. Mum

we shouldn't trust any of the others as we
don't know where they've come from. I thought
she was being picky, but when the Family
Liaison Officer, Nadia, didn't touch them either,
they went in the bin.

There's a knock at the door.

'I'll get it.' Nadia gets up from her place in the
kitchen. She sits near the doorway. We can't see
her, but she's close enough to hear what's being
said in the sitting room. Perhaps she's been told
to listen to what we say in case one of us knows
where Grace is. Whatever the reason for her
being here is, at least we don't have to answer
the door any more.

'Those bloody reporters,' says Matt. 'Can't
they leave us alone? If they've got nothing useful
to tell us, they should just keep the hell away.'

He still won't look at me for more than a few
seconds. Should I have replied to his message the
other night? What would I have said? Text
messages are terrible when discussing something
important, but we can't talk properly here. There
are too many people around us all the time.

'It's Detective Hines,' says Nadia. She stands
with her back to the fireplace and folds her arms.

'Morning,' he says. He looks as though he's
been wearing the same suit for days. His tie is
about three inches from the top of his collar.
There are bags under his eyes and stubble is
beginning to shadow his face. 'I want to make a
television appeal.'

Emma's sitting in the chair by the window, her
knees pulled up to her chest, her arms wrapped
around them. It takes her a few seconds to

acknowledge that someone has spoken.

'Pardon?' Her voice is cracked; she hasn't spoken for hours.

'An appeal,' says Matt. 'They want us to go on television.'

'You don't have to do anything you don't want to,' says Hines, 'but it might help jog people's memories if they've seen anything out of the ordinary.'

'Of course,' she says. She looks away from the detective and resumes gazing through the window. She's waiting for Grace. Any minute now she might walk back home. Emma wants to be ready for her, to open the door. 'If we do it,' she says, 'I want Stephanie to be with me.'

Hines writes in his notepad again. 'And you're Grace's aunt?'

Why does he keep asking me that? I thought detectives remembered everything.

'Yes,' I say.

★ ★ ★

Matt and I are on either side of Emma in the back seat. It's the first time I've been in the back of a police car, but it's not a panda, it's a BMW. You can only tell it belongs to a police officer from the oversized radio and the gadgets on the dashboard. DS Berry is driving; Hines is in the passenger seat. Voices continuously come through on the police radio, but the detectives ignore them, keeping their eyes on the road ahead. Being in this car is another part of this nightmare that doesn't feel real.

Mum has stayed with Jamie. Of course, she said she wanted to come, but Emma said, 'It's more important that Steph's with me.' I have no idea why she said that. Maybe she does remember something after all. Or perhaps she didn't want Mum losing it in front of all the cameras and journalists. Mum gave in easily though, which was surprising. *I don't want my picture all over the newspapers*, she said. *I've not had a blow-dry for days*. As though her looking her best was more important than finding Grace.

It's the first time in daylight that we're able to see all the teddy bears and tea lights in glasses left outside the gate. There are yellow ribbons tied in bows along the fence, and handwritten messages on the ground with stones on top to keep them from blowing away.

'Don't people usually leave candles for dead people?' says Emma.

'They're candles for hope,' I say, immediately realising how trite it sounds.

Matt's staring out of the car window. He doesn't seem to see or hear what we're talking about. He's wearing his work suit and his hair has gone curly, still wet from the shower. His reading glasses help to camouflage his red eyes.

After five minutes, we pull up outside the community centre. It's where they host youth club discos and table tennis tournaments. Emma's eyes squint when the car door opens and the strong September sun hits them.

The detectives get out and a uniformed policewoman drives the car away. Matt steps in front of me, taking Emma by the hand. I feel a stab of — what? Jealousy? Resentment?

Stop it, Stephanie. Get a grip.

There are a few photographers outside and several camera crews. One of the cameras has Sky News on the side. How did they get here so quickly? It was only in the paper yesterday, but I suppose most news is instant these days — they probably got here just after the story broke.

Detective Hines leads Emma and Matt towards the side door and I'm left at the front entrance. What am I supposed to do? Everyone outside is huddled in groups and I feel like a spare part. No one's here to tell me what I'm supposed to do.

Three journalists — well, I assume they're journalists; I've never met one before — are smoking cigarettes near the doorway. One of them narrows her eyes at me. She inhales the smoke like she's hissing and blows it out like a sigh.

'Are you a relative?' she asks.

The other two — a man and a woman — look up.

'No,' I say, and rush through the door.

9

'Won't be long now, kid,' I say to her.

She just nods, doesn't talk much. It could've been worse — she could have been a right mouthy little shit, but she seems to be keeping in line so far. I haven't told her my real name, not that I suppose it matters in the end. We are judged by our actions, not by our monikers. That's what the shrink said anyway. They say a man acquires more knowledge when he's inside, but I didn't just learn the bad stuff. I was guided towards the *right path*. All right — I did ask Tommy Deeks how things like this are supposed to be done. But that was serendipity. He was sent to me for a reason.

'Routines,' he'd said. 'Once you know someone's routine, then you can intercept them at any time you see fit. And I don't mean watching them for a few hours or a few days — you have to watch them for fuckin' *weeks*. Their lives should be more important than yours — you eat, shit, sleep and dream about them. Then, my friend, it's easy as fuck.'

All I needed was a name. And it just so happens that children have their own little routines too. Even in this day and age, kids are still allowed to walk the streets on their own. Their fuckwit parents should know better. There are too many weirdos out there. She's lucky it's only me that took her — there were some right

42

filthy perverts inside. Not that we got to see them. Most of them would be killed if they put them with the rest of us.

Anyway. I digress.

This is probably the biggest thing I've ever done. It will be my salvation.

And God anointed Jesus with the Holy Spirit and with power. He went about doing good and healing all who were oppressed by the devil. For God was with him.

And if the ends justify the means . . .

She will be so pleased with me. It would be like none of all that bad stuff ever happened.

'When will you take me to my mum?'

Her little voice almost made me shit myself. For a second I forgot she was there.

'Not long now.'

There's only so far I'm going to get away with that one. Another day or so, maybe. I've taken us the long way round, but we'll be there soon. She'll soon figure out that I'm not taking her to her mother. I look at her in the rear-view mirror — dressed in clothes I bought especially for her — her hair stuffed in a hat. Her cheeks look a bit red, but she'll live. She looks just like her precious mummy. Although that bitch couldn't even look me in the eye the last time I saw her.

She'll have to soon enough though, won't she?

10

Maggie

I've laid out all the cuttings from Zoe's disappearance on the coffee table. There are only a few — there weren't as many newspapers in 1986. Most papers used the photo of Zoe in her uniform — her first and last school photograph.

I try not to think about what she might have looked like if her picture had been taken every year after that. About how proud Sarah would have been of her. I try not to feel bitter every time I see her old school friends standing at the gates of the school down the road, adults now, waiting for children of their own. I simply let it stab me once, in the heart, before I bury it again. We used to talk about Zoe every day. I don't get to talk about her any more. No one else knows her now.

I look at the clock. Jim's late, but for once I don't mind. It gives me time to look at all the different versions of her little face in the cuttings: small and grainy; black and white and brightly coloured, of which there's only one. In the centre of them all I've placed the last photo of Sarah and Zoe together: my daughter and granddaughter.

I bury my face in my hands. It never gets any easier. It's not the natural order. I've said that to myself a thousand times. I wish God would just take me to be with them. It's too hard to be the only one left. Well, almost the only one.

Jim's taps on the kitchen window halt the flow of my tears. I grab one of the cushions off the settee and soak up the wet from my face. This is why I hardly ever look at these pictures.

'Where are you, Maggie?'

'Where do you think I am? I've only two rooms.'

I place the cushion back next to me, but reversed.

Jim appears at the threshold and shakes off his coat.

'You could've been in the lav,' he says.

'Well, you can't ask where a lady is if you think she's in the lav.'

'It was just something to say,' he says, 'so you'd know I was here.'

He sighs and the settee sinks a little as he sits next to me. We don't often sit like this together. I rub my right arm with my left hand to get rid of the tingling.

'So this is what you've kept all these years,' he says, looking at the pictures on the table.

He takes a folded newspaper from the inside pocket of his coat. The things he can carry in there. Last week he took out a tin of pease pudding because I'd never eaten it before. He should've kept it in there.

'It's today's,' he says. 'She made the nationals.'

My intake of breath gives away my surprise.

'Don't look so shocked,' he says. 'I knew you'd want to read it.'

I take it from him.

45

'I know. But don't you think you're indulging me? An old fool getting caught up in a story that's nothing to do with her?'

He shakes his head. 'You're not the only one. They were all talking about it at the shop. And anyway, it's not a story — it's real life. You more than most know all about that. Stop being so ashamed about it.'

I feel myself flush. Am I ashamed? Ashamed we couldn't find her? Guilty that she was taken in the first place? Or ashamed that I still think about her, that she might come back to me after everyone else has gone?

Jim picks up one of Zoe's articles. 'A sweet shop? Is that right?'

'Yes,' I say. 'Like where this girl, Grace Harper, was last seen.'

Zoe should've been in the paper straight away. Perhaps she'd have been on the news all day too — they have news channels playing twenty-four hours a day now.

'Have you been watching Sky News?' asks Jim.

He read my mind.

'I don't have Sky News. Why would I want Sky? All I watch is *Countdown*.'

That's a lie. I watch so much rubbish I couldn't say. Channel Five do a true-life film every day that I usually end up crying to. I'd never tell Jim about that.

He winces as he stands up. 'You're the only person I know who keeps their remote control next to the television. What's the bloody point of that?'

'Mind your language,' I say.

I wonder if Grace's mother is waiting at the window, like Sarah used to.

'You'll have Freeview,' he says. 'Everyone does now. News 24 — it'll be on there.'

I leave him to play with the remote control. I place all of Zoe's articles back in the folder, except for one. It was the one that broke us: *Search called off for missing Zoe Pearson.*

★ ★ ★

We heard it from the police first. Newspapers weren't as quick off the mark as they are now.

'Every lead has been exhausted, Sarah,' Detective Jackson said. 'If we receive any new information, we'll carry on the investigation. It's not closed, it's still open.'

I feel a drip on my hand and realise it's from my face.

Jim turns and glances at me.

'There you go,' he says, handing me the remote. 'It should be repeated any minute, it's nearly on the hour.'

He pretends not to notice, Lord love him. That's what we've always done, people our age: ignore things. Sarah used to tell me off for it. 'For fuck's sake, Mother, this isn't the 1950s. People talk about things now — important things.'

Thinking about it thumps me in the chest. I beat myself up about it every day: my hypocrisy. It was so hard to talk about Zoe then. But if Sarah were here now I'd be different. I'd talk about Zoe all the time.

47

'She used to sit by the window, did our Sarah,' I say. 'Waiting and waiting, never leaving the house. *I have to be here when she gets back*, she said. Every day. For years.'

'Aye,' says Jim.

I've told him many times and he always listens as though it's the first. He reaches over and pats my hand. I look into the little girl's eyes in the newspaper he brought me. Grace Harper's eyes.

'This one'll be different.' I say to her, 'They'll find you, love. Just you see. It's different nowadays. People have their cameras everywhere.'

Jim carefully picks up Zoe's article from the coffee table. 'Is it okay if I . . . ?'

'Of course.'

He takes his glasses, which are on a chain around his neck, and perches them on the end of his nose. He tuts several times, shaking his head. He removes his glasses and rests them on his chest.

'These sightings of your Zoe,' he says. 'Where were they?'

'Cyprus, France, Spain.' I reel off the list.

'Really? How could they have done that?'

'Who knows — they might have hidden her.'

Jim smiles at me kindly, like most people used to when I dared to believe Zoe was still alive. He looks up at the television.

'It's the appeal.'

A policeman in a suit is reading from a piece of paper. Next to him are, I presume, Grace's parents. The mother has her head in her hands; the father comforts her, his arm around her shoulders.

My heart beats too fast, I wrap my arms around myself — I'm so cold, I'm always cold.

'They look young,' says Jim.

'People do these days. Must be in their early thirties, I imagine. Though I can't see her face properly. My mother looked fifty when she was thirty.' My mouth is talking without my mind thinking. 'Those poor people.'

It cuts to a photograph of a school uniform laid out on a table.

'*These are the clothes Grace was wearing, although if someone has taken her, she might not be wearing the same ones.*'

Jim tuts. 'Course she wouldn't be wearing the same clothes. But you know, Maggie, I know I shouldn't say this, but what if someone's taken her, and just killed the poor little mite?'

I sigh loudly in the hope it'll shut him up. Even though I've thought the same thing myself.

The appeal must have been taped earlier as the news article cuts to a shot outside: a village hall or a community centre. I see the mother's face for the first time — her friend, or perhaps her sister, holding her by the elbow.

I get up slowly and walk to the television. 'She's a bonny one, isn't she?'

He doesn't answer.

'Would you pause it, Jim?'

He presses the button several times.

'Come on!'

'I'm bloody pressing it.'

He did it. The picture's frozen. I get closer to the screen, bending down to look at her face. My knees go weak. I drop to the carpet.

I can't breathe properly.

Jim's at my side.

'Have you had a turn? Shall I fetch the doctor?'

I take several breaths before I can speak and shake my head.

'I'm fine. Pass me that picture.' I point to the mantelpiece, but he picks up the one facing the wall — the one I rarely look at. 'Not that one, the one on the right.'

He grabs it and hands it to me. I hold it next to the pretty face on the television.

'Look.'

He squints.

'Put the glasses on your face, man.'

As he does, he brings his head next to mine, just a few feet from the television.

'Well, would you look at that,' he says. 'She's the double of your Sarah. But that's impossible, she's — '

'I know, I know. But it could be . . . '

Jim frowns. 'What are the chances of that? It can't be.'

My shoulders slump. 'I know. But it might. It might be Zoe.'

11

Stephanie

Grace has been gone for almost three days. If the police have any new information from the television appeal yesterday, then they haven't updated us.

Mum has been making a fuss of Emma, though I don't begrudge it of course, not now Grace is missing. She's indulged her ever since she came to live with us. Emma arrived with only a little rucksack. I had just turned eleven and she was ten and three quarters. Her hair was straggly, like it hadn't been washed for weeks, but it didn't smell horrible — it was sweet, like sticking your nose in a bag of pick 'n' mix from the cinema. Her knees were dirty though, and her skirt had food stains all over it. Mum had warned Dad and me that Emma might be *in a right state* because she'd been alone in the house for at least three days until her neighbours had noticed. 'Her mother ran away with a man half her age,' Mum said. 'All she had left in the cupboards was a tin of Golden Syrup and a can of prunes, which she couldn't even open.'

Emma and I didn't speak for four days. I was a little scared of her, plus she was given my bed under the window. It had been my favourite place to be. I could pull back the curtains and watch the stars when I couldn't sleep, imagining

I was somewhere else. It was only after I heard her crying for the fifth night in a row that I tried to talk to her.

'Do you miss your mum?' I whispered.

I heard the pillow move. I took that as a nod.

'Do you want me to turn the lamp on?'

'Yes please,' she said, as quiet as anything.

I flicked on the light and I'll never forget her face. The skin around her eyes was so puffy I could barely see them. Her hair was stuck to her cheeks from the wetness of her tears.

I opened my covers. 'Do you want to come in with me?'

She nodded and almost dived into my bed. Her head snuggled into my chest and she put her arms around me. I turned off the light, and put my arm around her shoulders. I looked to the window. The curtains were open and I could see the stars. Within minutes she was fast asleep.

The memory is so vivid, I almost forget where I am. I give myself a shake — now isn't the time to get lost in the past. I go into the kitchen to check on Jamie. I've kept him off school and he's been on his laptop all morning, reading what he can find about Grace.

'They've created a Facebook page,' he says.

'Who has?'

He shrugs. 'I don't know the names. Do you?'

He points to the screen. I haven't used Facebook for ages.

'I've no idea. They sound Scottish. How can they even create a page when they don't know us?'

'Anyone can create a Facebook page.'

'That's a bit creepy.'

He shrugs. 'It's just what happens.'

He scrolls down the page, which is filled with well-meaning messages: *I hope they find her. Praying she gets home safe.* Amongst them are comments from her school friends: *Missed you at school today, hunnie.* They're written as though Grace might actually read them. Who would let their eight-year-old child write on Facebook?

'What's that?' I look closer at the screen.

'Ah yeah. Just some random psychic woman.'

'Doesn't she realise how upsetting things like that are?'

'Things like what?' It's Mum.

'Don't sneak up on us like that.'

'What's going on?' she says. 'Is that Facebook? You know what I've said about that.'

'It's just some attention-seeking woman, that's all,' I say. 'Obviously on the sherry or something.'

'Let me sit down, Jamie.'

'Sure, Gran.'

He gets up silently. Why didn't she choose another chair? There are two spare. I rub Jamie's arm, but he flicks my hand away. Mum pulls the laptop closer and puts on her glasses.

'I thought you said ... ' I begin, but I shouldn't start.

'What?' She says it dismissively, but I know she knows.

She said Facebook was dangerous, that no one in their right mind should ever look at it, or write on it. 'You never know who's watching.' She's the same with mobile phones; I've bought her two now but she leaves them in the cupboard, switched off.

'Deandra,' says Mum. 'What kind of a name is that?'

'One created by fairies,' I say.

Mum gives me a sideways glance. In an instant her expression has said, *How can you be flippant at a time like this?*

Dad would have understood. Whenever something terrible happened, he would always cut through the darkness by saying something light. Three days after his own father died, Dad said, *I owed him a fiver, you know.* No one laughed, they just smiled. We could say anything to Dad. He'd know that it's my defence mechanism to try to remain in the present. Otherwise I might fall apart, and I'd be no use to anyone then, would I?

'*I have tuned in to my spirit guides,*' says Mum, reading from the screen, '*and requested their help. I believe that Grace is still alive, but she is being kept somewhere. I hear the sound of water . . .* ' She puts her glasses on the top of her head. 'Well, that's utter bollocks.'

My eyes dart to Jamie. 'Language, Mother!'

He rolls his eyes at me. 'Mum, I'm thirteen, I'm hardly a child.'

In ordinary circumstances I would have laughed, teased him.

'What's going on?' Emma stands at the doorway. Her brown hair is all over the place, her dressing gown is undone and her nightshirt buttons are done up wrong. She barely slept last night, but it looks like she hasn't had any sleep today either.

Mum flips down the lid of the computer.

'Nothing, love. How are you feeling?'

'I'm not.'

Nadia comes back inside — the breeze travels through to the kitchen as she closes the front door. She goes out whenever she gets a phone call about the case — probably because we'd listen in and second-guess the news from her responses.

Emma's hands are shaking. Mum stands and puts her arms around her. It's hard to read Nadia's expression — her demeanour has been measured and constant since she came to the house.

'Well?' says Mum.

'We've had no sightings of Grace, but . . . '

Emma bends over, as though she's been kicked in the stomach.

'I . . . I . . . thought you'd found her then . . . I thought you were about to say . . . '

Mum guides her to the other side of the table, pulls out a chair, and sits her gently down as though she were made of glass. She stands behind her and smooths down her hair. Why can't she just leave her alone? Emma raises her head and meets Nadia's gaze. My sister's jaw sets and she narrows her eyes.

'What is it? What have you found out?'

'We've had a big response to the appeal — a lot of people offering sympathy, many saying they've never trusted their neighbour — '

I clear my throat loudly. Why is she saying all of this — how long has she been doing this job?

'Anyway, there are some pieces of information

55

we are following up — '

'But what if someone's taken her out of the country?' I say. 'What then? How will you find her?'

'We alerted all ports — air and ferry — as soon as we knew of Grace's disappearance. But that's not what I wanted to tell you. We have an image from the CCTV camera outside the newsagent's on Monday, which shows a man and what appears to be a young boy. We're about to release the image to the press, but we wanted to show you first.'

She reaches into her rucksack and pulls out an iPad. She swipes it and places it on the kitchen table.

'Do you recognise either of these people?'

I lean over, as do Mum and Emma; our heads touch as we look at the screen.

'It's really blurry,' I say. 'You'd think they'd have better quality images these days.'

Mum gives me one of her glances and sighs. I can't say anything right.

'It *is* rather fuzzy,' she says, after a minute. 'How are we meant to tell by looking at their backs? They could be anyone.'

'Do you recognise any items of clothing on the child?'

'But it's a boy,' says Mum, rubbing her temples.

Emma looks up at Nadia.

'Do you think this child might be Grace?'

'We're not sure yet,' says Nadia, always talking in the collective, as though she has no opinion of her own.

Emma picks up the iPad.

'But I can't see the legs. This child has trousers on. And that coat — it's too big. Grace's only little, she doesn't eat much, you see. I try to get her interested, but she's not at all. The most food she'll eat is at breakfast. She'd rather listen to One Direction, or read books, or play on the console, or — '

She drops the tablet onto the table. My chair flips over as I rush over to her and pull her head into my arms.

'Oh, Steph. What am I going to do? I can't do this. I'm not strong enough. If anything's happened to her I won't be able to go on. I can't bear it.'

I stroke her hair and whisper in her ear. 'You *are* strong. You can do this. I'm here for you.'

She wipes the tears from her face with the heels of her palms.

'Where's Matt?' She pushes me aside as she gets up from the chair, and walks out of the kitchen.

★ ★ ★

Mum and I are still scrutinising the CCTV image when Matt walks in.

'Let me see,' he says, swiping it from under our heads.

Mum opens her mouth, but closes it again. Obviously she can bite her tongue when it's someone else.

Matt looks like shit. He slept in the same jeans and T-shirt he's worn for days, bar the press conference. He only went to bed in the early

57

hours of the morning after drinking the best part of two bottles of wine.

'Can't see a fucking thing,' he says. 'Haven't you got a clearer picture?'

I glance over at Jamie. Usually he smirks if an adult swears in front of him, but his lips are tight; he's staring at the table. I don't think he's heard Matt swear before.

'I'm sorry,' says Nadia. 'We don't.'

Matt rubs his eyes with one hand, and looks again.

'Jesus, it could be anybody. Do you think this bloke has dressed Grace up like this? Have you got any more pictures of them? Surely this can't be the only one of these two from the cameras in town.'

'We're working on it.'

'Are we?' he snaps. 'Well this is no bloody use to me.' He throws the iPad onto the table. 'Get back to me when you've got more than this shit.'

I sit down next to Jamie at the table.

'You okay, love?'

He nods. 'Do you think . . . ?'

'What?' I say, but he's looking down at the floor. 'What's wrong?'

'I know it's Friday tomorrow, but do you think it would be okay if I went back to school?'

I've been selfish keeping him here — making sure I can see him, so I know where he is. I should've realised that being here would be uncomfortable for him. His dad texted last night saying Jamie could stay there, which might not be a bad idea — if Neil didn't work all the time.

I put my hand over his. 'Of course it is.'

12

Maggie

I stand outside the bedroom door. I hardly ever open it, but I feel as though Sarah's telling me to go inside, to remember. I almost don't want to. The everyday thoughts are bad enough — those pangs I feel in my chest when it catches me by surprise, when I think I've buried it enough to go about my day. But it never goes away. I'm meant to be sad. Nothing will change that.

Sarah and Zoe moved in with Ron and me six weeks before Zoe went missing. Missing — it sounds so flippant. She was taken from us, murdered, vanished. *They* are the dramatic words that should belong to Zoe, because we don't know what happened to her. No, they're not the only words. She was kind, even at five years old, so kind. Yes, she could be challenging, but only because she was so bright — not that we said so at the time.

Sarah's husband, David, had been made redundant, but they'd been arguing long before that. She and Zoe moved in with us to give Sarah some space to think. But Zoe missed her dad.

Pull yourself together, Margaret. My mother's voice is tingling in my ears.

Easier said than done, Mother.

I turn the handle and push the door open. I always leave the curtains tied, so it's never dark.

59

There's not as much dust in here this time. What is dust, anyway? I once heard that it was about seventy per cent human skin. No one comes in here, so there can't be much. I wonder how many of the little particles left behind are from Sarah and Zoe. I want to gather them all up and bring them to life.

Next to Sarah's single bed is Zoe's little camp bed. Her three teddies are still on her pillow. One of them, her favourite pink elephant, Wellie (she couldn't say Nellie when she first got it, and it just stuck), is almost standing upright. The clothes they arrived with are still in suitcases under the bed. I couldn't bear to unpack, to look at them, to touch them, to smell them. Mother had a point when she said that some things are best left buried — it feels too painful to unearth them.

I still wonder if things would've been different if Sarah hadn't left David. They lived over twenty minutes away, so Zoe would never have gone to the sweet shop on the corner. I used to blame David for driving Sarah away, but that has lessened. I haven't seen him in over ten years.

I don't want to look to the left; I know what I'll see. The mahogany chest of drawers that Ron and I bought from a car boot sale in Blackpool. On top of it will be a twelve by seven photograph of Zoe in a beautiful carved frame; there'll be a box that contains a lock of Zoe's hair from her first trip to the hairdresser's; the candle, burned only once from her christening. There will be angels made from porcelain, plastic, wood; a stone Zoe picked from St Anne's beach; a jar of perfume she made with roses and Ron's aftershave; the conker she pickled in vinegar and made me bake for seven hours.

I know all those things are there and I can't look at them.

I stroke the cover of Sarah's bed — the place where my beautiful daughter died, and back out of the room.

13

Stephanie

Our secret has been easy to keep from Emma, as we'd only communicated through email. Emma, famously to everyone who knows her, never uses email outside of work, or Facebook, or any of that — she seldom even texts. She says she prefers to hear a person's voice.

Matt hasn't mentioned it since the text the other day. We can't talk about it here. It wouldn't just betray Emma, it would hurt Mum too. Somehow, I've got to access Jamie's laptop and delete whatever we put online. But I can't now — I'm frozen on the sofa. Matt is watching every news report about Grace — as is Mum, who's sitting in the armchair opposite me. Sky News has been running almost twenty-four-hour coverage since she went missing on Monday. It's now Friday. How has it got to the end of the week without her being found? Grace's face is everywhere; if someone saw her on the street, would they recognise her? Perhaps they'd ignore the feeling that they've seen her somewhere before.

I try not to imagine what that man in the CCTV image wants with her — even though it might not even *be* her in the picture. But if it is, and their picture is everywhere — on television, in the papers — then the man won't go out with her in public, he'll hide her away. We might never see her again.

There are reporters in town, and camera crews everywhere — interviewing the police spokesperson and the residents. It's like it's not real, that it's happening to someone else in a different town.

'I need to go and look for her,' says Matt. 'I should be out there, helping everyone else. They probably think I don't care. If I could just see a picture of this man's face — the man who was holding her hand . . . then I'll find him, find her.' He keeps saying the same things. He walks over to Nadia, who's perched on a dining chair near the door leading to the kitchen. She's been here every day, from early morning until late at night. 'Please let me help.'

Nadia has that same look on her face, the same tilt of the head she always uses to address him. 'Nearly the whole town is looking for her, Matthew. The whole town. We need you to be here in case we find her.'

'But what if it's not her in that photograph — what if someone *didn't* take her and she's trapped somewhere? She'll be waiting for me to come and get her. I'm letting her down just sitting here. What kind of fucking father am I, who just sits watching everyone else while they look for my daughter? It's my job, I should be there. It's been nearly four days. She's going to be really cold.' His voice is barely a whisper. Tears are streaming down his face. 'It's freezing at night.'

She guides him back to the sofa and I just watch, useless, an outsider looking in. It's the first of October tomorrow; the temperature might start to fall. I can't think about Grace being cold. I can't think about her being scared. My fears and my hopes are intertwined: I hope someone *has* taken her, but that they're looking after her, keeping her warm. It's wishful thinking, but better than what my imagination is trying to show me: the worst possible things that don't correspond with my lovely Grace. My thoughts trigger a rage I've never felt before. If anything happens to her, I will kill whoever did it with my bare hands.

The same thoughts go over and over in my head.

I sit up quickly.

Jamie.

Mum looks over at me.

'He's at school,' she says. It must be the first time she's ever read my mind. 'Do you want me to ring the school again — check he's okay?'

I look at Matt — he's not listening. Every time I talk about Jamie, I feel like I'm rubbing his nose in the fact that my child is safe.

'How many times have we rung?' I say.

'Three.' She's staring at the television now.

Three times? I can't remember the first time. Thank God it's Saturday tomorrow. When I escorted Jamie to the taxi this morning, there were flashes from the reporters' cameras. I wish I'd had a blanket to cover his face. Then whoever has Grace won't come for Jamie.

'Get me a drink, will you, Steph?'

I stand up automatically and grab the cup at Matt's feet.

'Not tea. Something stronger.'

I glance at the clock on the mantelpiece — it's twenty past one. I look to Mum. She raises her eyebrows and shrugs her shoulders. This from the woman who says drinking before six o'clock makes you either too rich or too common.

'Do you think it's wise at this time of day?' I say. 'What if . . .'

I don't know what to say — no one is listening to me anyway.

'There's some vodka on top of the fridge,' says Mum.

How does one person know where every single thing is in every house she visits?

I walk into the kitchen. My heart jolts when I see Emma at the kitchen table with Jamie's laptop in front of her.

'How did you guess the password?' I say, grabbing the vodka off the top of the fridge.

'I didn't guess it, did I? How the hell would I guess that? Jamie gave it to me.'

I don't even know his password. I stop my mouth before it opens and actually bite my tongue. I hate it when she goes behind my back like this, like she can do as she pleases, like she's — shit, stop it, Stephanie. I want to slap myself. Grace is not here and I'm thinking about myself.

I get a tumbler and pour the vodka halfway.

'What does Matt drink with his vodka?' I say.

'I wouldn't know these days.' Emma's eyes don't leave the screen. My heart beats faster at the thought of what she might be reading. 'You'd know better than I do.'

I say nothing and stride into the sitting room,

offering the glass to Matt.

'Am I supposed to drink it neat? What the fuck is wrong with you? Did you not see the coke in the fridge?'

I just stand there. I can't believe my hand isn't shaking. I don't know if I'm more upset than angry. I hear a noise behind me.

'Don't you ever, ever talk to my daughter like that!'

Mum is standing next to me and has her right fist held up. The tears well up in my eyes. Matt has never spoken to me like that; Mum has never stuck up for me like that. The air is charged for what feels like minutes. I look to Nadia; Mum's looking at her too.

'Perhaps now is not the time to get angry with your family, Matthew,' she says.

I can see the venom in his eyes as he looks at me. When he shifts his gaze to Nadia, his expression softens.

I'm shaking as I walk back to the kitchen and sit at the table next to Emma.

'What are you looking at?' I say to her.

She glances at me as though I'm a nuisance. Did she hear what just happened? Her eyes are bloodshot and there are tiny red blisters under them.

'That psychic on Grace's page on Facebook. I'm doing some research on her.'

'Oh.' I relax a little into the chair. 'I didn't know you knew your way around Facebook.'

'Just because you don't see me on the laptop at home, doesn't mean I don't use it all day at work.'

I should've realised — she's on a computer all the time at the recruitment agency. She didn't look at me when she spoke, but paranoia tells me that there was an undertone. What else has she been hiding from me?

'I've got to keep an open mind about these things,' she says.

'I guess.'

She tuts. 'My daughter is missing, Stephanie. Wouldn't you consider every possibility if it were Jamie?'

'Of course. I'd consider every possibility for Grace too.'

She glances at me and purses her lips. It's her way of saying we're friends again.

'Bring your chair nearer to me. You can help me look.'

She clicks onto Deandra Divine's Facebook page. I say nothing about the name. The profile photo is what I expected: a black and white shot of a woman in her fifties, black straight hair framing her face in a centre parting, her gaze off camera. Emma and I would have laughed at it any other time.

'I've read about other missing person cases she's given readings about, cases from years ago. She's been right most of the time.'

If she were the real deal, surely she'd be right *all* of the time. It's a thought I keep to myself.

'I've emailed her, Steph. If I manage to get an appointment with her, will you come with me?'

I pause for a second. 'Of course.'

★　★　★

I couldn't relax until Jamie was back from school. I didn't know how long it would take him to get here. At home he's usually back at 3.45 p.m., but I booked him a taxi to pick him up — no doubt he was mortified in front of his friends — and he didn't arrive until 3.55 p.m. In those ten minutes I experienced only a fraction of what Emma and Matt are going through. He's upstairs in his usual place now, in the spare room.

Mum is still hovering over Emma. It's her way of dealing with things beyond her control. I can tell that she's been crying because she spent ten minutes in the bathroom and the rims of her eyes are still red. I don't say anything. I never do. Once you start talking about feelings from the past, there's no way of forgetting them again.

When Dad died four years ago, she baked and cooked for twelve hours solid until she collapsed on the sofa at three o'clock in the morning. She would never let us see her cry. She tried to hide the noise in their — her — bedroom by putting the television on loud. Emma and I would sit at her door, both too afraid to open it.

It had all happened so quickly. Emma and I had been at Mum and Dad's house when the phone call came. 'You need to come to the hospital,' said the woman on the other end of the line to Mum. 'It's your husband. He's been in an accident.'

'What do you think it means?' Mum asked in the car on the way there. 'Why didn't your dad speak to me himself?'

She wouldn't stop talking.

Emma sat next to me in the passenger seat as I drove us there. While Mum spoke, Emma and I kept exchanging glances; I think we both knew what we were about to hear without us saying it aloud.

When I pulled up into the hospital car park I experienced a sense of doom — that I was walking into another life, another chapter. It was a feeling strangely familiar, like I'd been expecting it without realising.

The police officer was waiting for us in the relatives' room. He already had his hat in his hands.

'I'm very sorry,' he said to Mum. 'But your husband was taken ill this afternoon. He suffered a stroke while he was driving. There was no one else injured.'

'What?' she said. 'I don't understand. We're going out for dinner tonight . . . just the four of us.'

She looked to Emma and me as though we had the answers.

'I don't know,' I said. 'I don't know what's happened.'

'But I only saw him at midday,' she said. 'It can't have happened. He was fine.' She grabbed hold of my hand. 'He looked fine, didn't he, Stephanie?'

'I . . . I haven't seen him since last week.'

She put her hand on her forehead. 'Yes, yes. You two only came round an hour ago.' She looked at the policeman. 'Are you sure you have the right person?' She reached into her handbag,

69

took out her purse and flipped it open. 'Is this the same person?'

The police officer nodded. 'I'm so sorry.'

Mum buried her face in her hands. 'It can't be. It can't be.'

The room was closing in on me; the door, the walls, the ceiling. The tears fell down my face — a stream that came from nowhere.

Emma looked at me — her eyes wide, her mouth open. She shook her head. 'I . . . I . . . it's not right,' she said. 'Not Dad.'

My dad, my lovely dad, had gone in an instant.

He was pronounced dead an hour before we'd got to the hospital — just as Emma and I had arrived at our parents' house. For a whole sixty minutes, he'd been lying there, on his own. I couldn't imagine what it was like for him, dying alone. The suggestion that he'd have felt nothing was of little comfort.

I jump as Mum sets a platter of sandwiches on the coffee table. Being in this house now, with Mum and Emma, is making me think about the past too much. Emma is sitting in her chair, her eyes always locked on the window.

'I know you won't feel like eating it, love.' Mum places a small plate on the arm of Emma's chair, which contains half an egg sandwich, minus the crusts. 'But you need to keep your strength up . . . for Grace. She'll need you to be strong for when she gets home.'

It's like watching a switch activate in Emma's mind: she turns to the plate.

'Thanks, Mum.'

She stares at the sandwich for a few seconds before breaking it into four, placing one tiny piece into her mouth.

When she gets home. I so hope she's right — that Mum has more foresight than I have.

Emma's on her second glass of wine in thirty minutes. Matt phoned the woman at the off-licence and they were all too happy to deliver. Probably wanted to have a good look at the family in turmoil.

'At least she didn't charge,' I said.

'And so she shouldn't,' said Mum. 'Though I dare say they shouldn't be getting drunk.'

At a time like this, she didn't say. Six bottles of wine and two litres of vodka the shop had delivered. We shouldn't be drinking at a time like this, is what *I* had thought, until I'd finished my first glass of wine.

It hadn't taken Mum long to join us. Thirty-five minutes later and she's swinging her left leg, banging it against the bottom of the armchair. I want to dive on her leg to stop it moving.

Emma gets up quickly, glass in hand, and sways slightly. She collapses in front of the television, landing on her knees.

Mum sits forward on her chair, but doesn't get up.

'Emma. Are you okay? Have you drunk too much?'

I look at Mum through narrow eyes. What goes on in her head? Emma can drink as much as she wants; she doesn't need policing right now.

'I've got to find that DVD,' says Emma.

When I get up I feel dizzy. My glass clinks on the mantelpiece as I place it between the photographs of Dad and the one of Grace and Jamie last Christmas — their faces covered in pudding and cream after they'd pretended to be cats, eating from a saucer on the floor.

I kneel down next to Emma and flick through the DVD cases in the drawer under the television.

'The one from last year,' she says, but I know which one — it's the only one they had transferred to DVD from Matt's phone. We both have a copy. I thank God that Jamie is upstairs, so he doesn't have to see everyone like this.

'What are you doing, Emma?' Mum gets up and stands behind us. 'You're just torturing yourself.'

I can tell without looking that she's got her hands on her hips. Three sighs later, she leaves the room and stomps upstairs.

'Here it is.'

Emma wrestles the case open and opens the disc tray of Grace's Xbox. She doesn't move from the floor as the video of Christmas past takes over the television. The camera travels from the Christmas tree to the door to the hallway. Grace appears in her pyjamas, with strands of her shoulder-length hair in a golden halo around her head.

'You haven't started without me, have you?' she says.

'Course we haven't, sleepyhead.' Matt's voice booms through the speakers.

Grace walks over to the tree, which has at least fifty presents underneath it. She stands with her back to the camera, putting both hands on her head.

'He actually came!' She turns round, her eyes glistening. 'I told Hannah he was real and she didn't believe me, Daddy.'

The camera turns to the floor while her little feet run to Matt and she jumps onto his lap. The screen goes black for a couple of seconds before Grace is pictured sitting cross-legged on the carpet, yanking open a present wrapped with too much Sellotape.

'What is it?' It's Emma — the camera pans to her at the kitchen doorway, looking flushed and wearing an apron covered with smears of food.

'Socks,' shouts Grace off camera.

Emma rolls her eyes, turns round and walks into the kitchen.

The camera goes back to Grace, holding up the socks.

'They're Minions! I love them!'

She rips off the cardboard and puts them on. She stomps in a circle.

'I'm trampling all over my Minions,' she says, laughing.

Next to me, Emma grabs the Xbox controller and presses pause. It leaves Grace with one foot in mid-air and a huge smile on her lovely face. My hands are soaking wet and I realise that my tears have been dripping onto them.

Emma throws the controller onto the floor. I take the glass of wine from her hands just in time as she buries her face in them.

'Why didn't I watch her open her presents? I only saw her open the Xbox and that was it.' She sobs into her sleeve. 'I'm a terrible mother. I don't deserve her.'

I rub her back. It doesn't feel enough. I want to magic Grace from where she is now and back into this room. My heart hurts.

'But you had the dinner to cook for everyone,' I say. 'She loves your roast potatoes.'

It's such a shit thing to say. It makes her cry even more.

'When she comes back,' she says, 'I'll make them for her every day.'

Her cries are so loud and so heartbreaking. I pull her towards me and we cry together.

★ ★ ★

Mum is upstairs comforting Emma. Jamie went to sleep an hour ago and Matt's sitting on the sofa, his head resting on the back, his eyes looking to the ceiling. I step over his outstretched legs and sit next to him. I lean back into the sofa, feeling a brief flutter of comfort from the soft cushions around me. It's so quiet that the ticking clock is the only sound.

The times I have been here, when Grace has been watching the Disney channel, playing her dance game on the console or getting cross with *Minecraft* — stop, stop. Don't think about it. I can't go under too, not when they need me.

I wipe my face with both of my sleeves and try to muffle my sniffs with the tissues constantly balled up in my hand. I don't know what to say to Matt. He brings his head down.

'About that text,' he says. 'The emails . . . '

'It doesn't matter.'

'I don't want you to think that that was all I thought about when the police took the laptop — that I wasn't thinking about Grace. It's just that I'd been at work and — '

'I know. Don't give it a second thought.'

'I'm sorry about shouting at you before.' He breathes in, and his chest rises. He turns his head towards mine. 'We shouldn't have started all of that anyway.'

I say nothing in return, but my face flushes.

'I'd been at work,' he repeats. 'While Grace was being taken, or hurt, or God-knows-what — and for what? I work so hard for us, for our little family — and when it counted, I wasn't even here for them.'

Emma, and Matt's lives are so far removed from mine. Jamie's father sees him every Saturday night and Sunday, yet my son is never included in Neil and his new wife's holidays. They put on expensive birthday parties that always put my homemade meal and birthday cake to shame. They invited Jamie for Christmas the year before last and gave him at least thirty presents. I spent that Christmas with Mum. Jamie worried about me, but I couldn't show how I really felt — I had to be happy for him being surrounded by Neil and Joanna's families. It's something Emma and I never had — a big family gathering. It's something Jamie deserves.

Tears spring to my eyes again. Everything's making me cry. I'm being over-sentimental. I

75

wish I could be someone else sometimes.

Matt turns his head towards mine again. This time I turn and face him.

'You're always here, aren't you?' he says.

I frown.

'I don't mean that in a bad way. I mean, you're always there for us. You work, you have Jamie. I don't know how you do it on your own. You're so strong.' He reaches out his hand. With his index finger he strokes my cheek. 'So strong.'

I sit there for a few seconds. Feeling the warmth of his hand near my face. What must it be like to have that all the time, to have someone close to you with affection at the flick of a finger?

I gently move his finger away with my hand.

'I'm not as strong as you think.'

He brings his hand down and folds his arms. 'Emma's so cold.'

I don't know where to look. My cheeks are on fire. Emma hasn't mentioned any problems between them, but then she hasn't said much about anything for the past few weeks.

'Shit,' says Matt. 'I don't mean now. I mean before. Before Grace.' He leans forward and rests his forehead in his hands. 'What the fuck am I talking about? I'm so sorry, Steph. You always bear the brunt of my shit. Why am I even thinking about it, let alone saying it?'

I've known Matt longer than I have my ex-husband. It's only since last Christmas that I became nervous around him.

We were sitting next to each other at the table. Emma was flitting about, appearing busy when all the food was already laid out. I was wearing the red dress I'd worn to my work's Christmas party, and had my hair cut shorter so it rested on my shoulders.

'You're looking great today, Steph,' he said, smiling at me. 'I think being single suits you.'

He'd never commented on my looks before. It was such a harmless remark, but it surprised me so much that I didn't reply and my face burned. I was relieved when Emma finally sat down, but from that moment, whenever he talked to me, it was as though there was no one else in the room.

I don't think Emma noticed — she always seemed so preoccupied with other things. I can barely glance at him now when others are around us, in case they guess how I feel.

When I first told Emma that Neil had left, she came round to my house straight away, dragging Matt with her. When she went upstairs to talk to Jamie, Matt sat on the chair by the window — the one Neil usually sat in.

Matt looked around the living room — at the bits and pieces Neil and I had bought over the years; the mantelpiece that gave the impression of a happy marriage — the wedding photograph, the candles, that stupid figurine of a couple dancing that Neil's mother bought.

Matt clasped his hands together; he looked awkward, as though he didn't know what to say to me. He hardly ever visited my house, I was always the one going there. He didn't suit sitting in it.

'I don't know the details, Steph,' he said. 'But I'm so sorry.'

'Did Neil say anything to you about it?'

'God no! To be honest we don't really talk outside of family gatherings. I don't think he likes me that much.'

He was right. Neil never had anything good to say about Matt. 'Full of himself; I'm sure he's going a bit thin on top; putting on a bit of weight is our Matt.' Neil could be a right bitch. I wrote it off as harmless jealousy at the time; he was nice to Matt's face — overly so, to the point that it appeared a little obsequious. Neil hadn't attended the last few family meals; he was always working on some important project. I should've noticed him quietly removing himself from my family.

'I'm here for you, Steph,' said Matt. 'Anytime you need to talk.'

It was strange hearing him say *I*. Whenever Emma and Matt usually spoke it was as a collective: '*We're* getting this for Grace'; 'Are you coming round to *ours*?' Neil and I never talked like that.

I lean forward and look at him now — this man I have known for as long as Emma has. When I think about it, Emma had been rather distracted — she does that sometimes when she's having a hard time at work and doesn't want to bother anyone with her troubles. 'Everyone has better things to think about than my problems,' she always says, but she doesn't mean it. Perhaps she includes Matt in *everyone*.

My hand reaches over to him; it hovers for a few seconds before I pat his back. I can't do anything else.

14

The only words I've said to George since the ferry are yes, no and thank you. And we've been driving for over a hundred hours or whatever it is. I'm usually a *chatterbox* in the car — Mummy would have told me to *keep it zipped* at least twenty times if she were driving me. My bum is burning I've been sitting on it for that long.

'Come on, kid.' He keeps trying to talk to me. 'I'm getting bored driving, listening to bloody French radio stations. You're not still mad at me, are you?'

He was mad at *me*, but I can't say that. He'd tell me off again. He can just *turn*. I've seen grown-ups do that. I keep trying to guess to myself how old he is. He's older than Daddy, but not as old as Gran. His hair is black, but it has loads of streaks of grey, and he's either got a lot of hair gel in it, or it needs washing. That's what Mummy says about Daddy's, though he doesn't wear hair gel much these days.

Tears come to my eyes when I think of Mummy and Daddy. They'll be missing me by now. Are they really waiting for me in Belgium? George won't let me talk to them on the phone. It would be good to hear their voices, then I won't miss them as much.

I have to blink really fast to stop the tears. I daren't ask George about Mummy any more.

Every time I do, he shouts at me. *For the fiftieth fucking time, stop talking about Mummy and Daddy. I'll leave you in a field if you're not careful.* It was dark when he said that.

Out of the window, the land is flat. It's like I can see for miles, but I can't see England. We're nowhere near the sea.

'When are we stopping for food?' It's my tummy that told my mouth to talk. My brain didn't want it to.

'Ah, so it does speak.' He reaches over to the passenger seat and puts a cap on his head. It's not a nice cap like Abigail from school got from Disneyland, but a beige one — like a grandad would wear. 'Once we cross the border, we'll stop off somewhere. Promise. We just have to get past these bastards.'

He's the only man I've ever met that would do swearing in front of a kid. My gran would *have a coronary* if she heard him.

In front of us, cars are lined up in rows. There are little houses in the middle of the road that everyone is stopping beside. George turns round.

'Listen, kid. They might call you by a different name, but it's just a game. We're playing at pretend. If you win, and they don't guess your real name, then I'll buy you some sweets after your dinner. Deal?'

I nod. I just heard *different name* and *sweets*. I'm quite good at pretending. In my first school play, I was Mary — and I didn't have to say anything. All the grown-ups believed I actually was Mary. 'George' might not even be *his* real name; I said it twice ten minutes ago and he didn't reply. He was probably ignoring me again.

He can't sit still in his seat. He must have ants in his pants. He turns round again.

'Are you all right? Just be calm, everything will be okay.'

I am calm.

He wiggles his fingers on the steering wheel.

'Come on, man. You can do it. Ten grand, ten grand. All the booze I can drink. Come on, man.'

He thinks he's whispering, but he's not doing it properly.

The car stops. George winds down the window, and says something. It's not English.

He hands them some paper, but I can't see what's on it. He told me to look out of my side, so I can't peek too much.

A face appears at the window. A man with a grey beard. He's wearing a flat hat, like a policeman's. He points at me and makes circle shapes with his hand. It makes me laugh.

'He's telling you to wind the window down.' George doesn't sound mad, or happy.

I grab the handle with two hands and wind it round until the window is halfway down. The man squints at me. He's really close, but his nose doesn't come through the window. Is he a policeman? Shall I tell him that I've lost my mummy? I wish I knew how to speak the way George does. I'm trying to smile but my eyes are watering.

He stands back up and walks slowly round the car. He bends down to talk to George.

'*Die Kind ist acht?*'

He's talking like they sing in that song. I wish

I knew more words than *ninety-nine red balloons*.

'*Ja weiß ich,*' says George. '*Wir hören dass die ganze Zeit. Das arme Kind ist klein für ihr Alter.*'

The man in the uniform laughs, but I can't hear what he says back. I wouldn't be able to understand it anyway. The guard hits the top of the car twice and says, '*Willkommen zurück nach Deutschland.*' And we drive away.

After three minutes, George flings off his cap. He bangs the steering wheel three times with his fists. 'Get the hell in! We did it, kid. That was the worst one — they're right tough sods, those German border bastards. We've only gone and fucking done it. We're in Germany, little one!'

Germany? My mummy's never been to Germany before. Why would she be here?

I look out of the window, and it's raining.

So are my eyes.

15

Stephanie

Why have I woken?

It takes me a few blinks to realise where I am: on Emma and Matt's sofa. Another few moments and I remember why I feel so ill. I need water — my mouth is so dry and my head is pounding.

I sit up. A chilly soft breeze flutters over my face, through my hair. It feels so refreshing.

Shit.

The front door's open.

In the moonlight, I can see Matt asleep on the sofa by the window. I crawl towards him.

'Matt, the door . . .'

I stand up.

Grace.

She must be back. Why else would the front door be open at this time? I race up the stairs.

'Grace!'

I run into her bedroom — it's empty.

Matt and Emma's room — she's not there either. Neither is Emma. The bed is crumpled, but empty. The bathroom door bangs against the tiles as I storm in. Before I pull the cord for the light I know there's no one in here.

Jamie appears at the door of the spare room. 'Is Grace back?'

'No, love.' I'm trying to sound calm, but am

probably failing. 'Go back to bed.'

I wait several seconds to see that he does, before galloping down the stairs. All the lights are on, and Matt isn't in the house. I run out of the still-open front door, only wearing my socks. At the gate I look left and right, before making my way towards two people huddled together fifty metres away.

Emma is on her knees on the pavement; Matt has his arms around her.

'You can't look for her on your own, Em,' he says. 'It's three o'clock in the morning.'

I crouch down in front of her. She's still in her clothes from yesterday. It must have rained in the night; the ground is damp.

'But I have to find her.' She's clutching the giraffe from Grace's bed. 'I *have* to. What else can I do?'

She cries out as though someone is ripping out her insides. I inch towards her on my knees and wrap my arms around her shoulders.

'Let's go inside.' It's a voice from above. I look up: it's Nadia. Where has she been? Asleep in her car? She seems to come in and out of the house without me even noticing.

As we walk back to the house, neighbours' house lights flick on one by one, like uncoordinated street lamps. Curtains twitch and faces come to the windows.

Nothing to see here. Mind your own fucking business.

The tea lights outside the front garden have long since gone out — and the teddies and ribbons tied to the fence look sodden.

84

Inside the house, Matt wraps a blanket around Emma's shoulders and guides her upstairs. She's still sobbing. He rubs her arms as she's shaking so much, from the cold and from the shock.

'Are you staying here tonight?' I ask Nadia.

I hadn't noticed if she had the previous nights — I had just assumed she was always here.

'I'll sleep on the sofa. I'll grab a blanket from my car.'

I just nod. I expect she knows what she's doing — she must be used to situations like this. I feel myself shiver too. I don't know how Nadia does it — watching people suffer like this.

I head upstairs and tiptoe past Jamie in bed. I try to roll myself into the quilt, hoping it will soften the hardness of the floor or perhaps offer some form of comfort. But it doesn't. I close my eyes and pray for sleep.

★ ★ ★

When I open my eyes this time, I remember why I'm here. Daylight floods the spare room through the lightweight curtains. There's shouting coming from the kitchen below. I keep horizontal and try to make out who the voices belong to.

Footsteps.

Jamie is towering above me, dressed in his school uniform. I push myself up.

'Sorry, love. I didn't realise the time.'

He crouches next to me.

'It's okay, Mum. It's Saturday.'

85

I lift up my arm and glance at my watch. It's nine forty-five.

'How come you're in your school uniform?'

'They're the only clothes I have.'

I put my hands over my face.

'Oh, love. I'm so sorry.'

'No, it's fine. Is it okay if I go to Dad's? It's my day to go there after all.'

'But I wanted to keep you here, safe. I can pop home and get you more clothes — it's only ten minutes' drive.' I sit up and throw the cover off me. 'We can go now.'

'Mum, I'll be fine with Dad, won't I? Please let me go.'

It shouldn't sting, but it does. I look at him in his five-day-old uniform — I haven't even washed it for him in between. There's a pleading look on his face. I feel so ashamed for not thinking about his clothes. I've been borrowing Emma's — I didn't even think about his. What kind of mother am I?

'Of course. I should have thought of that before. I'll ring him now.'

I should have said that Neil had already suggested it the other day. For all I know, Neil has already texted Jamie with the idea. It's through habit that I always go into another room from Jamie when I telephone his dad. It stems from the days when I couldn't control how mad I got at him for simply sounding fine.

I sit cross-legged on the hallway carpet. It only takes four rings before he answers.

'I've left you about ten voicemails,' he says.

I don't bother with the sarcastic, *And hello to*

you too. That's for people who like each other. I rub my forehead to try to rid some of the frustration I feel every time I talk to him.

'I'm sorry. It's been . . . awful here.'

'Hence why I wanted Jamie here with me.'

I pinch the top of my nose. Who the fuck says *hence* in conversation?

'I'm sorry.'

He sighs. I can hear his bare feet padding around on his expensive kitchen floor.

'No problem,' he says, as though I were a work colleague. 'I was thinking, perhaps I could get Joanna to pick him up. She's shopping in town. She could pick him up after . . . about six-ish would suit us.'

Us.

Three years ago, he and I were *us*.

'It's okay. I can drop him off. I could use the fresh air. I don't suppose Jamie's left some clothes there to be going on with?'

'No, I don't think so. Joanna's mother used his room for a night this week — she would have said if his clothes were in there.'

'Oh.'

So they clear all traces of Jamie when it suits them. Poor Jamie having to carry a bag to and from his own father's house.

'Why hasn't he got a bag there?' he asks.

'I . . . I forgot. I can pick some clothes up for him on the way to yours.'

I get this sick feeling every time Neil hints that I haven't been the perfect mother — that I haven't been there for Jamie when he needed me. I was late once picking Jamie up from

87

school, caught up in traffic from an accident on the A153. The school office telephoned Neil. There is nothing like the worry that someone is going to take your child off you to initiate a feeling of dread. Even though he's never said it, the idea is always in my head. This notion means I'm always on my best behaviour in case my world falls apart. I wish I were more confident, less eager to please.

He tuts. 'It doesn't matter.' He sounds, as always, distracted, with far more important things to do than talk to me. He hasn't asked about Grace or how Emma is. 'I'll get Joanna to pick up a few things for him while she's shopping.'

'Are you working from home then? On a Saturday?'

There, I said it. Why can't *he* pick Jamie up? I'm not usually so confrontational. But then, that's hardly confrontational really, is it? It's the best I could do.

'Excuse me?'

You heard, I want to say, but that would be going too far. I'll bet he's not working at all — I can hear the television on. 'It's just I thought I heard *Top Gear* in the background.' I cover my mouth. What the hell has got into me?

'Er . . . I was just researching something.'

'Oh . . . I was just joking. I'll drop him off at six.'

I hang up. Now certainly isn't the time for me to start taking the piss. I must still be drunk.

My knees creak as I get up. In the spare room, Jamie's reading his mobile phone: he's probably got the text from his dad already. He's sitting at the desk, the light from the laptop glowing in the dullness of the overcast morning.

'What are you smiling at?' he says.

'Am I?' I sit on the edge of the bed. 'I was just thinking how grown up you are.'

He wrinkles his nose. 'Whatever.'

I stand up. 'Come on. Let's get you some breakfast.'

I follow him as we file out of the room. It's quiet upstairs. I look at Jamie in front of me. He seems so young from behind, his hair sticking up from the crown of his head. Poor boy, having to deal with all of this — and the commotion in the early hours of this morning. I'm tempted to call Neil back and ask if he can stay there for more than one night. I'm being selfish keeping him here.

He still has his phone in his hands when a message sounds.

'Toby said I could go round to his today — he said I could borrow some of his clothes. You know his mum, remember? I used to go round for tea when we were at primary school.'

'I'm not sure that's a good idea. I'd rather you stayed here for breakfast and the morning, until I can drop you off at Dad's later.'

'Mum, please. I'd only be sitting in the spare room watching YouTube on my laptop. I need to get out of here.'

I look at him, shadows under his eyes.

I reach down to my mobile.

'I'll ring a taxi for you.'

'It's okay, Mum. I'll walk.'

'You are not walking.'

I use my phone in the hallway. When I've finished, Jamie's sitting on the edge of the sofa.

'Taxi will be here in five minutes, no arguments.'

I say that, but he doesn't protest.

I sit next to him. 'I'm sorry about last night, by the way.'

He looks at me, like he did when he was little, with the big eyes, the freckles on his nose, the colour in his cheeks.

'Don't worry about me, I'm fine. It's not your fault — it's not anyone's fault.' He looks at his hands. 'Except the bastard that took her.'

I flinch slightly. It's the first swear word he's ever said in front of me. But I recognise those words as Matt's, not Jamie's.

A horn sounds outside. He gets up with almost a look of relief on his face.

'Shall I get you a hat or a scarf to cover your face? The reporters might have come back this morning.'

He rolls his eyes and bends down to kiss my cheek.

'No, Mum. See you later.'

He closes the front door carefully; it barely makes a sound.

★ ★ ★

The landline's ringing in the hallway, but the arguing from earlier starts again in the kitchen.

'Shall I get that?' I shout, but no one replies.

I walk towards it, but it stops ringing. I pick up the receiver and press 1471, jotting down the mobile telephone number.

In the kitchen, Mum, Nadia, Emma and Matt are sitting round the table.

'You've missed a call,' I say. 'I wrote the number on your pad.' No one acknowledges me. 'What's going on?'

'Matt, you can't go around questioning people. It's up to us,' says Nadia.

Emma's sitting next to her, cradling a cup of black coffee. Her eyes are barely open, the skin around them puffy.

'What are you talking about, *questioning people*?' I say. 'What's going on?'

Mum's rubbing her temples with her middle fingers.

'Matt wants to question Mr Anderson at the newsagent's.'

'But the police haven't questioned him yet, have they?' he says to Nadia.

'They're not reporting back to *me* with every line of questioning. What they *will* do is let us know if they have any vital information.'

Them and *us*. Nadia chooses her words and allegiances to suit the circumstances.

'That's not enough,' says Matt. 'That man . . . he's only lived here, what . . . three years? What does anyone know about him?'

'We would have searched the premises.'

'Oh, *we* would have, would *we*?' Matt puts on his trainers and stands. 'You can't stop me going for a walk, can you?'

'Of course not,' says Nadia, a lot calmer than I'd be. 'But I will have to call in help if you harass this man.'

Matt walks out of the kitchen.
'Call for fucking help then.'
The front door slams behind him.

16

Maggie

I'm nearly at the newsagent's. I need to see more pictures of her. It's been three days since I last went out. It's not raining, but I'm wearing my mac anyway. I don't know why I didn't look out of the window before I came out. It's sunny, bloody typical. It's never usually warm in October; I'm sweating in this stupid coat.

I shouldn't have come outside. It's making me think too clearly, but I need to see her in black and white, to feel the pictures between my fingers. It's not enough seeing the news on television. I'm getting the sickness again — that's what Sarah used to call it when she was obsessed with a boy at school. She knew it was happening, but couldn't do anything about it. It's how I feel about this; it makes me feel closer to Sarah.

I open the door to the newsagent's.

'Morning, Maggie. Not seen you in — '

'Morning. I've been ill.'

Hopefully my tone will put her off talking to me again.

'Are you okay? You haven't been yourself this past week.'

'How would you know? You haven't seen me for days.'

I wish she'd just shut up.

I pick up three copies of each newspaper,

placing each on the counter as I move along the rack. I've brought my shopping trolley so carrying them home won't be a problem.

'I'm sorry, Maggie. I should have realised. Sandra said you get awfully upset whenever there's a missing child.'

Sandra.

That bloody woman. I'm sure she was put on this earth merely to test my patience — to examine every single movement I make. I can feel it bubbling inside me. The rage is almost at my mouth. I have to stop and breathe before it escapes.

I slam the last three copies of the *Express* onto the counter.

'Just these, Mrs Sharples.'

'I'm sorry. I didn't mean to pry.'

I should have exploded while I had it in me — let her have every angry word I want to throw at the people who live in this village — all their pitying glances, their whispers of *That poor, poor woman, she's got nothing left.* But it would only give them something else to yak about. I've lived with this for too long. Once I let them have it, I'll know that I'll have finally lost it — and I came too close then, far too close. I'll have to keep myself in check.

'How much will that be?'

She pushes the stack of papers towards me.

'You can have them. Please . . . on me . . . no charge.'

Breathe, breathe.

I open my trolley and carefully lay the papers inside. I place the money on the counter.

'I do appreciate that, Mrs Sharples, but I don't accept charity. Never have, never will.'

I turn and pull my trolley.

'Maggie. Please call me . . .'

She doesn't bother to finish her sentence.

★ ★ ★

How has using scissors become so difficult? My stupid hands. It has taken me nearly an hour to cut out twelve pictures. Of course, it didn't help that the photos are so bloody small. The newspapers haven't printed many pictures of Grace Harper's family — they're not as important as the little girl. But they're important to me.

I've placed the grainy black and white ones — most of them duplicates — around the big picture of Sarah in the middle of the coffee table. It's like looking at lots of little Sarahs — the likeness is incredible. Is it the sickness clouding my thoughts — making me see things that aren't there? No. It can't be.

The photo in the middle is the clearest I have of Sarah. We didn't bother taking photographs after Zoe went missing — why would we? There was no happiness in this house after that — no good news to celebrate and document. With each year Zoe was absent, Sarah faded further away. I blamed the booze, but perhaps using drink was how she lasted so long without her daughter.

She only started drinking after Zoe was taken. I don't think she was depressed as such, just so desperately sad. I can't imagine my own child

95

being taken from me like that, the not knowing where she is. It's bad enough when it's your granddaughter — but your very own daughter who'd grown inside you. The thought is horrific.

I get up from the settee, using the coffee table as a crutch. I'm so tired: mind-tired, body-tired. Why am I still living? If I were still a religious person, I'd believe I was being tested, but I left God behind years ago — or did God leave me? I keep wondering what I did so terribly wrong in the past to make everything turn out like this, but I can't think of anything. All those petty little things I made up in confession as a child: thinking bad thoughts about my parents, not helping with chores. Maybe these weren't the sins they were looking for, because now I question my very being. Perhaps I just wasn't good enough as a mother.

In the kitchen, there's a bottle of sherry, half-empty, from a Christmas too long ago. How long does that stuff last? It's behind cans of prunes, peaches, and a little pile of tinned pies. Ron loved those pies, but I can't stand them. I don't know why they're still there. Comforting, I imagine.

The neck of the bottle is crusted. I put it to my nose: it still smells like sherry. It'll be fine. I grab a tiny glass from the cupboard and take it into the front room. I've never been a drinker; never had more than a tot at Christmas. I'm usually in bed by seven — do people drink in the evening to quash the loneliness?

I land further from the table than I thought and have to shuffle with the bottle and glass in my hands. If anyone could see me, they'd think me ridiculous, a lush. The lid grates on the crust as I unscrew it. I hold up the glass after it's filled. It still looks like sherry. It still tastes like sherry — or what I remember sherry to taste like.

It doesn't take long to feel its heat. A fake warmth, but a warmth nonetheless. That's why this stuff is evil. I stroke Sarah's cheek on the photograph. My poor darling girl.

I refill my glass and take another sip. I feel a calm I haven't felt in years. I pick up her photo and hold it to my chest. I close my eyes. I often talk to her in my head. I used to speak out loud in case her spirit, her essence, could hear me, but the silence that followed was too much.

I miss you, Sarah.

That night — that New Year's Eve — I thought you'd turned a corner. Even though your dad, my Ron, had died that August, even though our little Zoe was still out there in the world or worse (we never talked about the worse). But no. It was a show you put on just for me, for one night only.

I hold the picture to my heart as I top my glass up a third time, and lean back into the sofa. New Year's Eve, 1999.

We still had your dad's ashes on the mantelpiece, didn't we? Couldn't bear to see him leave us too. We wanted to know where he was at all times, not to be blown away in the wind. But that's what he wanted, cremation. He didn't want to rot away in the ground. What had he imagined happened to Zoe? He never did talk about it, did he?

You sat in the chair you always sat in, next to the window, but you could see the television. You'd taken up the cigarettes again, but I let you smoke in the house — it was the least I could do. The bottle of vodka was next to you on the little green table, alongside the ashtray and two packets of cigarettes.

'Do you believe in heaven, Mum?' you said.

Not this again, I'd thought. This time though, because it was New Year, I thought I'd humour you.

'You know, perhaps I do. Maybe Dad is waiting for me.'

'Maybe he knows where Zoe is,' you said. 'Maybe he's even *with* Zoe.'

You weren't looking at me; you were watching the telly. A smile slowly spread across your face. 'Wouldn't that be wonderful? If they have each other? They'd be waiting for me. Dad pointing to his watch, frowning and swearing.'

'Don't forget me. I'll be going first,' I said.

I was going to add, *That's the natural order of things*, but something stopped me just in time.

'Those psychics,' you said. 'Some of them said Zoe's still alive, but others believed she's with the angels.' You picked another cigarette from the packet and lit it. 'Which one do you believe?'

You'd never asked me that before. Well, not for years at least, not since she first disappeared. And for years I thought Zoe was just waiting to be found. But the longer it took, the more my hope dimmed.

'I think she's out there somewhere. Waiting for us to find her.'

I couldn't tell you the truth about what I thought.

You sat with your vodka, and it was only when you stubbed out your cigarette did you say, 'Yes. I think you're right. After tonight, I'm going to look for her.'

'What do you mean?' I said. 'Like David is?'

You never replied.

By the next morning I knew what you meant. When I found you on the bed, another bottle of vodka on your bedside cabinet and the empty pill bottles next to your lifeless hands. Your note was simple.

Mum, I'm so sorry. But this is the only way I can think of to find her. I'm sorry for leaving you. I hope you understand.

You were only thirty-seven years old. I will never get over what you did, Sarah. But I know why you did it. If I had the nerve, I would do it too. Perhaps if I drink enough of this sherry I'll put an end to it all.

I can't believe I'm still talking to you, and you're not here.

I refill my glass, again.

17

He keeps ringing my mobile, but I'm ignoring it for now. I know what he'll say, but he'll just have to realise that it's for the best. And when I see her face, it will all be worthwhile. If I have a chance to get back at *her*, then that's fine with me. I dial the number on my mobile and it rings about ten times before she answers.

'Hello?'

That can't be her. She sounds different. Probably got other people in her house.

I hang up.

I should think of the right things to say first. I was stupid for even trying without having prepared something. I'll think about it while I get me and the kid something to eat.

I let her come to the table, but she's not even smiling. You'd have thought she'd be grateful for something to eat.

'Do you want any sauce with that?'

She shakes her head.

'Fair enough.'

She sits there for ages. I hate it when people watch me eat.

She winces when I stab my sausage with the fork. I can't help but laugh. She looks scared shitless.

'Come on, kid. You must be starving. Eat some of your chips. Bought them special for you — and they weren't cheap.'

She grabs her fork and picks up a chip. She turns it round, looking at it as though it might come alive and bite her hand off. She moves it slowly towards her mouth, which she opens as though she's forcing herself to. She chews it and her throat gulps as she swallows, like in cartoons.

'See — that's better, isn't it?'

She nods slowly.

We eat in silence for a few minutes.

She places her fork down — she's only eaten about five chips.

'When are you going to take me to my mum?'

'Not long now, kid.'

I wish she wouldn't ask me questions like this. It's not in my nature to lie.

18

Maggie

My eyes don't want to open. I had it again. I haven't had it for years. Those few moments when nothing was wrong in the world — when it was just me, and nothing bad had happened. Then it came rolling in one by one. Zoe, Ron, Sarah. Given to me, then taken away in a couple of seconds. At least I didn't dream about them. When that happens it's like I've actually been with them again, it makes waking up such a wrench.

My shoulders and neck are stiff from being asleep on the settee, and my mouth is so dry. The sherry. Three glasses and I was drunk. Three glasses and I thought I would die from alcohol poisoning. *Amateur*, Sarah would say. All I've had is an afternoon nap.

'Maggie? Maggie? Why's your back door locked? Are you there, Maggie?'

So that's what woke me. Bloody Jim shouting through the letterbox.

'For God's sake, Jim, stop shouting your mouth off. I'm going to change my name if you keep blaring it out.'

'Sorry, love.' He lowers his voice. 'Thought you might be dead or something.'

'Charming.' I say that, but it's a fair comment: death is usually the reason why a person of our age wouldn't come to the door.

I take a deep breath before getting up. God, my head. I unlock the door and dart my head outside. In the front garden of one of the posh houses opposite, Mrs Cooper is gardening again — are those scissors she's doing her edges with? Mr Austin is buffing his old Citroën, even though he only drives it on a Sunday.

Jim walks in, rubbing his hands like he's arrived from the Arctic.

'I reckon we're in for snow this evening,' he says. 'The clouds look full of it.'

'It's too warm for snow. Stop being so dramatic.'

I follow him through to the living room and he spots the bottle.

'Bloody hell, Mags. Have you been on a bender?'

He laughs.

'Yes, very funny. I just had a thimbleful.' I sound like my mother.

'But you don't drink.'

'Well . . . no. Not usually. I was just toasting Ron's birthday.'

He takes off his cap. 'Right you are.'

Typical. I knew he wouldn't remember when Ron's birthday is. I grab the bottle, take it into the kitchen and pour what's left down the plughole.

'I was in the newsagent's this afternoon,' he calls from the living room. Can he not wait until I'm back in there? Why does he have to shout so much?

'And?' I come back in and sit down in the

armchair. I should offer a brew, but my manners have taken leave.

'Mrs Sharples said — '

'Oh, here we go with the old gossip-mongering. You could tell them anything and they'd believe it.'

'Don't be like that. They care about you, that's all.'

I fold my arms.

'Well, anyway. She said you seemed out of sorts. And I haven't seen you myself in a few days so I've come round to see if you want taking out.'

'Are you going to shoot me?'

'Eh?'

'It was a joke.'

He still looks confused. I don't blame him; I'm not usually one for jesting. I've probably still some sherry in my bloodstream.

'Anyway.' He's rubbing his hands. 'They've got bingo over at the Hills at six. I've ordered a taxi. It'll be here in a few minutes.'

Orange Tree Hill he means — the retirement home in the next village. *Over the Hill*, Ron used to call it.

'That's a bit presumptuous, isn't it?' I say. 'What if I say no?'

He rolls his eyes. 'Then I'll go on my own, won't I? Come on, you used to love bingo.'

He must be getting me mixed up with someone else.

On the coffee table, the little photographs have blown with the draught from the front door. Some have escaped to the floor. What was I thinking?

'Go on then,' I say. 'Wait while I put on my face and my coat.'

Yes, that sherry must still be working.

* * *

I'm in the bathroom, dabbing my face with powder, when the phone rings.

'I'll get it. You get yourself ready,' Jim shouts.

A bit of blusher and a touch of lipstick. I look at myself in the mirror. I've not worn make-up in ages. I peer closer. How long have I looked so old? My eyes are the same, but those wrinkles . . . I zip up my cosmetic case. Bother it. No one looks at me now anyway.

Jim's waiting for me at the bottom of the stairs.

'What's with your face?' I say. 'You haven't seen my resident ghost, have you?'

'No, Maggie.' He's not even smiling. 'I picked up the phone and he started talking before I could say hello.'

'He? Who's *he*? What did he say?'

'I don't know what he meant.'

'Spit it out, Jim. What on earth did this man say?'

'He said . . . *Maggie, it's me. I did it for you.*'

19

Stephanie

Matt managed to talk to Mr Anderson for a few minutes before the police escorted him out of the newsagent's. Apparently, he remembered a man with a hat coming into the shop shortly before Grace, but didn't see either of them leave. How could it be possible not to notice? It's such a small shop.

The police left ten minutes ago, with a warning to Matt to leave the investigating to them.

'I can't believe you went storming in there,' says Mum.

'What do you care, Milly?' Matt's shouting again. 'You don't even know him — how many times have you been in that shop? He's a quiet one, but it's always the quiet ones, isn't it?'

'You can't go accusing innocent people. Who's next? The milkman?'

'There isn't even a milkman round here any more.' He walks closer to Mum and my heart is beating through my jumper. 'Grace was last seen in that shop, walking out with a man. How can both of them have avoided CCTV *in* the shop?'

'The CCTV was only on the till.' My voice is so quiet.

'Oh, really?' Matt says it accusingly.

'Yes.'

'Right, well.' He waves his arms about, walking up and down the length of the room and sits heavily into the sofa. 'We've had no news. I just wanted to do something.' He puts his head in his hands. 'Oh God. What have I done?'

Emma gets up, looks at him and walks out of the room. It's Mum who goes to him, sits down and puts a hand on his.

'There, there. You did what you thought was right at the time. Don't think about it any more.'

She's touching his head now. What the hell is she doing? It's like she doesn't know how to comfort him. She never was the most maternal of mothers. I've often questioned in my mind why she had me, and took Emma in, when she's not really that bothered about us at all. She's always been preoccupied with something else.

At least Emma and I had each other. We started high school together. A new town and new school. Mum had let us go into town to pick our own uniforms. I wouldn't have let Jamie into town that young, but perhaps that's the way the world is now — or maybe it's just me. There are a lot of things Mum did or didn't do with us that I vowed I'd do differently when I became a mother myself.

She wasn't happy, of course, when we came back from our shopping expedition.

'Pink skiing jackets? Pink? Since when do you ski at school?'

'It's the fashion,' said Emma. 'They had all sorts of ski jackets in C&A — white ones, yellow ones. We picked the less obvious colour.'

Mum folded her arms. 'Hmm.'

107

I smiled at Emma in thanks. Mum wouldn't have been placated so easily if I had said it.

'What do we have here, then?' It was Dad, climbing through the patio doors after *mending* in his shed. 'A pair of Anneka Rices, I do believe.'

'Is that slang for something?' Mum said.

'No.' He walked towards us, taking off his glasses. 'They'll certainly notice you two at school next week.' He was still chuckling as he walked into the kitchen. Emma and I looked at each other, and laughed all the way up the stairs.

He was right, Dad. They did notice us at school. Mum and Dad had changed Emma's surname by then, so we were both Atkinsons. The same name, the same age — we told everyone we were twins. 'Not identical, obviously,' Emma would say before anyone would mention the fact that she was at least six inches shorter than me. Actually, thinking about it now, I'm not sure if we ever confessed that we *weren't* twins.

'What are you smiling about?' Mum hisses to me.

'Just remembering,' I say.

'Remembering what?'

She's looking at my face so intently, I daren't tell her the truth.

'About Grace of course.'

'Well make yourself useful and get a cup of tea for Matt. Poor man's in bits.'

She says this even though he's right next to her. I thought at a time like this, Mum would be kinder, softer. But she's being worse to me than she's ever been. What have I done that's so bad?

I get up to go to the kitchen, but the phone rings in the hall.

Mum gestures for me to get it, like I'm her own personal housekeeper.

'Hello?'

There's no answer.

'Hello?' I repeat. But whoever it is has already hung up.

The banging on the front door makes me jump. The smell of fresh air hits me first, then the sound of heels on the laminate hallway, the bustle of long coats as they pass in front of me. DI Hines and DS Berry dominate the sitting room as they stand in the middle of it.

Mum gets up and stands at the bottom of the stairs as she shouts for Emma to come down.

My heart's thumping. Are they not speaking to us until Emma gets here? Their expressions are neutral. DS Berry holds a folder, which is black and thin. What have they got in there? What have they found? My legs are starting to shake. The detectives stand aside to let Emma further into the room.

'What is it?' she says. 'Have you found Grace?'

Detective Hines puts a hand up. 'No, no. We haven't found Grace.'

Emma breathes in and out, loudly and quickly. 'Oh God.' In, out, in out. 'When I saw you both standing there . . . ' She's hyperventilating. I put my arm around her and sit her on her chair. 'Steph, I thought they were going to tell me — '

'I know, Em. I know.'

My heart is still beating so hard; I'm surprised

it hasn't jumped out of its place.

'We have another CCTV image,' says Hines, 'that we've been able to enhance. We can see their faces now.'

Emma stands straight up. 'Give it to me.'

Rachel Berry opens her folder and hands over one of the copies, and another to Matt who's been quiet since they arrived. Emma holds the image inches from her face. The tears gather in her eyes before rushing down her cheeks. She strokes the piece of paper.

'Oh, Grace, my baby. Where are you?'

I daren't look.

But I have to.

It really is Grace.

I want to sink to the floor and cradle the picture in my arms.

I thought it would be grainy — that we'd think it looks a little like Grace, that it could be another child, but not this. It *is* her — in different clothes: dark trousers and a large hooded coat. Her face is so clear, but all of her hair has been taken up — or been cut — underneath a black hat. This was why they thought it might have been a boy in the first image.

Matt is holding the piece of paper in front of him, but the other hand is over his eyes as he sobs silently.

'Let me see her,' says Mum, the other side of Emma. 'Oh my God. It's Grace.' She covers her mouth with a hand.

'Do any of you recognise the man holding Grace's hand?' says Detective Hines.

Holding her hand? I hadn't noticed — I

hadn't even looked at the man.

'Why is Grace smiling?' says Matt.

It's like we're all looking at the photo for the first time again without our blinkers on. She *is* smiling — how had I not seen that?

'But the man — do you recognise him?' The detective sounds impatient.

Mum takes the photo from Emma, and looks at it closely. She narrows her eyes, shaking her head. 'I don't think so.'

'Emma, Matt,' says Hines. 'Is he familiar to you?'

'I've never seen him before,' says Matt.

'Not even with work? Could he be a client of yours?'

'We only meet clients briefly, but I've definitely never met him before, I'd remember.'

The detective turns to Emma and me. Mum passes the paper back to us and we stand, heads together, as we look at it.

'I think I have,' I say. 'He looks familiar, but I can't remember where from.' I look to Emma, and I don't know why I feel scared, but I do. 'Em?'

She nods her head imperceptibly. Her eyes are wide and her face is pale. The paper starts to ripple as her hands shake. 'Yes. I have seen him before. He was at the office a few weeks ago. I work as an accounts assistant at a recruitment firm. Oh God. I might have even spoken to him.' She's starting to panic again. Mum takes her to sit down.

'What was he doing at your workplace?' asks Hines.

'He said he was there for a job. We advertise for temps for local businesses ... drivers, warehouse assistants, waiting staff, that sort of thing. We must interview at least twenty people a week, but he seemed different; he wore a suit — dark green, old-fashioned. He was a bit cold — stared at me. I couldn't look him in the eye properly.'

Emma gives the details to the detectives and I walk slowly into the kitchen. If she knows him from work, then where the hell do *I* know him from?

20

Maggie

'We should telephone the police,' says Jim.

The taxi driver looks at us in the rear-view mirror. I bet he's listening to every word. He should keep an eye on the road — there's sleet coming down hard. I'm surprised he can see out of the windscreen, the speed he has those wipers going.

'What would we say, that some idiot has the wrong number, talking gibberish?'

'But he said your name, Maggie.'

'That's what *you* say. I didn't hear for myself. Did you have your hearing aid in?'

'You know I don't wear a hearing aid. Stop being so flippant. Are you not worried?'

'It'll be something or nothing. I'm not worried at all.'

Of course, that's not true. I've been wracking my brain to think who it could be. A man who knows my telephone number, who knows my name. Ron's brother? I haven't heard from Alan since Ron died and he wouldn't telephone me with such a strange message. Could it be Zoe's dad, David? No, it won't be. He couldn't wait to remove himself from our family. Only waited three years after Zoe went before leaving Sarah for good, the coward. The deserter who shacked himself him up with a new family — three kids, I

113

heard. He should be ashamed of himself.

'Keep the change, mate,' says Jim, handing over a five-pound note. The fare was four pounds seventy-three pence. Last of the big spenders. I put my hand in my pocket and give the driver a pound coin before following Jim out of the car.

'I've got my lucky socks on,' he says. 'Come on. Let's get you out of the cold.'

'I'm not that cold.' There's a blast of warm air as we walk through the door. The place smells of roast dinners. 'How did he say it?'

'How did who say what?' Jim turns round and looks at me funny. Ron always complained that I could continue a conversation three days after it finished.

'On the phone. Was it a menacing *I did it for you*, or a kind *I did it for you?*'

'Don't give up your day job, Mags.' He holds the door open for me, and almost pushes me into a communal lounge. All these years it's been here and it's the first time I've stepped inside the place. 'I suppose it was kinder than not. I didn't feel threatened by it. It was just . . . what's the word . . . perplexing — the way he just hung up.'

'Are you sure it was a man?'

'I may be a bit daft, but I'm not stupid. It was definitely a man.'

'Did he sound old or young?'

'I don't know — I can't tell a person's age from their telephone voice. Anyway — you're probably right — it'll be nothing to worry about.' He's trying to make me feel better, but his smile isn't reflected in his eyes. He takes out his wallet. 'I'll get our bingo cards. You sit yourself down

114

here,' he pulls out a chair at the nearest empty table to us, 'and we can at least *try* to forget about the phone call for a few hours. After that, we can figure out what to do about it.'

I sit where I'm told to, while he wanders over to a man of about fifty standing behind a table with a bingo machine on it. Around me, residents are sitting in groups at various-sized tables. It's the quietest bingo 'hall' I've ever been to — though I've not been to many, contrary to what Jim seems to think.

The table next to ours is far too close for my liking, but I suppose I don't have to talk to them.

'Have you been here before?' I whisper to Jim. He sits down, placing eight A4-sized bingo cards in front of us. They're for the partially sighted I imagine, though I could probably read the numbers from outside.

'Welcome to bingo at Orange Tree Hill!' The booming voice makes me jump. 'And let's get this show on the road. Are you ready?' There's silence. 'I said, *are you ready?*'

'Get on with it, lad,' shouts Jim.

My face flushes as the few people who heard Jim turn to look at us. I want the ground to swallow me up.

'Right we are then! Dabbers at the ready. Two fat ladies, eighty-eight.'

As the man announces the numbers — and he can't even do *that* properly — I can't shake the feeling that someone's looking at me. As I cross my numbers out, I glance around the room.

A lady next to us, wearing a pastel blue fine-knit, waves her ticket in the air.

115

'I think I have a line.'

'Give it here,' says the man next to her. He picks up a magnifying glass and squints as he scrutinises the ticket. 'You've only got three numbers — at the very maximum — on any one line, Eileen,' he says. 'You need five in a row to shout *house*. Do we really have to do this at every third number he shouts out?'

'But you know my eyes are bad,' she says.

'Well, you shouldn't play if your eyes are that bad. How can anyone else enjoy it if we're interrupted every two minutes?'

'Eh, Jack, leave Eileen alone,' says another woman. 'Let her have her fun. You never know, she might be dead tomorrow.'

Oh God, this evening is going to drag. Why do they have to talk so loudly? I must have a bad head from that sherry earlier. Someone shoot me now and put me out of my misery.

'I said, how's your card looking?' shouts Jim.

'Did you?' I look down. 'Fine.'

I glance towards the door and spot the eyes that have been staring at me on and off since we got here. I look back at my bingo card, but I can still see her from the corner of my eye. She's not as old as the residents — younger than Jim and me too. She must be a visitor. Although she's sitting on her own, with playing cards or something laid on the table in front of her. Perhaps she's with the bingo caller.

'Here, let me take over, Maggie. You're too slow.'

Jim takes control of my numbers; I can't concentrate. I keep thinking about the man on

116

the phone. Sitting here in the warmth, amongst people I don't have to talk to, I feel safe. I almost don't want to leave and be alone in my house — the home I've lived in for nearly sixty years. I don't feel confident about answering the telephone any more. I can't think about it.

'Come on,' says Jim. 'Shout bingo!'

'What?'

'You've won, love.' Jim's almost jumping up and down in his seat. He grabs my hand, lifts it and waves it in the air. 'Bingo! Over here.'

'Oh, Jim, just pretend it's yours. Please.'

'Don't be daft, you've won fifty quid.'

The man from the front jogs slowly to reach our table and checks my ticket.

'Congratulations, my lovely,' he says, almost shouting. Does he think I'm deaf? 'If you'd like to take your ticket to my dear wife over there.' He points to the lone woman at the table of playing cards. 'Don't worry,' he leans closer and winks, 'she's not as scary as she looks.'

He jogs back over to the front.

'Well done there, Mags,' says Jim, grinning to his ears.

'It's not like I've won *Mastermind*.'

'Don't rain on it. Fifty quid's fifty quid.'

'Will you get it for me? I'll split it with you.'

'Tell you what . . . we've got three games left . . . I'll come with you after it's finished.'

'Thanks, Jim.'

The bingo restarts, but I still can't concentrate. Without saying, Jim has taken over my next card. I look at him from the corner of my eye. He never was a looker, bless him, but he looks better now he's older. What's it they say about growing into your face? It must be the case with Jim. I think about what's happened over the last couple of days and I don't know what I'd have done without him.

'Come on then, let's get your winnings,' he says.

'They can't have played three games already.'

'They have indeed. You're away with the fairies. But I don't blame you. You've enough on your plate.'

Jim's up and ready in seconds. He kept his coat on the whole time we've been here. He must have cold bones these days. He stands waiting, patiently. I know I'm being slow, but there's something about that woman that unnerves me. I'm in no rush to get to her.

He almost drags me there; my feet are so heavy. She watches us while we walk and stands when we reach the table.

'It's nice to see you, Maggie.'

She holds out her hand. I've never seen her before in my life. Her hair is too dark for her age; she must dye it — there's not a grey in sight. She's wearing a velvet blouse in maroon that reminds me of my great-grandmother's curtains.

'Do you two know each other?' asks Jim.

'I've never met you before,' I say to her.

'Sorry about that, love,' Jim says to the stranger. 'Not one for niceties, isn't Mags.'

'That's okay. Sorry,' she says. 'I could've sworn we'd met before.'

She sits back down. I look at the table and what I thought were playing cards have strange pictures on them, rimmed with gold.

'I'll just get your prize ready.'

She counts out five ten-pound notes and puts them in an envelope. Before she seals it, she puts in what looks like a business card. She looks up. 'Just in case you need to contact me.'

I've never heard anything so ridiculous. Why would I need to contact *her*?

Jim rubs his hands, again. 'I'm just off to the gents while we wait for the taxi. Won't be a min.'

I want to follow him, but that would be a little undignified.

'I'll wait in reception,' I say, trying not to look at her.

I only get a few feet away when I feel a hand grab my elbow.

'Wait, Maggie.'

I turn slowly, knowing it's her. 'How do you know my name?'

She glances at the floor, before looking me straight in the eye.

'I'm sorry,' she says. 'My name's Dee. I remember you from years ago. When your poor granddaughter went missing.'

'Right.'

I don't know why I didn't think of that before, but strangers haven't approached me for years. I knew they meant well, but it was mortifying, heartbreaking. It was why we hardly went out.

'I'd better be going,' I say.

'Maggie, please wait a minute.'

'Hang on. Why do you keep calling me Maggie? I was always Margaret in the newspapers.'

She comes closer to me; I step back.

'I know you probably think I'm insane — I get that a lot. But . . . ' She takes a few breaths and taps her chest. 'Zoe's still alive.'

21

We've been driving for days and days. It might even be weeks. I haven't been home for a long, long time. We had dinner at a café on the *autobahn:* sausages and chips, or *bratties und frits* — that's what George called them to the man behind the counter.

'Not long now, kid,' he said. 'Should be there in an hour.'

'Be where?'

He tapped his nose with his fork. 'You'll see.'

'Is it somewhere scary?'

He almost choked on a frit. 'Course it's not. Lovely people. Probably.'

He wiped his mouth with the paper towel, and that was the end of our meal. There was another girl with a man sitting at the table near the window. He was probably her daddy. She kept looking at me, but I pretended I didn't see as I'm not to look at anyone any more. There were lots of people around. I should have shouted or screamed, or asked someone where my mummy is. I wasn't very brave at all.

I don't know how long it's been since we were at the café, nearly three hours I think. Or was it yesterday? I can't tell if I've been asleep or not. I don't want to get to where we're supposed to be going, but I don't want to stay with George either. At least I know he won't hurt me — not without me doing something to make him upset anyway, and I'm trying really hard to be good.

'Almost there, kidder.'

I don't think he knows my name — he hasn't used it yet. I'm not sure if he knows my mummy either. If he did, he'd have let me talk to her by now. She gets worried if I'm quiet upstairs for too long. She's going to be really worried now I'm not even in the house. I can't remember our telephone number, not in the right order.

Lovely people, he said. If these people *are* nice then I can ask *them* when I'm going to see Mummy again. I clasp my hands like Gran does and whisper a prayer. *Please, God. Make these people kind. Please get me to my mummy soon.*

★ ★ ★

We're slowing down and George has a giant map on the steering wheel. I hope we don't crash.

'Bloody German streets,' he says, but they look like any other street I've ever been on.

It takes a few minutes, but we're near another border — with a barrier this time. It seems to go on for miles and miles. Behind the gate are loads of houses that all look the same — little grey boxes in rows.

He drives round the corner, so we can't see them any more, and opens the passenger door.

'Right, kid. You need to trust me on this one. Another game. Have you ever been in the boot of a car?'

I shake my head. I've never heard of *getting in the boot of a car*. It doesn't sound very fun.

He flicks his head: this means I have to get out

of the car. I do, and he crouches down in front of me. 'You need to be really brave now, okay? I'm going to put you in a bag, then put you in the boot of the car — but it will only be for five minutes tops. Okay?'

I nod my head, but inside it, my brain is shouting, *No, it's not okay — I can't get in the back of a car — I'm too big to be in a bag.*

He opens the boot. I look round, but there's no one here. He knows that, doesn't he? He pulls out a light blue suitcase, lays it on the floor and unzips it.

'Come on.'

I stand in the case and look up into the sky. The clouds are fluffy here — there aren't many of them. It's always cloudy where I live — it's always raining. I keep the picture of it in my mind as I lie down, just in case I never see sky again.

22

Maggie

'What did that woman say to you?' says Jim as we head off in the taxi back home. 'I've never seen you look so angry.'

'Nothing important. What is it with some people? They think they know everything about you, about your family, but they've never met you. It's ridiculous. People like that should be arrested for the hurt they cause. I've a right mind to call the police.'

Over the years, we had at least twenty mediums telling us that Zoe was alive, but over thirty said that Zoe was dead or *no longer with this world*. I don't know what makes them think they can just come out and say whatever they like to someone they've never met.

When the first medium approached us, it offered us hope — that somewhere out there, Zoe was waiting for us to come and find her. *I see her with a man*, she'd said. We'd invited her round to the house after she'd sent us letter after letter. She was an older lady — in her sixties I think. Old enough to know better. *I see her in the country — in a house, with a grandmother figure.* Sarah had been desperate enough to believe that the first time. The police, however, were less convinced.

'We don't deal with mediums,' Detective

Jackson said. 'There's not enough proof that they work. Every one we've encountered contradicts another. They've never been right in any of my investigations.'

'But what if he's wrong?' Sarah said later. 'He can't possibly know every tip-off in the history of police work. What about other regions — what about other countries?'

'He might be wrong,' I said. 'But we can't travel to every house in the countryside on the off chance Zoe's there.' I felt heartless for saying it.

I didn't intercept the next letter quickly enough when it arrived. It was six months after Zoe went missing. I came downstairs to find Sarah sitting on the hallway floor, in streams of tears, holding the piece of paper.

'He says Zoe's dead . . . says she's with her grandfather.'

I knelt on the floor next to her.

'He's talking rubbish, love.' I stroked her hair. 'Both her grandfathers are still alive.'

'But what if he means great-grandfather?'

I took the letter from her. I remember the words to this day.

Dear Sarah,

I am sorry, but I feel compelled to write this letter. I have tried to get in contact with you, but the police would not supply me with your contact details.

I feel like I know you so well — Zoe has told me so much about you. Forgive me for saying that straight away, and I write this with a heavy heart, but Zoe wants you to know that she is on the other side, and that you don't have to worry about her any longer. She has her grandfather with her, taking good care of her.

'Till we meet again, Mum,' Zoe says.

If you would like a further reading from me, please find my contact details below.

Love and peace,

Brian Tadcaster (Registered Medium)

As soon as I read it, I tore it up into tiny pieces.

'Registered Medium, like hell he is — I'll bet there's no such thing.' The pieces dropped to the floor, and I put my arm around Sarah's shoulders. 'Love, Zoe never calls you *Mum* — she always, always calls you Mummy.'

She wiped her face with both palms. 'She does.' She used me as a crutch to push herself up from the hall floor, and held out her hand to me. 'Come on, Mum. Let's get a cup of tea.'

I'll always remember her pulling me up from the floor that day. I feel like she's doing that now, from wherever she is. I know that's a contradiction, given the experience of mediums we've had so far.

'Are you crying, Maggie?'

It's Jim. Why is he noticing things he should ignore?

'Course not. It's from the wind before. And stop staring at me, will you?'

He rolls his eyes and shrugs. Poor man. I don't know why he keeps coming back for more.

When the taxi's gone, he walks me to my gate.

I can see them from here, even though the sun has almost set, and my doorway is in semi-darkness.

'What the . . . ' says Jim. 'Is it your birthday and you haven't told me?'

'I don't *think* it is.'

I daren't walk up to them. My feet are frozen to the path. It's not the most attractive bunch of flowers I've ever seen: yellow carnations and orange lilies.

Jim gently pushes me aside. 'There's a card. Do you want me to have a look?'

'I don't know.'

He's already bent over. He grabs the card.

'Shall I open it?'

My mouth is open, but no sound comes out. I walk slowly to the front door. Jim's still bent over, rubbing his back. 'Bloody hell, I hate getting old.'

I open the front door. 'Let's get in. And mind your language.'

We leave the flowers on the doorstep and I close the door behind us.

'I'll put the kettle on. I'll make you up a hot-water bottle for your back.'

'Thanks, Mags.' He stands next to the settee. 'If I sit down there, I doubt I'll be able to get back up.'

'I'll get you a chair from the kitchen.'

I walk as slowly as I can. I don't want to know what's written on that card. Whoever left it was actually here, at my door. Interflora doesn't leave orders on the doorstep — anyone could pinch them. My hands are shaking as I flick the kettle on. I rub them together in the hope the warmth stops my jitters.

'Won't be a sec with your chair, Jim.'

'Right you are, Maggie.'

He's always so polite is Jim; he wouldn't hurt a fly. Which is a bit of a problem. What if someone's watching me and wants to hurt me?

I drag the chair through to the living room, and grab Jim by his elbow.

'Eh,' he says, 'I never thought that in my life I'd be helped to sit by an old lady.'

'Less of the cheek.'

If I wasn't feeling so out of sorts, I'd have shoved him right off the bloody chair.

After he settles, he picks at the envelope, his hands shaking.

'I think you'll have to do this,' he says. 'Damn hands. I think my body's giving up on me.'

I take the envelope from him.

'Give over. Stop being so melodramatic.'

'I'm not.'

I get my glasses from the mantelpiece, and glance at the photograph facing the wall. If Jim has ever been curious about it, he's never mentioned it. Perhaps he's had a peek when I'm not looking.

I perch on the settee I take the card from the envelope. There's no picture, just a handwritten message. I read it out to Jim.

'*I've got a surprise for you, Maggie.*'

It gives me the shivers.

We sit in silence.

'Why didn't they just knock at the door?' says

Jim after a few minutes. 'Speak to you face to face without all of these silly games.'

I get up and walk to the window and look through the net curtains. I scan the street, but there's nothing unusual. There's my neighbour, John, having a smoke in the front yard — showing up our side of the road as usual. I daren't ask him if he saw who delivered the flowers; I don't want him asking questions.

'Is anyone outside in a mac and balaclava?' asks Jim, his shoulders shaking at his own joke.

'You laugh now, but someone might be out to harm me.'

'Then why don't you call the police if you're that worried? Who can you be so scared of to get you into this sort of state? Is it Sarah's partner — David, was it? Could it be him?'

'He was her husband. He was a bit . . . how should I say it . . . sensitive. I don't think he'd try to intimidate me. I've not wronged him.'

'Then who have you upset?'

'What do you mean?'

'You said you haven't wronged him. That implies you've offended someone else.'

I look at the ordinariness of goings-on outside my front door. Why couldn't I have had all of that? I'm too old for all this nonsense.

'Yes,' I say, walking to the mantelpiece. I grab the photograph that I haven't looked at for years, and hand it to Jim. 'I have. My son, Scott.'

23

Stephanie

It's getting too claustrophobic in Emma and Matt's house. I miss my home and it being just Jamie and me. I didn't get out of the car when I dropped Jamie off at Neil's. I wasn't in the mood for talking about Grace when he plainly doesn't give a shit — even though he's known her since she was born. Besides that, I didn't feel like seeing Joanna swanning around on their white carpets, with red toenails and silk nightgown. She probably wasn't wearing that at all, but that's how I always imagine her. I waited until Jamie was safely behind their closed door before I set off. At least Neil had agreed to have Jamie for a few days, so I don't have to worry about him being in such an oppressive atmosphere. I didn't want to come back inside Emma and Matt's myself — it was a wrench getting out of my car after a few minutes of freedom.

Mum's in the kitchen, heating up a lasagne one of the neighbours brought round. I'm not usually one for food when I don't know the source, so I'm already anxious about that. Why am I nervous about the stupid little things? I'm trying not to think of Grace. Has she eaten? Is she happy? Who's looking after her? The man in the CCTV photograph with Grace doesn't seem the fatherly type — but what is that anyway? I still can't think where I've seen him before. His face looked so familiar, but in the way someone on television would. I close my eyes and I can still picture his face in my mind, but there's no context — no surroundings, no one with him.

Oh God, it's too much. How could someone take a child? There's something wrong with them.

'Washing,' says Emma, breaking the silence. 'I need to do her washing. I can't have her coming back to a mess. Grace wouldn't want to stay if her room was a shithole, would she?'

She walks out of the sitting room and up the stairs.

Neither Mum nor Matt attempts to follow her.

'I'll go.' I try to walk but sprint up the stairs. I don't know what's going through her mind. I can't know what she's thinking; how can anyone unless they've been in this situation?

She's transferring clothes from Grace's laundry basket and floor into another basket. She's doing it so fast it's as though she's possessed.

'Emma, wait a second.'

She doesn't stop.

'Emma.' I walk round Grace's bed, grabbing hold of the basket in Emma's arms.

'What are you doing?' she says. 'I've got to do it — to make it nice for her.'

I pull the basket towards me. 'You can do it tomorrow. You need to rest.'

She's tugging it back. 'Rest? How can I rest? This is something I can do for when she gets back.'

'I know, but I don't think now is the right time.'

'Why? What else can I do? The police have already searched her room — they've tainted it. They've looked through every single thing that she has. How would she feel about that? She'd be mortified. Not even *I* have looked in her diary, yet they've taken it. They've taken pictures off the photo collage on the wall — they've taken her comb for samples of her hair, her skin — they've taken her toothbrush. It's like she's not mine any more — she's everyone else's. And I don't know what to do to change that. I don't know what to think. I don't know what to do.' She sits down on Grace's bed. 'I don't know where she is.' Tears are streaming down her face. 'I want her to tell me what to do.'

'But washing these . . . '

'What?' She leans closer to me, her eyes searching my face. 'You think she's dead, don't you?'

'I never said that.'

'You don't need to. Why else would you say to leave her things? Unless . . . ' She stands up and tips Grace's clothes onto the floor. 'Unless you think *I* did something to her.'

I stand up quickly. 'Of course I don't think that. How could you — '

'No, how could *you*?'

'What's all the noise — why are you shouting?' Matt's standing at the doorway.

'Stephanie thinks I shouldn't wash Grace's clothes because she thinks she's dead!'

'I never said that, Matt. I just said that maybe

132

she shouldn't be washing her clothes . . . '

Matt strides over, picking up Grace's things and putting them back into her laundry basket. 'What are you thinking, Emma? Just leave them.'

Emma puts her hands on her hips. 'Well I should have realised you'd side with her. I should have bloody known.' She turns to me. 'You want everything I have, don't you?'

'What? No. What are you talking about?'

'Why don't you get your own boyfriend, eh? Instead of fawning over my husband?'

'Emma!' Matt shouts. 'You're talking shit now.'

'What the hell is going on?'

Great. Now Mum's come to give her two pennies' worth.

'Steph and Matt are ganging up on me as usual.' Emma's shouting, her face is red and her eyes are wide. 'I just wanted to wash Grace's things.'

'You wanted to wash them?'

'Oh, not you as well. So none of you think she's coming back? How could you think that?' She collapses to the floor.

'Oh, Emma.' Mum puts her arms around her shoulders and guides her up. As they walk slowly out of the room, Mum says, 'I'll get you one of my Valium. You need to get some sleep. You're so tired you can't think straight.'

Matt and I watch them leave in silence. I try to suppress my sniff so as not to draw attention to my tears. Where had all that venom come from? Does Emma really think that of me? We walk out

133

of Grace's room to go downstairs just as Mum is leading Emma into her bedroom.

Since when did Mum take Valium?

* * *

The first time I met Matt was when Emma brought him home to meet Mum and Dad in 1998. We were in our second year of college and it was the start of Emma and I doing our own thing. After being nearly inseparable until we were seventeen, it had been a shock when Emma started to distance herself from me. The school friends I had pushed aside in favour of my sister hadn't wanted to know me any more. I had to make new friends, while Emma spent all her time with her new boyfriend.

'Matt's coming round tonight,' she'd said, coming into my bedroom. She was wearing a long jumper over a flowing green skirt, with cherry-red Doc Martens — trying to appear arty probably. She'd met him in her ceramics class. 'Try and be nice, won't you?'

'Course I'll be nice,' I said. 'I'm a delight.'

She looked at my vest top and tracksuit bottoms.

'You're not wearing *that*, are you?' she said.

I shrugged. 'Yeah. I'm not leaving the house, am I?'

She tutted, rolled her eyes and flounced off.

We'd just finished supper when the doorbell went, and Emma rushed to the door. She was beaming when she brought him through to the kitchen. Of course, I recognised him from

134

college, but had barely spoken to him — she had her friends, I had mine.

Matt was so confident, even then. 'Hi, Steph,' he said, as though he'd known me for years.

Dad got up and shook Matt's hand; he was always so proper and polite.

'So what are your intentions with my daughter?' he said.

Matt's eyes widened. 'Umm.'

Dad laughed.

'Don't worry, Matthew. I'm just joshing with you.' He stood there, his hands clasped behind his back. He was always slightly awkward in front of our friends — as though he should think of something witty to say.

'So, love,' Dad said to Mum. 'Shall we leave these young people to it?'

'But we were about to have dessert,' she said. 'Matt, would you join us? We have plenty.'

'Mum!' Emma's eyes almost bulged out of their sockets. I was surprised she didn't drag the two of them out of the room. 'You promised . . .'

'Did we?' said Mum.

'You know very well we did,' said Dad. He opened the fridge door and brought out the cheesecake. 'We said we'd give them privacy in exchange for them doing the washing up. And because we're being evicted, we get to eat the whole cake.'

'But I couldn't possibly eat half of that,' said Mum.

'Course you could,' said Dad, winking at us as he closed the kitchen door.

'God, he's so embarrassing,' said Emma.

'No, he's not,' I said.

As soon as I started the washing up, Emma had appeared at my shoulder and whispered, 'I'm just going to make myself look beautiful. You don't mind, do you?'

'Of course not.'

I did.

But only until Matt joined me at the sink. He stood so near to me, it was as though I could feel him if I closed my eyes. He grabbed a tea towel and waited as I scrubbed a pan with a Brillo pad. I'd never looked closely at his face before; I'd only ever seen him at a distance. He had little freckles on his nose and on the top of his cheeks. His eyelashes were the longest I'd seen on a boy — not that I'd seen many close-up. I hadn't been on a date since high school. A late bloomer, Dad called me.

'I can't believe you two are sisters,' said Matt, catching me staring at him. 'You couldn't look more different. You, tall with blonde hair, and Emma — she's what? At least five inches shorter than you with dark brown hair. It's crazy.'

Matt took the pan from my hands, my face burning with embarrassment. He didn't look as though he was joking.

'She's six inches shorter than me,' I said. We'd measured our differences for years. 'But she's not really my sister though. You do know that?'

He looked up, startled. Then a grin slowly appeared with a twinkle in his eyes. He playfully slapped my arm with the tea towel. 'Yeah, good one. You almost had me there. Though, no

136

offence — you do look totally different. Did your milkman have dark hair?'

It was then that I realised that Emma might not remember as much as I do. But surely she was old enough to? Perhaps she blocked everything out. It's not the sort of thing you start discussing when it's not been mentioned since she came to live with us so long ago. I'd always assumed she'd told Matt everything — but she didn't, not for ages. I left it when we were teenagers, assumed that Emma would tell him in her own time. It was only a few weeks ago that I realised she hadn't told him the whole truth.

I first brought up the subject of Emma's biological mother to Matt when we were both drunk together last month. I shouldn't have — it was one of those late nights when daylight is emerging and the birds start to sing.

I just wanted to know if Emma had ever mentioned any details. I only remember bits of the conversation. Jamie was at his dad's and Emma had gone to bed. Matt and I were sitting cross-legged on the floor in front of the fire — looking at stupid YouTube videos of dancing cats, our tongues loose after drinking too much wine.

'Has Emma ever tried to find her real mother?' I said. 'She must remember bits about her.'

I don't know what made me just blurt it out like that.

'Eh?' said Matt, squinting like he always does when he's had too much to drink.

'Doesn't matter.'

I flapped my hand, trying to make the words disappear into the air.

'What do you mean, remember?' He swayed slightly. 'She can't know anything about her birth mother, can she? Emma was only a baby when your parents adopted her.'

I looked at my hands. Why had I said anything? It wasn't my place to tell him anything so important. It was up to Emma to decide what she told people about her past.

'Steph?'

I looked up. 'What?'

'I said, how old was Emma when she came to live with you?'

'Did you?' I was stalling for time. Could I take it back, say I didn't mean it? 'You should talk to Emma about it. It's not for me to say.'

He leaned closer, his hands in fists on the carpet.

'Just answer the question.'

His eyes were wide and fixed on mine. He wasn't going to let it go.

'Okay. But please don't tell her I told you,' I said. 'She was ten years old.'

He pulled away, falling back against the chair behind him like he'd been punched in the stomach. He looked into the fire, frowning.

'Why wouldn't she tell me that? She told me it was at birth. That she never knew her real mum.'

'I don't know,' I said. 'From what I remember, her mother didn't treat her very well — perhaps Emma didn't want to upset you. She might think you'd feel differently towards her.'

The memory of that night jumps to Matt and

me going onto the missing person's website.

I shouldn't mix with people when I've had a drink — I don't know what I was thinking. I felt such shame when I remembered the following morning.

'Is that okay, Steph?' Mum's standing behind a chair at the kitchen table opposite me. Emma's upstairs, still asleep. Her voice jumps me back into the present. Mum, Matt and I have just finished a meal of reheated lasagne from one of the more 'trusted' donations. I should keep my mind in the here and now and not keep drifting off into the past.

'Pardon?' I say.

'Daydreaming again, are you?' Mum looks so tired. She smiles at me. 'I said I've ordered a taxi. I'll spend the night at home and be back in the morning.' She walks over to me, brushes a strand of hair from my face and tucks it behind my ear. 'My beautiful girl. Always so strong.' She bends over and kisses my cheek. 'Night, love.'

When she leaves, Matt shakes his head. 'She's certainly unpredictable, your mum. I don't know how you deal with her being so contrary all the time. One minute she's snapping at you, the next she's sticking up for you.'

I don't say that his behaviour towards me has been the same.

'It's always been like that between Mum and me. I can't remember when it started — it might've always been this way. It's like we couldn't get along — I felt she was always disappointed with me just being myself. She's worse now that Dad's not here, though. He always stuck up for me.' I look down at my hands. 'Not that I need someone to protect me now — I'm a grown woman. Ignore me. Everything's insignificant now that Grace is missing.'

He stands up and reaches over for my plate. 'It feels like we're living in a nightmare.'

I put my hands over the dish. 'Leave this — I'll see to them. You go to bed, be with Emma.'

'She'll be out for the count with the tablet Milly gave her. I didn't know she took Valium.'

'I didn't either.' I get up and take the plates over to the sink. 'I've been thinking. That thing we were doing; I think we should stop. I think we should delete it. We were drunk.'

He frowns, rubbing his forehead with his hand. 'I know. I can't stop thinking about it — if that's what started all of this . . . Shit. If Emma found out she'd kill me.'

'She'd kill me first.'

He smiles a sad smile. 'That's probably true.'

I fill the sink with hot water and leave the dishes to soak. 'I'll get my work laptop from upstairs.'

24

Maggie

'You don't look surprised,' I say to Jim.

He's looking at the photo of Scott as a child. He's wearing his school uniform; fourth year juniors, last year at primary. He was such a lovely boy — cheeky, but charming. 1976 it must've been — he still went out with his dad then, on Saturdays when the weather was nice. The pair of them would head out to the canal carrying their fishing rods. They'd leave early morning and not come back until teatime — starving as they'd eaten their sandwiches at eleven o'clock. 'I caught one and it was *this big*,' Scott said one time, holding his arms out wide. I looked to Ron, and he nodded. 'Aye, he did, Mags. I got the moment on film.' He pulled the camera out of his pocket and placed it on the kitchen table.

I can't remember seeing that picture of Scott and the fish he caught. The film could be upstairs, still in the camera.

Tears spring to my eyes as I think of that time, before everything went wrong.

'It's not that I'm not surprised,' says Jim. 'When we worked together, Ron didn't talk about his family much — a photo on his desk of the four of you, that's all. You know what he was like — he liked to keep work and family separate,

141

and I wasn't one to pry. But he did mention Scott — just briefly — at the pub one time, years ago.'

'He did? He never mentioned it to me.'

'He didn't go into details. He thought he saw Scott from a distance . . . shouted his name across the bar. It wasn't him — or if it was, he made a sharp exit.'

I try to remember a time that Ron might have behaved differently after his and Jim's trips to the pub — three pints in the afternoon without fail after he'd retired — but I can't. He was a lot quieter after Zoe anyway, but he never once mentioned Scott and what he did.

Some experts say that addictions are hereditary — could that be the case? Ron's three pints in the afternoon, Sarah's dependence on drink to get her through the day after Zoe. And Scott — well, he took it to another level.

'I'm guessing you don't want to talk about what happened,' says Jim.

'No, not really,' I say. 'I'm ashamed of what I did to Scott. That's not to say it wasn't the right thing, but that was the end for him. He wanted nothing more to do with us after that. Who could blame him?'

I handle the card from the flowers in my hands.

'But, it can't be him,' Jim says, nodding to my hands. 'The card says *Maggie*, not *Mum*.'

'He stopped calling me Mum a long time ago.'

I slump back against the settee, not caring if I'm able to get up again. Why is everything coming back to me now? Sarah, Scott. And the feeling that I'm connected to every child that goes missing. Am I having to confess my sins now, because it's nearly the end for me? Perhaps that's wishful thinking.

I sit up and shuffle my bottom to the end of the settee.

'I'll make us some tea.'

★ ★ ★

We're both sitting at the kitchen table after I'd busied myself making drinks with proper teacups and getting out the fingers of shortbread that have been in the cupboard since Christmas.

'So Ron didn't mention anything to you about what Scott did?' I say.

'Nothing. We talked about the football, the old times. If Ron didn't want to talk about a particular subject, then he stayed quiet.'

'That's right.'

I thought Ron and I might have had a conversation about our son at some point in our lives, but his heart attack came so suddenly, in the end we said nothing. I merely held on to him for dear life.

'Shall we not talk about this any more, Mags? You're getting upset.'

I shake my head. 'I think I have to. It's like a confession, I suppose.'

Jim slurps from his teacup, but says nothing.

'Where to start? He was such a good little boy, but most children are, aren't they? When the world hasn't spoilt them. He started smoking at high school, but we didn't mind then. He used to

143

love to go fishing with Ron until he was about fourteen.

'But then he got in with a bad lot — it always sounds like passing the buck, but he wouldn't even listen to his dad. Ron didn't usually have an input with raising our kids, but he had to step in. After Scott left school he had a few jobs, but nothing that lasted more than a couple of months. He was only twenty-one when Zoe was abducted. A few months after, I could tell he was going downhill. He wouldn't wash for days, weeks. He'd spend the whole day in his room, only popping out for a few hours, then rushing back up there.'

I drop two lumps of sugar into my lukewarm tea, and stir it. I don't even take sugar.

'It was the nineteen eighties; Ron and I were in our fifties. We didn't know anything about drugs or stuff like that. Perhaps we should have kept a better eye on him, tried to talk to him, but our heads were somewhere else.'

I rest my hand on the table. Perhaps it doesn't need to be said out loud, all of this. Maybe I just have to revisit it in my mind.

'I understand, Mags,' says Jim.

It's these words that bring tears to my eyes. That someone can comprehend what Ron and I went through. I've never described this to anyone before. And there's nothing but kindness in Jim's eyes.

I take a deep breath.

'Fast-forward to three years after Zoe disappeared. Sarah was drinking, Ron was putting his brave face on everything, even though at night I knew he lay awake. I never saw or heard him cry, but he must have done. What else is darkness for if you can't shed a tear? Anyway . . . one of those nights we heard banging downstairs. We didn't have mobile phones in those days. What were we supposed to do? Ron went to the top of the stairs and shouted for them to get out. He got brave, and went down. I heard a terrible noise — I actually thought we were all going to die.

'I was shaking when I went to the landing. I turned on all the lights, though of course, nothing woke Sarah — and from the top I could see the telephone in the hallway. It was so quiet. I tiptoed downstairs, and halfway, I saw Ron just lying there on the hallway floor. Without thinking, I ran down. His face was bloodied — I was so scared that he was dead. The voice in the darkness made me jump. It was Scott. He was holding a cricket bat. *You weren't supposed to wake up*, he said. He'd wanted to make it look like a burglary, to get money for drugs.'

I drink the rest of the cold, sweet tea. My hands are shaking, as though it were still that night — the last time I ever saw Scott in our house.

'I had to call the police on him, Jim. I had to.'

I can't stop the tears that are pouring out. My shoulders won't stop shaking. I bury my face in my hands.

I feel Jim's hand on my arm.

'That's it, Maggie. You let it all out, love. There, there, now.'

'He was sentenced to seven years for

aggravated burglary. I hadn't known what that even meant before then.' Jim tears me off a piece of kitchen roll and I wipe my face with it. 'I felt numb when I heard his sentence. None of it seemed real. Everything was falling down around me.'

'Have you not heard from him since?' asks Jim.

I shake my head. 'Ron never talked about him — or anything to do with him, and I never pushed it; he was the one who ended up in hospital, not me. But Scott was my son — I felt another part of me had died. I expected to get a letter, a phone call, something from him to say that he was sorry, but there was nothing. After Ron died, I didn't know what to do for the best; should I search for Scott? I couldn't find an address for him. It was like he didn't want to be found.' I dab my face again and scrunch the damp kitchen towel into a ball. 'What if it's him now? I can't call the police on him again. He's my son.' I wipe the wetness from my face with the back of my hands, and look at them while I rub them dry. Such old hands. Scott will be fifty now — I can't imagine him that age. And Sarah, she would have been fifty-three. The same age I was when Zoe was taken.

Jim sits down.

'But we don't know it's him who's been contacting you.' He pours some fresh tea into my cup. 'The internet's your answer. I'm taking you to the library on Monday and we're going to find out where Scott is.'

I take a deep breath. I should have been a

146

better mother to them both. I don't deserve to still be alive. Perhaps this is my purgatory. Or perhaps this could be my chance to make everything better.

'Thanks, Jim.'

You're a good friend, I want to say, but something — impropriety, shyness maybe — stops me. I hope he knows.

25

I can feel my breath coming back at me, like it's bouncing from the sides of the suitcase and blowing into my face. It's so dark in here; it's like my eyes are closed.

The car's stopped.

'All right, fellas,' says George.

'Hello, George. You visiting again? I bet you know nearly everyone on this base.'

George laughs. 'I like to earn a living.'

'Just hang on while we see if you're on the list for today.'

I can hear him tap, tap, tapping on the steering wheel. Someone's shouting, but I can't hear what they say.

'Thanks, Geoff,' shouts George. I can hear *him*.

We don't drive for long before the car stops again. His door shuts and I hear his footsteps. Why's he walking so slowly? For all he cares I could be dead.

'Won't be a minute, kid.' He's talking funny — like how Daddy speaks when he's got a sock monster on his hand. 'I'm going to pick up the case, so you might bang around a bit, but I'll try to be gentle.'

My heart is banging so bad and the tears haven't stopped since he put me in here. I think he's going to kill me. Oh, Mummy, where are you? I really need you. Please come and find me, please.

There's a knocking sound — like a front door. My knees are up so tight against me it feels like my chest might give up breathing soon.

The front door opens.

'George?' It's a man's voice. 'Can I help you?'

'I've a delivery for your wife.'

'Excuse me?'

'Oh, George, you're here!' It's a lady's voice. 'I've been waiting by the window for days.' A pause. 'She's not in *there*, is she? Don't tell me you've put her in a suitcase. You haven't hurt her, have you?'

'Of course I've not hurt her. What kind of person do you think I am?'

The other man makes a strange noise, like he's coughing.

I feel the ground on my back, then I'm lying down on my side. The zip sounds so loud next to my head. When the lid opens I daren't move. I can't stop myself from shaking.

Oh no. I think I've wet myself.

I start crying again.

The woman bends down. She's wearing a light green skirt. Mummy never wears skirts.

She starts to stroke my head. 'There, there. No need to cry, you're home now.' She takes hold of my hand, and tugs it slightly. I get up, and I'm standing there — my trousers soaking, and my face wet with tears. I'm still shaking — it won't stop. This isn't my home — why did she say that?

The woman grabs me in a big hug.

'I'll make you all better. Let me run you a bath.'

The man — her husband I think — is staring

149

at me. His eyes are wide open like he can't believe I'm here — that I've been magicked from nowhere.

'Dear God, Catherine,' he says. 'What the hell have you done?'

26

Stephanie

'I always thought it was strange,' says Matt, 'that there were no photos of her as a little kid, next to the ones of you at your mum's house.'

The screen is shining blue light on his face. It makes the shadows under his eyes look worse.

'I had no idea that she'd never explained it all,' I say. 'Emma and I don't talk about it either. I thought it would upset her if I brought it up — that she'd speak to me about it if she wanted to. I don't know if she's spoken to Mum about it either.'

'It's not strictly true that's she never talked to me about her past, though,' he says. 'Sometimes, after a drink or late at night when she couldn't sleep after Grace was born — she came out with the strangest things.'

'Like what?'

'Things like, *I'm tainted, you know, Matt.* Then sometimes she'd say, *If you realised who I really was, then you wouldn't want to know me.* If I asked her about it, she'd cut me off, or leave the room almost in tears.'

'When did this start?'

'I suppose she's always said these kinds of things — I just thought she was being over-dramatic . . . you know how she can be. Over the years, she's gone through phases where

151

she's shut me out, pushed me away. But after Grace was born, I wondered if Emma thought of her birth mother even more — and questioned why that woman gave her up for adoption when *she* was a baby. But actually, Emma wouldn't have thought about that at all. It's so much worse that her mother left her as an older child, isn't it?'

'Oh God. Poor Emma,' I say. 'I always thought she'd buried the memories of that time, but it's been just under the surface for all of these years.' I dab my tears with my sleeve. 'This was a stupid idea. Putting a search out that anyone could've seen was reckless.'

'I know,' says Matt. 'I feel like I'm betraying her, going behind her back.'

Who did I think I was, meddling in her life when she wanted things to stay just as they were? Of course she wouldn't want to find the person who didn't care for her — the mother that Emma thought had tainted her. I wish she'd spoken to me about it — that everything hadn't been so secretive. I used to blame Mum: when I wanted to talk about Emma's mother, it would upset her. Dad used to be the one to shield Mum from everything. *Let's not talk about this now*, he'd say, his arm around her shoulders. *Some things are better left unsaid.*

I enter the password into the website: *JamieGrace123*. A few clicks and we are at the post we created.

'Oh God — why did we put a picture up?' says Matt. 'Anyone could have seen that.'

'I doubt it. You'd have to be really specific in

152

searching to get to this site — they'd have to know our names. We'll have to delete the post from the official website, plus the photo we posted to that other forum.'

I read the post through again. I can't believe we uploaded it without telling Emma.

Searching for friends and family of Emma Harper (née Atkinson). Emma grew up in the village of Coningsby, Lincolnshire. Please contact Stephanie Palmer at StephPalmer125@email.com.

Below it, we'd posted a photograph from last Christmas of us all. We look so happy: Grace and Jamie sitting at the grown-ups' feet; Matt with his arms around Mum and me, and Emma, wearing a purple paper hat from a Christmas cracker — her cheeks flushed from her first glass of champagne after cooking all day. I feel so guilty looking at it that I feel sick.

'What if Emma comes down?' I say.

'She won't if she's taken Valium.'

All it takes is a few clicks and the posts are deleted. I lean back into the chair.

'Thank God for that. I just hope no one's seen it.'

'I doubt it. We only put it online last week.' He folds his arms, but after a moment he sits up straight, resting his hands on the table. 'You don't think there's a connection, do you? What if her mother saw it . . . then traced us . . . and took Grace?'

I wrinkle my nose. 'Surely she couldn't have

managed to do it that fast. We gave an email address. She would have just contacted us.'

'But what sort of person was she? Sometimes kids are put up for adoption against their parents' will, if they can't look after them properly. Maybe she thinks your parents stole Emma.'

'Don't be silly,' I say, but I'd already thought of that. Something inside me is shouting something, but I can't hear the exact words. Perhaps her real mother wants contact with her grandchild, but then, who's the man on the CCTV? 'I don't know. The only things Mum said was that Emma's biological mum couldn't look after her any more — that her new boyfriend didn't like children. So Mum and Dad looked after her. I don't know if they kept in contact with her mother or not.' I put my elbows on the table, and my head in my hands. 'Which is why we were so stupid to put anything on those websites. It'd seemed like a good idea after too much wine. We should've deleted it the day after we posted it.'

Matt puts his arm around my shoulders. 'It's gone now. Chances are no one saw it.'

I sit up, but Matt doesn't move his arm. 'Should we tell the police that we uploaded that photo?' I ask him. 'I mean — even if there's a remote chance — it's still something the police don't know.'

'Is it?'

'What do you mean?'

'The police always know more than they let on. They'll be digging into every one of us. They might even think *we* have something to do with Grace's disappearance.'

'Really?'

'Of course. Don't be naïve, Steph.'

'I'm not. It's just — '

I look at him and he's already looking at me. He strokes my face. 'You're so beautiful, Steph. You've always been there for me.'

He leans closer to me. When he's only inches from my face, I stand up quickly.

'Matt! What the fuck are you doing?'

He blinks quickly as though someone's just slapped him. 'Shit. I'm so sorry. I don't know what happened then. I'm so sorry.'

I walk towards the door.

'Steph. I'm really sorry. You won't tell Emma, will you?'

I turn round to look at him. It's like I'm looking at a stranger.

'No, I won't tell her. But I'm going home tomorrow.'

'Wait, no, you can't! Emma needs you here.'

'No she doesn't. She shouted at me a few hours ago. It's for the best.'

I walk up the stairs slowly, then open the door to the spare room. The bed Jamie slept on is empty. I get into it and can smell the Lynx he's used all week still on the bedding. I miss him so much.

What the hell happened tonight? Matt trying to kiss me; Mum taking tablets; Emma shouting in my face. I pull the covers to my neck. It's like I don't know any one of them.

27

She'll soon get one of my messages. I left them with a friend. Although that *friend* wanted paying. I should've known better than to trust anyone Tommy Deeks put me in contact with. A bloke with the nickname The Panther, which he gave himself, was always going to be a bit of a liability. His real name's Kevin Tranter. But still — we all have our price, and his was relatively cheap. Half upfront, half on delivery. I just hope he's *compos mentis* enough to post it through the right bloody letterbox.

I wish I could be there to see her face when she reads it. Would it make her tell the truth? Probably not. She's kept her secret for so long now. The next message should do it though. Wait till they find out where their precious little girl is now.

Looking at them playing happy families in the photograph nearly made me vomit. How dare she get to have all of that when I have nothing left? It was a Christmas photo by the look of the posh Christmas tree in the background. Bet that cost them a fair bit. Rich, smug bastards.

It's pouring with rain outside. I try not to stand for long at the window. People round here don't like me, so I keep myself to myself. A woman passes by with her dog. She always has a good nosy. I had to put up net curtains so she wouldn't keep looking in. She uses her dog sniffing round the fence as an excuse to stop, even in the rain. I keep my eye on her — if that dog shits in my front garden, I'll go out there and —

There's a bang from upstairs. A dragging sound along the floorboards.

Shit.

28

Stephanie

I can't sleep any longer. The sky is violet. Soon everyone else will be awake and I'm dreading it. Last night keeps running through my mind. All these years I've often imagined what it would be like for Matt to like me back, yet when it came to the reality, it filled me with shame. Blood or no blood, Emma is my sister. Had I told Matt about Emma's mother to subliminally distance myself from her should he and I get together? I've behaved like a schoolgirl with a ridiculous crush. My cheeks burn with the embarrassment of it. Did Emma know? I wasn't the most talkative of people, but she's the closest person to me.

Matt said I'd always been there for him, but it's Emma who's always supported me. When my marriage to Neil broke down after he left me, Emma stayed with Jamie and me for a week. I could barely get out of bed, it was like I'd been floored. Mum, on the other hand, said, *I'm glad your dad isn't around to see you like this.*

Dad wouldn't have minded at all. When Neil and I told my parents we were getting married all those years ago, Dad reacted to the news with a smile. But a few hours later, after Neil had left and Mum was out of the room, he said, 'If you're pregnant, you don't have to get married. People don't have to stay together these days. You're only twenty-one — you could do anything with your life.'

I laughed and said, 'I'm not pregnant, Dad. And I know it's not the nineteen fifties any more. Just because I'm getting married, doesn't mean I can't do something with my life.'

He just nodded and said, 'Okay.'

He was right. I was pregnant by the time I was twenty-two, and gave up the idea of training to be a teacher to stay at home and look after Jamie. I didn't begrudge those years — it was just a different path to what I'd planned. Although working in a call centre is the total opposite of my dream job.

Dad had been dead just under a year when Neil told me it was over. He probably stayed with me for those twelve months out of guilt — I'm sure he would have ended it sooner had my father not died. It was three days after what would have been Dad's sixtieth birthday, though Neil wouldn't have remembered that — I'd have to remind him of his own mother's.

He told me to meet him in a café in town. 'So we're in neutral territory,' he said, as though we were about to enter battle.

'I've met someone else,' he said.

The rest of his sentence was a blur. Twelve years of marriage, over in a second.

'Someone from the office,' he said when I asked him who it was.

Neil and his colleague — I didn't even know her name — were only together for six months after he left me. It would be laughable, had Neil's leaving not broken Jamie's heart. Mine was already numb after Dad died.

When they'd both come to visit, Emma had sent Matt back home after seeing how distraught I was, and he left a little too quickly. She held my and Jamie's hands as we talked through what was going to happen now that Neil had moved out. Jamie had tried to be brave in front of me, but when I came into his room after being in the bath that Emma had run for me, he was crying into her shoulder.

'He'll be okay,' she mouthed above his head, gesturing for me to get into bed.

She was there for Jamie when I was a wreck. She watched daytime telly with him when he had that first day off. For the rest of the week, she took him to school, making sure he wore a clean uniform. She helped him with his homework.

During the day, she brought me up cups of tea and bowls of soup. 'You could open a shop, the amount of tins you have in your cupboard,' she said.

It was as though I'd always known he was going to leave and had planned ahead. It was the first time Emma had taken care of me. Since she had Grace, we had become far closer than we had been at college. It was like our childhood roles had been reversed. She became strong for me.

'Whenever you're ready, Steph,' she said, after I'd been in bed for four and a half days, 'I'll take you to a solicitor. We need to make sure you keep what you're entitled to. We don't want that bastard trying to make you sell this house to get his share.'

When she left the room, her words echoed in my head. I loved our house. I had made the spare room into a guest room, which had been my sanctuary. I used to sleep in it so Neil wouldn't have to listen to me crying at night after Dad died.

Had he said something to Emma about our house? I'd not taken any calls from him — I couldn't bear to listen to him, trying to make it sound like everything was my fault. *You were so depressing to be around. I needed a lover as well as a friend.* What a prick.

Emma was right. I had to stop wallowing in self-pity. It was down to her that I gathered the courage to fight back. After that week, she phoned every night at nine o'clock after Jamie had gone to bed so I didn't feel so alone.

I must be here for Emma now.

There's a tap on the door.

It opens slowly.

A head bobs through the gap: it's her.

'You awake, Steph?'

If I wasn't, I would be now. She's never been the quietest of whisperers.

I sit up, even though I don't want to. She beckons me out of the room and we walk as softly as we can down the stairs.

In the kitchen, she lifts the chair so it doesn't scrape on the floor.

I pull back a chair and sit adjacent to her. I don't know what to say, so I say nothing.

'I'm really sorry about shouting at you last night,' she says. There's no change of intonation in her voice — there hasn't been since Monday.

'I was just so tired. I don't know what Mum gave me, but I was asleep in seconds, at least I think I was. I don't think I even woke in the night.'

'It was Valium. She did say, but I don't think you were listening.'

'Really?' She leans back in her chair. 'Shit. Did you know she took that?'

I shake my head.

'I don't even know if it's legal any more,' she says. 'She must have started taking them after Dad died. I know she's quite headstrong, but she depended on him, didn't she? Three years has it been?'

'Four.'

Emma looks out of the kitchen window. 'It's been nearly a week. Where is she, Steph?'

'I don't know. I wish I did. I'd go and find her myself.'

She looks back at me. 'I know you would.'

Silence.

'That man you recognised on the CCTV photograph,' I say. 'You don't know anyone with a grudge, do you? Or someone connected to one of your colleagues?'

'Of course I don't! What a strange thing to say.'

She turns her back to me again.

'It's not a strange thing to say,' I say gently. 'You said you recognised him from work. I'd be wracking my brains to think what his connection to Grace is, if it were me. It's too much of a coincidence.'

'I . . . I can't even remember his name.' She turns around. 'And it's not you, is it, Steph? I'm trying to get through all of this the best I can.'

'I know. I'm just saying what's been going on in my head. I'm sorry.'

She starts pulling at the skin around her thumb. Sometimes when she was younger she'd do it till her fingers bled. She wouldn't realise until I'd point it out. She hasn't done it for years.

'I need to ask you a favour,' she says. 'That medium. She left me a voicemail last night. I know it's Sunday, but she said she'd fit me in, as it's an emergency.'

My laptop is still on the kitchen table from last night. I close the lid.

I know what's coming next — on the day that I was going to go home, I'm going to drive Emma to this medium, wherever she might be. 'All right.'

'How did you know what I was going to ask?'

I raise my eyebrows, and she gives me the tiniest of smiles. 'Thanks, Steph.' She gets up, forgetting about the chair scraping on the floor and it makes a screeching sound. She winces. 'She lives in Yorkshire. Is that okay?'

'Of course it is.'

What else could I say? At least Jamie is at his dad's so I don't have to tell Neil where I'm going.

'We'd better set off soon then — her earliest appointment is at midday.'

Emma rushes out of the kitchen before I can say anything, but I can't be mad at her — even though she's dodging questions about the man she saw on the CCTV. She knows something and she's not telling me what it is. If there were

163

answers to find, I want them too. I just hope that whoever we're going to see isn't some ambulance-chasing charlatan.

My shoulders feel heavy as I stand. Of course she's going to be a charlatan — there's never anything more than lies and guesswork involved in these sorts of things. But I'll go — it'll be good for Emma to get out of the house, to give her mind a break, even for just a few hours. I might get a few answers out of her, too.

★ ★ ★

We're only half an hour away according to the satnav. The further north we travelled, the cloudier it got.

Mum came to the house just minutes before we left.

'Where on earth are you going at this time?' she said. 'Emma, shouldn't you be staying here?'

'If you hear anything, Mum, I've got my mobile.' Emma pulled out a phone from her handbag.

'Where did you get that from?' said Mum.

'Ah — it's my work phone.' She rooted in her bag and pulled out another. 'I have both. Just in case.'

'Well, don't worry. I'll look after Matt.' Mum waved us off as though we were going for a jolly day out.

'Mum's acting really weird,' says Emma now, from nowhere. We're in the car. It's been three hours since we left the house and she's barely spoken. 'I don't know what she's going to say from one minute to the next.'

'She's always been like that.'

Emma's wearing sunglasses; I can't see the expression in her eyes.

'Has she? I don't think I've ever noticed.'

Because she was always nicer to you, I want to say.

She leans over and presses the button on the stereo. She pushes each channel until she finds a golden oldie station. 'I don't want to find anything out from the radio.'

Why are we driving so far away? What if Grace comes back and we're not there?

A song by Nena sounds on the radio.

'Emma, you used to sing this all the time. Do you remember? You used to sing it in German.'

She looks out of the window. 'Did I?'

'Yes. Even Grace knows some of the words.'

Emma just hums in reply. Perhaps the Valium is still in her system. She's not herself today, but then that's not surprising. It does, however, make me wonder how long Mum has actually been on the tablets. I'm not sure I want to know.

There's a sound coming from Emma's handbag in the footwell — a mobile phone vibrating.

'Aren't you going to get that? It might be urgent.'

She bends down, and reaches into her bag for the phone. 'It's just work. I wish they'd leave me alone.' She throws the phone on top of the bag.

'They're probably just wondering how you are, Em. I think they might have been trying to contact you on the landline as well. It's rung a

165

few times, but no one's been on the other end.'

'Really? Who uses a landline these days?'

'Someone who's not having much luck with your mobile I imagine.'

She shrugs.

We drive for a few minutes before Emma breaks the silence.

'Steph?'

'What?'

'Do you think the police know more than they're telling us?'

'What do you mean?'

'That they know everything about us — all our secrets.'

My heart starts to beat faster. Does she know what Matt and I did? Does she know about her mum? Has she been in contact with her without telling us?

'I've no idea,' I say. 'If I stopped to think about everything I've ever done, I'd go mad.'

Emma lifts up her sunglasses and turns to look at me. 'You're not worried?'

'No. Why should I be?'

She puts her glasses back on her face. 'No reason.'

If I wasn't driving now, I'd probably be sick.

29

I'm on the bed near the window, sitting upright with my hands hugging my knees. It's bigger than my room at home, though Catherine doesn't like me mentioning Mummy or Daddy. She starts to cry and it makes me feel bad. The curtains are blue, the walls are blue and the bed sheets are blue. Dark blue. The cover on the bed opposite is the same colour. It's the strangest-coloured bedroom I have been in, though I haven't been in that many. The girl who normally lives in here must really like blue.

There aren't many toys: three teddy bears, two Sindy dolls, and a house that looks like a teapot. In the corner on a wooden table is a pretend record player with plastic records. I want to play with it, but it might be too loud; Catherine hasn't said if I can touch anything yet.

The sun is rising, but I've been awake for hours. I've never felt this tired — like I haven't slept for days. What are Mummy and Daddy doing now? Are they worried about me? Do they think I've disappeared — or do they even think I'm dead? I don't ever want them to think that. I don't want them to ever stop looking for me.

An alarm sounds in the other room.

My tummy feels a bit sick, and a bit sore, but I daren't use the toilet in this house. What if they listen at the door? What if they're spying on me? I look around the room, but I can't see any cameras. Though they can be pretty small — the size of the tip of my finger, Daddy said.

I can hear someone moving in the room next door — or is it outside this one?

Tap, tap, tap.

It's outside this one.

Am I supposed to say anything?

'Hello?'

'Ah, you're awake.' It's Catherine. I don't think she's looked in the mirror today, as there are black lines down her face from her eye make-up. 'How did you sleep?'

'Okay.'

She walks on tiptoes to the side of the bed and kneels down on the floor. She's still in her nightclothes; her housecoat is dark pink with bits of lace around the edges. Mummy would never wear anything like that, not unless it was to a fancy-dress party. She wears Daddy's old t-shirts at night-time. I wish I had one of them with me; I'd wear it and smell of her.

'Seeing as you didn't want one yesterday, shall I run you a bath now? Well — when Michael's finished in the bathroom. He's got to be at work for eight.'

'No, thank you.'

'I can put some Mr Matey in — I think we still have some of that. And maybe some bath salts.'

'No, thank you.'

She frowns and tilts her head to the side.

'You can have a bath on your own. I won't be there. I can get some clothes ready for you and put them on the chair next to the bath. I'll make sure the towel's nice and warm on the radiator.

168

Does that sound better?'

I nod.

This makes her happy.

'Then after that,' she says, 'I'll make you some nice bacon and eggs.'

I nod again, and she almost skips out of the room.

Bacon and eggs and it's not even a Sunday. At least I think it's not. I can't actually remember what day it is.

★　★　★

Catherine was right, I do feel a bit better after that bath. I don't smell as bad now. Their dining table is dark wood and really big. Michael is sitting at the opposite end, reading the paper.

When Catherine pours his tea, she says, 'Anything?'

He shakes his head, but he doesn't speak.

'Probably won't be for a few days,' she says. 'And certainly not if we cancel the English papers.'

Michael lowers his paper to give a nasty look to Catherine. I know those stares well, because I do them to Thomas Babbington when he pulls my plaits. Michael's hair doesn't look long enough to pull on though — I wonder if Catherine put salt in his tea instead of sugar.

He closes his paper and looks up at me.

'So. How are you enjoying your holiday so far?'

'It's okay.' My mouth is full of toast. 'When am I going home?'

He dabs his mouth with a cloth and stands up. 'In a few days I should think. Don't worry about it. I'll try to get word to your — '

'To who?'

Catherine is standing at the door to the kitchen with her hands on her hips.

'She can't stay here, Catherine. How on earth would we explain that? And what about her poor parents? How could you do that to someone else?'

They don't realise I know they're talking about me. Michael might ask George to take me home again, though I've not seen him since the other day. We won't be able to tell Catherine about it. I think she'd be upset if I left, though sometimes she likes me; sometimes she doesn't.

Catherine throws the tea towel she was holding onto the table, and follows Michael out into the hallway.

I can only pick up little bits from there, Catherine's voice is the loudest. 'Posting . . . authorities . . . that you knew all about it.'

The front door slams. It's nearly all made of glass. It could have broken into a million pieces. Catherine walks back into the dining room with a wide smile — her eyes are wide too.

'Who are these photographs of?' I ask her, pointing to the two in frames on the wooden dresser. There are three more of the same girl in the living room. 'Is she your daughter?'

She looks at them, as though she's never seen them before either. She looks the same age as me, the girl in the pictures. She's got blonde hair too.

'She's very pretty,' I say.

As she walks back into the kitchen, she pats me on the head. 'That's very kind of you to say.'

She's sniffing in the kitchen. I think she's crying because Michael shouted at her.

I dip my last bit of toast in my egg. As I'm chewing, I notice the picture on the tea towel is of Big Ben. That's near where I live — well, nearer than where we are now. Maybe Michael wasn't telling lies. Maybe I will be going home in a few days.

I swing my legs under the table and stab a piece of bacon.

I'd better make the most of it. I wonder if they have bacon and egg every day here.

30

Stephanie

We pull up outside a white cottage — the only house within a mile. It's surrounded by farmland and it has a cattle shed at the side filled with rusting machinery. The clouds look heavy with rain or even snow, and the white-topped Yorkshire moors in the distance give the place a dramatic, almost eerie atmosphere.

'If this is what you can afford working as a medium, then I'm in the wrong business,' I say, getting out of the car. My role as a team leader in the soulless call centre feels so far removed — so insignificant — from where I am right now. My boss has given me compassionate leave this week — I just hope she remains as understanding with my having time off if we don't find Grace soon.

'It might be rented,' says Emma, taking off her sunglasses and placing them on her head. She rubs the tops of her arms. 'It's freezing cold here. It's like we're in a different country.'

'Have you ever been to one of these people before?'

'Course not. I'd have told you if I had.'

A few months ago she would have. I feel sad for that time, a pang of nostalgia. It's funny, the little things we take for granted.

I take in a deep breath. It's so pretty here in

the middle of nowhere. I could imagine losing myself in a place like this, in the open space.

The red front door of the cottage opens. The woman looks less intimidating than her profile photo. I expected her to be wearing purple velvet and no shoes, but she's wearing jeans, long boots, and a red chenille jumper. Her long hair is twisted up in a scrunchie at the side of her head.

'Come in out of the cold,' she says in a soft northern accent.

We do as she says, and she stands aside as we go in.

Inside, it's exactly how I pictured a little country cottage to be. The ceilings are low and the carpet in the hall is red with mustard-yellow flecks and grey swirls. She leads us through to a sitting room that's deliciously warm. Crammed bookcases line the back wall, with extra books stuffed in every available space. To the left is a real open fire that's crackling with burning logs.

'Please, come sit.' She holds her arm out to four armchairs, three of which are made from the same material as the hallway carpet. I'm guessing that the slightly grander, but threadbare gold chair is hers, so I push Emma gently to the seat nearest the fire. She hasn't stopped shivering since she got out of the car.

'Are you okay?' I mouth, as we shake off our coats.

'I don't know,' she mouths back, her eyes wide.

She's scared. I'm scared.

'I'll just get you two girls a nice cup of hot chocolate. Won't be a sec.'

I rub my arms and look around. Under the window to our left is a mahogany sideboard. On the top of it are twenty, maybe thirty, photographs of people in various-sized frames.

How did we get here? *What* are we doing here? Even Matt doesn't know what we're doing. He doesn't believe in all of this spiritual stuff, especially after reading what this woman wrote on her Facebook page about Grace: *I believe that Grace is still alive, but she is being kept somewhere.* 'It's too general,' Matt said. 'It doesn't mean anything. These people are vultures, preying on the vulnerable.'

Where has Emma told him we are?

I turn to her and she still has a panicked look on her face.

'Are you okay, Em? We can leave if you're not sure about this.'

'I don't know what to do. This is the only thing I've done for days. I can't think straight.'

Deandra walks backwards through the door and turns round with a cup in each hand. She puts them on the small coffee table in front of us.

'So, shall we get straight to it?' she says. 'I know you must be extremely worried about Grace.' She sits forward in her chair and takes hold of Emma's hands. 'I have a gentleman here, a father figure.'

Emma glances at me from the corner of her eye. 'Our dad?'

Deandra narrows her eyes, as though distracted. 'It would appear so. He's showing me a poster.'

'Is Grace with him?' says Emma, her words tumbling out. 'Please say she isn't. Tell me that I'll find her.'

The medium tilts her head slightly, still holding on to Emma's hands.

Why isn't she replying? The wait is agonising. The wood in the fire sounds as though it's hissing at us. My whole body is shaking. If I weren't sitting down, I'd have sunk to the floor.

I want to grab the woman by the shoulders and shake her. *This isn't some sort of game — this is our lives; this is our family!*

'She's not,' the woman says eventually.

'She's not what?' Emma almost screams the words.

'She's not with her grandfather.'

'Oh my God.' Emma pulls her hands away from the medium's and covers her face. 'Oh my God. Oh God. This is unbearable.'

Deandra plucks a tissue from the box on the table. When Emma drops her hands she takes it and wipes it across her face.

'I know you might not believe in my work, but Grace's grandfather is showing me some images. Can I share them with you?'

Emma nods, her left knuckle white as she grips the tissue.

'Firstly, I'd like to give you some facts about Grace, so that I can . . . authenticate, if you will, the information I am receiving.'

Just get on with it, woman.

'I can see a picture on a wall. Is it a pop band? I'm not familiar with them, but one of the faces has been crossed out — or perhaps covered with

175

something. Did Grace dislike this person?'

'Zayn,' I say, quickly. 'Zayn left One Direction. Do you remember, Emma? She scribbled his face out with a black felt tip.'

More tears are streaming down Emma's face, down my face.

'I remember. She was so upset when they split up.'

'I've got another strange image, but do bear with me on this one. It's of Grace, and a boy . . . I don't know if this is right . . . but they're dressed as cats and eating out of a bowl on the floor? I know it sounds strange, but — '

'That's right,' says Emma. 'That's completely right.' Emma narrows her eyes. 'You haven't been in our house, have you?'

Deandra shakes her head. 'Only through your father.'

'Where is Grace now?' I can't help myself. This is why we came here after all.

The medium looks to the side of us again, nodding at thin air.

'He's giving me the picture of a cottage — bigger than this one — in a small village. Not a northern one, perhaps it's in the Cotswolds, the stone of the houses is light — they're all the same colour. There's a little face at one of the windows — the curtains are a light blue colour. There's a car parked in the front, on the gravel. It's a Volvo, also light blue.'

Deandra sits back as though exhausted and closes her eyes.

'So what do we do with that information?' I say. 'It's not much good if we can't do anything with it. We can't drive to the Cotswolds and check every little village — there are too many.'

She opens her eyes again; it makes me jump a little.

'You need to find her as soon as possible — the man she's with is unstable.'

'You don't think we know that already?' Emma reaches for her coat. 'We've got to let the police know.'

I put my coat on. Now is not the right time to tell her that the police might not take this as seriously as we are. The information is so vague — we don't even have a name.

Deandra stands up.

As we run out of the door, she shouts, 'It is important that you look deeper into your family.'

I'm not sure which of us she's talking to.

31

Stephanie

We're twenty minutes from home and the sun is almost set. Every word the medium said is running through my mind and it drowns out the conversation Emma is having with Matt on her phone. Emma presses the end call button and flings her phone on the floor of the car, for the second time today.

'Matt's going mental,' she says. 'He thought someone had kidnapped me too. Didn't Mum tell him we were going out?'

'You know what she's like. You never get the full story until you ask her the right questions. She's like a teenager.'

Emma leans back into her seat. If there had been news about Grace she would have mentioned it. She didn't tell Matt about what we heard from the medium, but does that count as news?

There's a vibrating sound coming from Emma's bag.

'Is that work again?' I say.

'Probably.' Emma's looking out of the window — I can't see her face.

'I can't believe they keep ringing you. They should know you're going through a terrible time. Shall I pull over? Do you want me to talk to them for you?'

'No, it's fine. They won't ring again.'

She's wrong. Five minutes after it stopped, it starts again. Emma's trying to ignore it, but the skin around her thumb is red raw as she picks at it.

It stops. Then starts vibrating yet again.

'Oh for God's sake. Why won't he leave me alone?'

She grabs the phone and presses a button. I can't see if it's the red or green one out of the corner of my eye.

'Hello,' she says, her voice flat.

The voice — a man's — on the other end is loud, but I can't hear what he's saying. It sounds as though he's shouting at her.

'You have to stop calling me,' she says. 'Now is not the right time, you should know that without me texting you.' I feel her eyes on me. She clears her throat. 'I will catch up on the paperwork when I get back in.' She turns to the window. 'We have to stop. It's not what I want any more, I told you.' She's whispering, but her words bounce off the windows and into the space between us.

Whoever she's talking to — it's not about work.

⋆ ⋆ ⋆

When we pull up there's another BMW parked alongside Nadia's. My car has only just stopped when Emma opens the door and gets out.

I follow and she stops at the gate.

'Do you think they know something?'

I go past her and run to the door. I feel, and smell, the claustrophobia inside the house: the smell of people barely washed, mixed with the warmth of central heating. The oppressive atmosphere of a home with the presence of police officers.

In the sitting room, the detective is holding a clear plastic wallet.

'So you've no idea what this could mean?'

Matt's kneeling on the floor, his arms folded across his body.

'For the third time — no. I don't know anyone who could have said that.'

Mum is perched on the armchair, hands on her knees, rocking back and forth.

'What's going on?' I'm standing in the middle of the room. It's like we've walked into another time zone. I'd expected Mum and Matt to be waiting for us, so we could tell them what the medium said.

Matt looks up. 'I've been trying to ring you.'

Emma grabs her phone out of her bag. 'I'm sorry, I switched the wrong one off.'

'What?'

She runs her hands through her hair. 'What the hell is going on?'

The detective is holding up the plastic wallet. Inside it is a piece of paper.

'We were called here about twenty minutes ago. Your husband found this on the doormat. It had no name on the front, no stamp, no address. Inside is this.'

He hands it over to Emma. She wrinkles her nose. 'But what does this mean?' She looks around the room — at the walls, at the ceiling. 'Oh God.' Her knees start to shake. She's going to fall any second.

I grab her elbows and guide her to the nearest seat — the room is full — so I take her into the kitchen. I sit next to her.

'What does it say?'

'It's all my fault, Steph,' she whispers. One hand is supporting her forehead. Tears are dripping onto the table. With the other hand, she slides the plastic sheet to me.

'*It's payback time.*'

★ ★ ★

I thought Emma was going to talk about her mum, and how she thought this woman had taken Grace to get back at us for taking Emma, but she didn't. She wrote a name on a piece of paper and handed it to Detective Hines.

'This might be the man who wrote the letter. He might have taken Grace.' Her hands were shaking. 'He's been stalking me at work.'

Hines narrowed his eyes at her. He didn't ask why she hadn't told them before. He didn't shout at her for keeping secret an important piece of information that might help find Grace. He just took it and left.

'What the fuck, Emma?' Matt's standing at the kitchen doorway, his face flushed and sweat pooling above his top lip. 'Someone's stalking you and you didn't even fucking tell me?'

She says nothing in return.

He turns to me. 'Did you know?'

I shake my head. What is she thinking? Is she telling the truth?

'Is it the same person that's been ringing the landline?'

'What?' says Matt.

'No, that was work,' says Emma — her eyes wide as she looks at me.

'What's his name?' says Matt.

'It doesn't matter,' says Emma.

'Course it fucking matters.'

'Could you stop swearing and shouting.'

'Why should I? Grace isn't in the fucking house, is she? I can swear if I want to.'

'He's been calling my mobile, harassing me at work. I've told my manager. I didn't think he'd do anything like this. He must be getting back at me.'

'Getting back at you for what?' says Matt. 'If you've done nothing wrong, then there's no reason someone would feel they had to take our daughter. What could you possibly have done to warrant you worrying about it?'

'*If* I've done nothing wrong . . . ' She looks to the floor as she says it.

'Emma,' says Matt, frowning as he glances at me. 'What have you done?'

I crouch at her feet. 'Why didn't you tell us, Em? We could have helped you. You must have been going through hell. Do you think he's the type of person who would take a child off the street?'

She shakes her head, her mouth slightly open.

'I . . . I suppose he might be.' She looks up at Matt. 'I don't know him that well — he could be capable of anything.'

'What's his name?' says Matt, louder this time. 'I'll find out where he lives — he might be keeping Grace there.'

'You can't,' says Emma, almost pleading with him.

'Why not?' he says.

'He might be dangerous. I've given the details to the police. They'll deal with it.'

'Have you told them what he's like?'

She stands. 'No,' she shouts, as she rushes out of the kitchen. 'I need to speak to Nadia.'

Matt looks at me, expecting me to say something, but I can't find the words.

The man on the other end of her mobile phone in the car was shouting at Emma. If he were a stalker, why would she talk back to him? And if Emma thought him capable of snatching her daughter, she would have said something before this. We're only getting half of the story. She's hiding something.

'I don't know anything,' I say to Matt. 'She's hardly talked to me about anything recently.'

He shakes his head at me. 'I don't know what's going on. Everything's falling apart.'

He pulls out a chair and sits, resting his head on his arms. I walk over to him, and put my hand on his.

'I'm sorry, Matt.'

I look at the clock on the kitchen wall. It's nearly nine o'clock. Jamie should be in bed. Why aren't I keeping track of the time?

'I have to say goodnight to Jamie.'

Matt raises his head, and nods as he wipes the tears from his face.

I run through to the sitting room. As I pass the telephone table, I notice that the phone number I wrote down has gone.

I rush up the stairs. The door of the spare room is closed. I open it quickly. But it's empty. Jamie's at his dad's. Why can't I think straight? I reach into my pocket and pull out my phone, sitting on the edge of the bed. I almost cry when he answers it after three rings.

'Mum? Are you okay?'

'Yes, yes. I'm just phoning to see if you're all right.'

'Course I am. I only saw you yesterday.'

'I know, but with all of this going on — '

'It's okay, I understand.'

The tears fall down my face, but I try to keep my breathing steady so he doesn't know I'm crying.

'Are you all ready for school tomorrow?'

'Yeah. Joanna showed me how to use the washing machine. You'd have thought it was rocket science the way she was describing it.'

I allow myself a giggle. I shouldn't enjoy him mocking her, but I do.

'You're growing up fast.'

'Whatever, Mum.' I can hear the smile in his voice.

'I'll let you get some sleep. Love you, Jamie.'

'I love you, Mum.'

I press the end call button on my phone and lie down on the bed, burying myself in the pillow and finally letting myself sob.

32

Maggie

I barely slept the past two nights. At first I thought I could hear noises downstairs — like that awful night twenty-seven years ago, but these noises must have been in my head. I didn't bother to check downstairs — if someone was going to get me, I wasn't going to make their job easier. I kept expecting Scott to walk into my bedroom, but of course it's morning now, and this very idea is ridiculous. It's surreal what my night-time brain imagines could happen.

Jim's not due here till half past eleven. The photo of Scott is still on the kitchen table. I don't know what to do with it. I regret not asking Ron if he'd forgiven him for what he did. I'd always believed there was plenty of time for us all to make amends. What a fool. What if I died tomorrow and hadn't spoken to my only living child?

When Scott pleaded not guilty, I believe, in his mind, Ron disowned him.

'What kind of person does this to their own family?' he said, when he realised he had to speak in court.

It was like Scott was a different person standing up there; he didn't react to anything his father said. I had expected to see my little boy, and feel pity, but it was like looking at a stranger

185

who only replied in single-word answers.

When Ron stood in the dock to give evidence, Scott wouldn't even look up.

'It was almost midnight,' he said, his voice trembling. 'We — my wife and I — heard a noise from downstairs, like glass breaking. I got up — tried to make myself heard, that's what they tell you to do. I turned the hall light on from upstairs, but I couldn't see anything, so I went down. I shouted, 'Is there anyone there?'

'There was no reply. It all went quiet. I thought whoever had been in our house had gone, so I went to turn the living-room light on. Then I heard this crack, and I fell to the ground. It took a few seconds for me to realise the pain in my head was caused by the noise I heard. Then I saw him — he stood over me. 'You're not supposed to wake up,' he said to me. He was holding a bat in his hands. Then everything went black.'

On our way home, Ron turned to me and said, 'You're not supposed to wake up — that's what that boy said to me. What do you think he meant by that?'

'I thought he said, You weren't supposed to ... That we weren't meant to catch him stealing our things,' I said. 'He didn't want to hurt you; it was the drugs.'

But Ron shook his head. That was the last time he ever spoke about Scott.

Scott hadn't even appeared remorseful. Was that pride? Shame? Indifference? I will only ever know if I face him again. Perhaps he wants to say he's sorry — or he might need me desperately.

Why else would he make contact after all these years? What if he has children and something's happened to one of them?

Grace.

I switch on the news. I can't believe I haven't thought about her for a whole day. I type in the number Jim wrote down for the Sky News channel. There's nothing on the main news, but there's a ribbon along the bottom. *New photo released of Grace Harper with her alleged abductor.* How have I missed this?

The bang on the front door makes me jump.

I glimpse through the curtains first, before opening the door to Jim.

'Why are you coming to the front door?'

'I didn't want to startle you, what with everything that's been going on.'

'Have you brought me the paper?' I say as he steps inside.

'Did you ask me to?'

'It has a picture of the man who took her.'

'Took who?'

'The girl — Grace.'

'Oh, that.' I'm sure Jim just rolled his eyes. 'I thought today was about Scott. I've booked us on the computer for midday, so we'd better get a move on.'

'Don't let me forget.'

'As if you would.'

* * *

We're walking at a rate of about nought point five miles an hour, but at least it's not raining.

'I thought you said we had to get a move on,' I say. It's only when I turn to get his reply that I see he's rubbing his back. His face is scrunched up until he catches me looking. 'Have you been to the doctor with that?'

'Aye, aye. I don't want any fuss. I'm just getting old, is all.'

'What do you mean?'

He waves his hand at me, which means, *Shut the devil up, woman.*

The automatic doors to the library open slowly, which is just as well, the speed Jim and I are going. He waves a card in the air.

'We have a reservation, my lovely.'

'Morning, Jim.' I've never seen the lady behind the counter before. I thought I knew everyone in this village. Her hair is a huge blonde bouffant — I reckon it would explode if I put a match to it. And her blouse is gaping across her bosom. I don't know where to look. I thought libraries were meant to be respectable. Everything's going downhill these days. 'I'll show you to your machine.' She gives Jim a smile as she turns round to look at him. She's bloody shameless.

She pulls out a chair for him and when he's seated, she rests her hands on his shoulders.

'Right, you've got half an hour, but if no one else comes in, I'll turn a blind eye.'

'You're an angel,' says Jim, putting on his glasses.

I go to the spare chair next to him. 'Well, that's charming.'

'What is?'

'She pulled out a chair for you, and left me standing like an idiot.'

Jim's shoulders shake as he laughs. 'I don't think you're her type.'

'Give over.'

I watch Jim as he takes control of the computer, opens the internet screen and goes straight onto a site called Whitepages.

'You're quite the expert, aren't you?'

'I'm a member of a few of these sites now. I've got to pass the time somehow. And anyway, there's a few people I've wanted to get in touch with recently — you know, just to have a catch up.'

'Like who?'

'No one you know.'

He leans closer to the screen, squinting through his glasses.

'Where did you say he lived last?'

'At Her Majesty's Pleasure — in Manchester.'

He types in Manchester, and his year of birth. Scott Taylor is a common name, but he's the only one with Beckett as his middle name in the area.

'Well I never,' says Jim. 'I didn't think it would be that easy.'

I shuffle forward in my seat. 'But what if he's in prison again?'

'He can't be — it's got 2015 on here. If he were in prison, he wouldn't be on the electoral roll, would he?'

'What if he's been in trouble since?'

Jim turns to me. 'What are you scared of, Maggie? That it's best not to know? Look, I'll

189

google his name and see if we get any results.'

I hadn't expected this search to be so fast. I thought we would have to scroll through rolls and rolls of film — what do they call it? Microfiche. That's how they do it in the films. They don't just type in a name and find it like this.

Jim clicks on the button called news.

I'd expected *No results* — that Scott's learned his lesson after years of being in prison, but the headlines were, *Manchester's Most Prolific Petty Criminal* and *Manchester Man's 100th Offence*.

'Bloody hell,' says Jim. 'I wasn't expecting that.'

'How could all of this be available, yet I've never heard of it? Did you type in the right name?'

Jim clicks on one of the articles and a photograph pops up of a man: unshaven, in a white, grubby t-shirt. It's him. It's Scott.

Career criminal Scott Taylor has today been sentenced to eighteen months for assault with intent to resist arrest. This conviction marks Taylor's 100th offence. His previous crimes include driving while disqualified, possession of a sharp object in a public place, and being drunk and disorderly. The most serious of his offences — aggravated burglary — was in 1989 when he was jailed for seven years.

Before his most recent sentencing, Taylor told the judge residing at Manchester Crown Court that he was planning to 'retire' from a life of crime as he was 'getting too old for it'. A Ministry of Justice spokesperson said: 'Reoffending in England is at an unacceptably high rate — rehabilitation in our institutions needs to be overhauled.'

I touch the screen of the computer and run my finger down the side of his face. How did it get to this? How did I let him down so badly? Scott didn't have to become this broken person.

'A long time ago,' I say to Jim suddenly, wanting to recount the memory, 'I was laid up with this awful stomach bug — I couldn't move for the sickness I felt. Scott must've only been about ten or eleven and had to make his own sandwiches for tea — he even made Ron's.

'I had a bucket next to me — sorry to be so descriptive — and little Scott didn't half look worried. *Can I borrow fifty p?* he said. I didn't have the energy to question what for. I felt guilty I couldn't cook his dinner, so I just pointed to my purse. He took the money and ran out of the back door. I thought to myself, *Well, he'll be gone for a while then*. But he came back five minutes later. He placed a bottle of Lucozade next to my pot on the floor.' My hands grip the arms of the chair. 'Oh, Jim. Why do things have to change? It must be my fault he's turned out the way he has.'

'Don't torture yourself,' he says, like he's read my mind. 'What he did to you and Ron was shameful. There's not a bad bone in your body,

Mags. There's no way he learned that behaviour from you.'

'Do you think the whole village knows what's become of him?'

'Do they heck. It can't be the first secret they've ever kept — we'd have heard about it. Well, I would have heard about it at least.'

I stare at the photograph. What type of person is he now? Does he have a wife? Has he turned his life around? Is he still alive?

'Jim, what's the latest date on the article?'

'2012.'

'That means he's had time to change his ways, doesn't it?'

Jim doesn't look at me. 'I don't know, Maggie.' He gets out a notepad and jots down Scott's last known address. 'I know it's not the quickest way, but given that we don't have his email address this is the best we've got.' He hands it over to me. 'Do it today, will you, Maggie?'

Since when did Jim get all savvy with emails and the internet? I look at the computer and press the button next to the green light. I suppose it's too late for me to start.

Jim puts his hands on his knees and turns to me. 'Can I show you something?'

I can't help but frown. 'It can't be anything as bad as seeing my son has become the most prolific criminal in Manchester, can it?'

He shrugs, leans over to the keyboard, and instantly a page called *MissingKids* is on the screen.

'*One every three minutes,*' says Jim, reading the headline.

'There never is.' My hand goes to my mouth, the other rests on the desk. 'It can't be that many.'

'I know. I started looking the other day. When you were so affected by — '

'Grace.'

'And I found this . . .'

Jim types in a name, and there she is.

A picture of Zoe. In her school uniform. The light from the sun makes a halo on her fair hair. It's a photo I could recall without looking at it — a picture I can see when I close my eyes.

'How did they get Zoe onto the internet?' Both of my hands support my chin, my fingers touching my lips. 'So anyone in the whole world can see her?'

I look to Jim and he nods, slowly.

It makes the world seem a little smaller. If Zoe were alive and saw this picture, would she recognise herself? She might question where all her baby photos are; or the thought may not have even crossed her mind.

Last seen in Bilton, Preston. Age now: 36. DOB: 5th January 1980.

It's so hard to read the age she would be now. Somewhere, our Zoe could be thirty-six years old, with her own husband, children, family, and not know a thing about us. I used to think I'd be okay if I just knew she was safe, if I knew she wasn't dead. But now, looking at the screen, I just want her back with me.

'Hey, Mags, I'm sorry.' He puts his arms around my shoulders and hands me a tissue. 'I never meant to upset you. I just wanted you to know that in some place . . . even cyberspace . . . people are still looking for her. Her face is still out there.

'But that's not all I found. I've been looking at these sites for days, hours. As you can imagine, missus over there has given me free rein, so I've sort of taken advantage a bit. Well, this . . . I had to email it to myself, just to make sure I wasn't seeing things.' Jim clicks on another page, and another photo fills the screen. 'This!' Jim leans back and holds up his right hand to the screen.

I lean towards it. 'It looks just like her.'

Jim's nodding. 'It's not there for coincidence, Mags. We were meant to find it.'

I lean in closer. I don't believe in all that superstitious nonsense.

'But who else has seen it?'

★   ★   ★

My heart sinks as I open the front door: the phone is ringing. I had wanted to contact Scott first — to show him that he didn't have to make the first move, that I — as his mother — was interested in him too.

'Do you want me to get it?'

'No, thanks, Jim. It's got to be me. It can't go on like this.'

I'm talking to deaf ears — Jim is already sitting on my settee. I dash as fast as I can to the telephone.

My hands are shaking as I pick up the handset.

'Scott? Scott? I've been trying to find you.'

194

'Maggie? Can you hear me?'

'Scott?'

There's a silence. For a moment I think they've hung up again like last time.

'It's not Scott, Maggie,' says the voice. 'It's me — David.'

33

They don't have bacon and eggs every day. Yesterday and the day before that it was cornflakes and boiled eggs, which isn't too bad. They have those little cereal boxes that Mummy won't buy me, but we've not finished the big box. Catherine doesn't like wasting things. She said the cornflakes'll go soft if we leave them. I think it's a waste having the mini boxes if no one's going to eat them. I'll be going home before they open one.

I haven't been outside yet. Not even in their back garden. It has a swing and a tree house. It's a bit mean to not let me play on them really, but I haven't said that. Catherine cries if I say something she doesn't like, which is most of the time.

I've tried really hard not to ask about Mummy. Last night I did, when Catherine turned the light off in the room I sleep in. I thought Catherine wouldn't be too mad; I helped her dry the pots before bed. I was wrong.

'Am I going to see my mummy tomorrow?' I couldn't help saying it. I'd been trying to say it since we got here and the words fell out of my mouth.

'What did you just say?'

I covered my mouth with the quilt. 'Nothing.'

She walked slowly towards me. In the dark, her eyes looked quite scary — wider than they usually are — brighter, darker.

'I'll tell you one last time. If I ever hear the word mummy come out of your mouth again, I'll make you wish you hadn't said it.'

She slammed the bedroom door shut — even though Michael was in the room next to me *having an early night.*

It took me ages to get to sleep after that. I kept the middle of the curtains open so I could see the sky. Everyone's underneath the same sky; Gramps told me that. I pictured Mummy and Daddy watching telly, with me on the stairs peeking through the living-room door as they watched *Coronation Street.* That was when they were happy. It wasn't like that when I left them. Now, they shout at each other like Catherine and Michael.

'I was thinking.' Catherine speaks to me now as though she's singing, making me jump. We're sitting round the dining table. Our empty shells are in front of us in Humpty Dumpty eggcups. I've still got the milk to drink from my cornflakes — it's the best bit, with all the sugar at the bottom. 'Perhaps I could take you out today.'

'Really?' I don't want to get my hopes up. She changes her mind so fast.

Michael has gone to work, so he isn't here to say if it's a good plan or not.

'I've said that I have a niece visiting from England. Actually . . . I told my friends that weeks ago . . . just in case we had a real visitor. And it *is* school holidays here. Perhaps you could play with children of your own age. We need to

197

see if you'll be all right mixing with others anyway. Did you have many friends?'

'Yes. At school.'

I want to say that they're *still* my friends, but she won't like that.

'Very good,' she says. 'So, you'll be a good girl if I let you out?'

I don't know how much happiness to give away. Usually when I let her know my feelings, she gets angry.

I just nod.

'Would you like that?'

I nod again.

'Well, if you don't really want to go, then we shan't. I can't force you to go.'

She turns her back on me and goes back into the kitchen.

'I'd love to go,' I shout.

It takes her ages to come back in.

'Well. There you go. It's not hard to be nice, is it?'

I shake my head, to agree with her — even though I thought I *was* being nice.

'Before we go, I think we should do something about your hair. It's a bit too long for this heat, don't you think?'

'Maybe.'

If she cuts my hair, my mummy will go mad — she really will. *I've been growing her hair since she was born*, she always says. If Catherine cuts my hair, will Mummy recognise me?

I've only just finished my breakfast, and Catherine drags the chair I'm sitting on into the kitchen.

'Easier to sweep up the mess,' she says. 'Wait there.'

She comes back a few minutes later with a towel and a pair of scissors. They're not like scissors I cut things out with, or the orange ones Mummy uses for wrapping paper, but long, silver ones. She fills a cup with water, dunks a black comb into it and uses it to brush my hair. When she gets to a knot, my head burns, but I try not to make a sound. She puts her hand on the top of my head and she pulls the comb through it, again and again and again. My ears are throbbing.

'He wouldn't let me touch her hair,' says Catherine.

I want to ask whose hair she means. The girl in the photos? I want to ask when she's coming back from holiday. It would be so much nicer being in this house if she were here too.

By the time she's combed my hair, drips are running down my face.

'Don't you look pretty with wet hair?'

No one has ever said that to me before.

She puts the towel on my shoulders too late. The dark blue t-shirt I'm wearing is already soaked at the back. She pulls the towel tight around me and fastens it with a clip at my chest.

Catherine combs my hair forward over my face. The scissors scrape together as she snips me a fringe. *Rrrpp.*

'Close your eyes,' she says.

I do, and she blows into my face. I feel the hair drop onto my hands; I try to keep them still in case it falls to the floor.

'You look nicer like that,' she says, still bent in front of me. This is the closest I've looked at her. Her freckles are hiding under the powder on her face, and her eyelashes are like thick spider legs. Mummy doesn't wear much make-up — I've only ever seen her wear lipstick on parents' evening.

She stands back up and cuts the rest of my hair so it only comes down to my chin. It's the shortest it's ever been. She snatches the towel away; it scrapes my neck.

'What a transformation!' she says. She's in front of me, her hands resting on her hips. Her eyes narrow as she looks at me. 'Would you like to see yourself?'

'Okay,' I say.

She tuts and walks away, coming back moments later with the big mirror off the living-room wall. She turns it around.

It's not me any more.

Mummy won't know it's me — I look too different.

There must be hair in my eyes; they're starting to water.

'Do you like it?' she says.

'Yes,' I say. Catherine doesn't like me nodding.

She turns round, taking the mirror back to the other room.

I stare at the girl in the photograph on the cabinet. I look just like her now.

★ ★ ★

We're in someone's back garden. The mums are sitting round a plastic table on a patio and me

200

and *the kids* are on a blanket on the grass. Catherine comes up to us all the time. 'Everyone getting along? Are you all talking nicely?'

A boy with dark hair (he likes jumping into the round paddling pool and splashing everyone) is sitting opposite me in his swimming trunks. He's called Mark. On each side of us are Faye and Beth, who are the quietest people I have ever met — they only talk to each other.

'So,' he says, chewing on a giant hot dog sausage that he's holding up to his mouth, 'have you ever been to London and seen Big Ben?'

'No.'

'What a bumpkin,' he says. 'I bet you're not even from England.'

I see a yellow-coloured bottle on the blanket and pass it to him.

'In England, everyone loves this.'

He reaches over and squirts it into his mouth. I have to cover mine as he spits it out.

'Bloody hell!' He wipes his tongue. I've never heard a boy that young say a swear word, but I suppose he's allowed. His mummy makes him call her by her first name. 'That's goppin'.'

The girls next to me laugh, which seems to make him happy.

'You eat it then.' He's holding out the bottle to me.

I grab the bottle from him. 'All right.' I get one of the rolls and split it open with my fingers, like Mummy does. I place a hot dog inside it then squeeze a line of yellow along it. I take a bite.

'Mmm,' I say. 'Mmm, mmm, mmm.'

Mark picks up a roll and throws it in my face.

'Blah, blah.' He smiles at me. 'I bet you have to wear a uniform at school. And I bet you don't have harvest festivals. Where you can make your own bread. And butter.'

I throw the roll back at him. 'We have harvest festivals.'

'Everyone all right here?' It's Catherine again. 'What are you talking about?'

'Harvest festivals,' says Mark.

I smile at him, because he hasn't said about the mustard.

'What about them?' asks Catherine.

'They have them in England,' he says.

The smile on her face is still there as she turns to look at me.

'Is that right?'

'Mark asked if we had them. That's all. That's all I said.'

'*We*? If *we* had them?'

I use the smile that I use when Daddy isn't feeling well, to make him think that everything is all right.

'We. Me and you and our family, Auntie Catherine.'

I remembered what she'd said to me in the car. *Auntie Catherine.*

She looks at me with one of the stares she must have practised from Michael, and I make my smile go away. I'm not going to be allowed to play outside ever again. She thinks I'm too naughty to do anything fun.

Why have all the grown-ups in the world turned mean?

34

Maggie

I fell asleep on the settee again. My dreams these past few days and nights have been so vivid. This afternoon, I was chasing Sarah, like I did a few days ago, but when she turned round, she had Zoe's face. A child's face on an adult body. Obviously I was running faster than I can in real life. Why can't it have been Sarah? It's not as if it were real.

Last night I dreamt of Scott. It was possibly a memory. We were walking back home from playschool, just him and me. He must've only been three or four.

'I've just learned skipping,' he said, hopping on each foot.

'I'm glad they're teaching you all the important things,' I said. 'How else would everyone know you're happy as you walk?'

He giggled, his little eyes squinting from the glare of the sun.

'Can I stay with *you* tomorrow, Mummy, instead of being at big playschool?'

I loved the name he called it. I didn't tell him it was Saturday the following day; that would've spoilt it.

'Of course you can, Scottie.'

He skipped off into the distance — too far away. He disappeared into the bright sun on the horizon.

The dream had ended too quickly, as anything good does.

My heart physically aches when I remember him as a little boy. I want to go back to then, and start again. If I could dream of Sarah, Ron, Scott and Zoe every time I went to sleep, I'd never leave my bed.

Since little Grace Harper's disappearance, my life has been shaken up, and not for the better. I've seen photos of someone who looks like Sarah, contacted Scott, and been telephoned by David. What is happening? I feel like it's building up to something I'm not ready for.

The sun is warming my ankles from the window. The weather doesn't suit my mood, but I suppose it can't rain every day, can it?

I push myself up. David. He's coming here the day after tomorrow. He has some news he wants to tell me face to face — news he didn't sound happy about. If it were about Zoe, the police would've told me. Otherwise, I can't think of anyone else alive that I care about. Unless it's about Scott. I care about him as a son, but as the twenty-one-year-old lad he once was.

The last time I spoke to David was two years after Zoe disappeared. Obviously he and Sarah were separated before, which was why she and Zoe were staying here, but he used to come round every day to ask for news, even though he knew we would have contacted him if there were any. We liked David then — he hadn't had an affair or anything, they just didn't get along.

That day, he came round as usual — at the same time, nine thirty. Sometimes Sarah would still be in bed after being awake until the early hours of the morning. She never came down if she heard him arrive. I suppose I didn't blame her. Seeing the face of Zoe's father, reminding her of the child who was lost. Zoe looked so much like him — her dark eyes and blonde hair. But when I looked at Sarah, I could see Zoe in her as well.

He was carrying a folder — a pale green one, I remember. When he sat down on the settee, he opened it. There were all sorts of things in it — pictures, maps, newspaper articles. The file looked a little grubby round the edges already.

'Do you want a cup of tea?' I said. He used to have tea: strong, three sugars.

'Not today, Maggie. Thanks.' He took out a notebook — orange. It clashed with the green folder. 'I've listed all the sightings of Zoe. See.'

I looked to Ron, sitting in his armchair next to the fire. He frowned. After a year, the police had stopped telling us about sightings of Zoe; they always came to nothing: Ireland, Germany, Cyprus — even one as far as Australia. It seemed that if anyone — usually from England — saw a blonde girl about Zoe's age, they would report it. One even took a photograph of some unknown child — it didn't look anything like her up close. There weren't cameras on phones in those days. Perhaps if there were we might have found her. That's if she were alive.

His list was long. It included countries and cities that I'd never heard reports of.

'How have you got all of this?' I said.

'From the library. I've gone through nearly

every newspaper that they have microfiche for.'

'Leave it to the police, lad,' Ron said. He called everyone younger than thirty *lad*.

'But the police aren't interested any more. There have been too many sightings, too little evidence. What am I meant to do? Just sit and wait?'

'It's a crazy idea,' said Ron. 'How on earth are you going to pay for it? You've no job, no money.'

David put the notebook back in the folder.

'I've got a couple of hundred saved — that should get me into Europe. Then I could get work when I'm there. I've worked in bars; I could pick fruit.'

Ron sat back in his chair. 'Pick fruit!'

'I'm serious, Ron.'

Ron looked at him, his eyes narrowed. 'I know you are, son. That's what worries me. You going all across Europe on a wild goose chase. You haven't been well as it is.'

Not being well. That's what Ron called David's depression. It was what he was signed off work with. But this was the most animated I had seen David for years. He had a purpose.

'Will I fetch Sarah down?' I said.

'Don't bother her,' said David. 'I'll write. I'll try to phone when I can.'

Ron got up to see him to the door. Just before he closed it, he said to David. 'I'm proud of you, son.'

It had brought tears to my eyes for two reasons: because David was doing something that Ron wanted to do himself, but couldn't; and because he'd never said that to our own son.

I'm waiting for the kettle to boil and there's an aeroplane outside. It's one of those ones with a tail with a message on. Sarah used to love those. 'Is it someone proposing, Mum?' or 'Is it someone looking for their lost love?' She was always sentimental. She used to read the lonely hearts columns in newspapers too, trying to guess what the person in the advert looked like. 'I like reading them, Mum,' she said, before she met David. 'But if I ever get desperate and consider putting one in the paper, shoot me.'

She could have been a romantic, had she had the chance at love again. But her life was snatched away when Zoe was. How was she meant to have a normal life after that? How were we all?

I put on my glasses, but I still can't read the message in the sky. I have this desperate urge to find out what it says. Ron's binoculars are in the pantry. I grab them and rush outside, and hold them up to my eyes.

MARRY ME KIM — I ♥ YOU

It takes my breath away a little. I don't know why.

* * *

Sarah's grave is only ten minutes' walk away. I go at least once a week, but I haven't been since the news about Grace Harper. I shouldn't get caught up in things all the time. Is it time to let go? I stop at the card shop. I always buy Sarah something.

Before I get to Sarah, I stop at Ron's. I take a tissue from my pocket and dust the flakes of mud off the base of his headstone. I kiss my fingers and place them over his name.

'I'm having a strange old time of it, love,' I say.

I glance across the cemetery. There's no one else around. The sky is darkening as it's close to teatime; I imagine families sitting around their kitchen tables, or having dinner on their laps in front of the telly, all safe and warm.

I feel a spot of rain on my cheek.

'It's nearly fifty-six years since we got married here, Ron,' I say, glancing at the church to the left of me. 'Can you believe that? When I was a girl, I didn't think I'd even get to fifty-six years of age.'

I pick out a couple of honeysuckle stems from the ground next to me. They're not the nicest looking plants — you don't get many flowering at this time of year — but they smell good. I place them into Ron's vase.

'I'm so tired, love.'

I pat the top of his headstone and start the short walk to Sarah's.

I can see before I get there that there's a small bunch of flowers that I don't recognise next to her gravestone. For years, I've been the only one to place something here. Could they be from David? I only saw him in the distance at Sarah's funeral. I couldn't believe that he hadn't come over afterwards to speak to me. I understood that it was over thirteen years since he and Sarah had been together, but they'd been married, had a child. I'd considered him part of our family. The least he could've done was come over to me after I'd just buried my daughter.

The day before that, I'd heard about David's move to Hull and that he'd stopped looking for Zoe. My world had crumbled beneath my feet.

It was also at Sarah's funeral that I last saw Detective Jackson, the lead on Zoe's abduction. He was in his fifties when the case was closed, but looked as though he'd aged twenty years by the time of the funeral. He'd come to the house after the service, and sat looking uncomfortably hot, pulling at his shirt collar.

'Thanks for coming, Detective.' I handed him a cup of tea on a china saucer.

'It's just Robert now.' He managed a smile. He took a sip of the tea and sighed a weary sigh. 'The day Zoe went missing, I always thought we'd find her, you know?'

I perched on the settee opposite him.

'I know. I thought the same.'

'And now, this has happened. I am so very sorry, Maggie. About Zoe, Sarah, Ron. What you've been through. Only half of it would break a person.'

'It's not your fault.'

'Perhaps it is — there might have been things we missed. I think about it every day. If we'd found her, then everyone's lives would have been so different.'

'I suppose we'll never know if that's true.'

I thought of his luxury — that he only thought about it every day; I had a job to stop myself thinking about it every minute.

'How's Mrs Jackson?'

He looked up, surprised. 'Oh, yes, she's fine. Had a list of all the things she wanted us to do when I retired — think we've managed one of them.' He drank the last of his tea and placed the cup on the coffee table. 'I heard David was in Cyprus. Is he still looking for Zoe?'

I put my cup on the table next to his. 'No. He's living with a girlfriend in Hull now — think she's got kids too, apparently. It appears men move on more quickly than women.'

'I wouldn't be too sure about that.'

'About what?'

'All of it.'

The wind blows across my face and into my hair as I tie the balloon I've bought next to Sarah's headstone. I wonder if Detective Jackson's still alive — he must be in his seventies now, probably looking like a centenarian.

I look down to the vase on the ground. There's no card with the flowers, but they're daisies. Sarah loved daisies. She painted them on her black boots when she was at college. I stroke the softness of the petals, and pick one of the flower heads off, putting it into my pocket. I wish I still had the boots that she painted.

The past is always part of my present.

35

Stephanie

I'm waiting outside Emma and Matt's, sitting in my car in silence, not wanting to go in. I can't pretend I'm going to the shop every time I want to be alone. I'll tell them that I'm going home just for tonight to give them, and me, some space. Mum does it all the time.

It's nearly dark now — the time when I worry more for Grace. I don't know why; she's been missing for days. It's at bedtime when she should be tucked up safe and warm.

It's payback time, the note said. Emma is convinced it's her stalker — the stalker she had never mentioned before. She'd not even hinted at it or appeared frightened. All I've witnessed is the constant phone calls in the car, and she replied to whoever it was calmly, too easily.

I linger at the gate. Their shouts are coming through the window.

'Stephanie!'

His voice makes me jump.

I turn around.

'Karl? What are you doing here? How did you know — ?'

'I just asked at the shop. I think everyone knows where your sister lives at the moment.'

He glances at the tea lights, soft toys and the ribbons at the garden fence.

His hands are in his jeans pockets. I've never seen him in jeans before. On our two dates, he's worn smart casual, or his mum's definition of that. He looks much better in jeans, younger.

'I thought you might need a friendly face — maybe go for a drink or something. Unless you have Jamie?'

I cringe at the *friendly face* cliché, but then paranoid thoughts jump into my head. Has he been following me? How does he know Jamie isn't with me? If I didn't work with him, if he were a stranger I'd met online, I would have run into the house.

'Actually, that sounds like a good idea,' I say despite myself. Anything would be better than going back into that house. 'It'll have to be just one though.'

He smiles and looks less like a nervous teenager. 'Great.'

★　★　★

The noise in the pub quietened for the briefest of moments when we walked in. When I looked round, eyes went to the floor or to the drinks in front of them. I felt bad, briefly, for being in the pub. What had these strangers thought? That I should be with Emma waiting for news?

Karl brings the drinks over. Mine is only on the table for a second before I pick it up and take a large sip. So crisp and cold I almost shiver. I place it in front of me, drawing a line through the condensation with my finger.

'It feels trite to ask you how everyone is,' he

says. 'But, how are you?'

I lean back against the booth. People around us are no longer staring, but talking amongst themselves. If they're eavesdropping, they're doing a great job at pretending they aren't.

'I'm doing well if I haven't cried in thirty minutes. I can't imagine what Emma and Matt are going through.' I grab the glass and take several gulps. 'Actually, I can. And it's . . . it's unbearable. The worst thing that can happen to a parent.' I put the heels of my palms against my eyes in the hope it will stop the tears coming out.

'I'm really sorry,' he says.

Poor bloke. We've been seeing each other for a month. I can't actually believe he's here. Neil wouldn't have been, I'm sure of that.

'I've been following it on the news,' he says.

'Really?'

He pulls his stool nearer to the table. 'Shit, not in a stalker kind of way — in an interested kind of way. God, I'm not explaining it very well.'

I put my hand on his. The wine is emboldening me. 'It's okay. I know what you mean.'

'It's because it's your niece. And because I care about you.'

I take my hand off, and clasp it with my other on my lap.

'Oh God, you think I'm a weirdo now, don't you?'

He looks around the pub, his knees are bouncing up and down.

'Chill out, will you?' I say. 'I don't think you're a weirdo.'

I smile at him to let him know I'm not just saying that, and his knees stop moving.

'Good.'

'How are they coping without me at work?'

He rolls his eyes. 'Well, Nicola keeps saying that we're fine, but she's shouting at everyone. Sandy's taken over your accounts, and obviously not doing as well as you, so she's having a ball.'

'Shit, sorry.'

'Don't ever apologise, Steph. Everyone understands. It's making them see the bigger picture.'

I raise my eyebrows.

'Bloody hell, I'm talking in clichés again, aren't I? I need to get a new job.'

I smile and pick at the beer mat under my glass.

'I think Emma's having an affair. Some bloke keeps ringing her on her work phone — even though I never knew she even had a work phone. It can't be just a colleague if he's ringing her constantly at a time like this, can it?' I don't wait for Karl to reply. 'But what I'm really scared of, Karl, is that Emma's real mum might've taken Grace. Emma hasn't seen her since she was a kid.'

Karl spits out the beer he was drinking.

He wipes his mouth with the back of his hand. 'Sorry.'

I take my glass and drink the last of my wine. He asks if I want another. I said I only wanted one before we got here, but nod anyway.

'So,' he says, putting the new drinks on the table, 'you think all of this, but have you told the police?'

'No. I'm not sure Emma knows about her mum.'

He's frowning. 'But surely she was old enough to realise. It's too important to keep from the police.'

I fold my arms; it's cold in here.

'She's already given the police the name of this man. She said he was stalking her.'

'I didn't mean that. I meant about her mum. What if she hired someone to get Grace?'

'I keep thinking that, but she wasn't even bothered about her when she gave her away, was she? Why would she be bothered now?'

'People change. Clarity. She might have been searching for her for years.'

'But Mum said she didn't give a shit. People like that never change.'

He tilts his head to one side; the thing people do when they either feel sorry for you, or think you're stupid.

'People can change.'

I push my glass further away from me.

'I need to go.'

★ ★ ★

'I'm sorry you had to see me like this,' I say.

We're outside Emma and Matt's and I'm still dreading going inside.

'Don't say you're sorry. I'd be an absolute mess if it were one of my nieces.'

'You have nieces?'

He puts his hands in his pockets again. It's actually cute the way he does it. That wine must

215

have gone to my head.

'Three. My brother has one daughter, and a son, and my sister has two girls.'

'It's strange that I'm just learning these things about you.' I rub my forehead. 'Sorry, I think I'm pissed already. I thought I'd become a hardened drinker after these past few days.'

Shit, what am I saying to him?

He takes a hand out of his pocket and rubs my left arm. 'I'd be pissed all the time.'

He leans over to me, I'm worried that he's going to kiss me. I can't do this, not now.

My shoulders relax as he kisses my cheek.

'Just ring me or text me if you need me. I'll be here.'

'Thank you.'

I stand with my back to the gate, watching him walk away. I can't believe he came. He's braver than I am. That's what I need in my life, someone fearless.

When I step inside the house, the warmth is suffocating. I wait outside the sitting-room door, listening for the sound of news. I breathe in and push down the handle.

'You're back at last!' says Matt. He's pacing the carpet again. 'Perhaps you'll get some sense out of her.'

Emma, sitting in the chair by the window, winces at the word *her*.

'I'm not talking to you when you're like this,' she says.

'So what did you expect me to be like, eh? *Okay, Emma, love of my life. Who is this man that was stalking you for months? Who is this*

216

man *I could have put in his fucking place?* Eh?'

Emma looks to the window. It's dark outside and the curtains are open.

'Do you think he's taken Grace? Do you?' He's kneeling next to her, his face just inches from hers.

They must have had this conversation too many times since I left.

'Where's Mum?' I'm standing in the middle of the room; I feel helpless.

Matt stands up. 'Now, where *is* your mother? She's on the patio having a fucking cigarette. Said she'd had enough and she's going outside for some fucking fresh air. Bet she thinks we don't know, but we do. Probably on her third by now, with a bottle of wine next to her. That's where your bloody mother is.'

I turn my back on him, and walk slowly into the kitchen. He's lying. Mum smoking? As if.

As soon as I get into the kitchen I can smell it. I pull open the door and step outside, sliding the door shut behind me. Mum is sitting on a white patio chair, a bottle of wine and a half-empty glass on the plastic table in front of her. She holds up her hand — the one with the cigarette in it.

'Don't say a word about the ciggie,' she says. *Ciggie?*

I pull out the chair next to her and sit down. 'Okay.'

'Shall I get you a glass?'

'No, I'm fine.'

She shrugs. 'Fair enough.'

I think she's had more than what's gone from

217

the bottle. She would never have smoked in front of us. Or would she? I can't remember.

I put my hands under my thighs to try to warm them. I need to say it. While she's like this — it's the only chance I might get.

'Can I ask you something, Mum?'

She nods, but doesn't look at me. Instead she takes a drag on the cigarette. It's so weird seeing her like this.

'This note. *It's payback time*. Do you think it might be Emma's mum? Is she the type of person to take Grace?'

She's frowning when she turns to face me. She stares at me for what feels like five minutes before she opens her mouth to speak.

'Jean?' she says. 'You remember Jean?'

'I couldn't remember her name, but I remember Emma coming to live with us.'

'Hmm.' She turns back to looking at the concrete garage. 'I thought you girls had forgotten about her. She was no good for Emma.' She picks up her drink.

'What do you mean?'

'I mean that she used to go off drinking for days and leave that poor little girl on her own in that disgusting flat of hers.'

'Did you call social services?'

Mum puts her drink on the table and turns to face me again.

'Social services? Have you any idea how they treated children? No? Well, it wasn't good back in those days. One of the wives — in one of the villages we stayed in a long time ago — had experiences of being in care and it was horrific.'

218

She grabs the glass, downs its contents, and pours another. 'Jean came to me a few weeks after we took Emma in — her husband had died in a car accident years before, though I never asked around to see if it were true. She asked if we'd look after her daughter permanently. She'd met a new man . . . he didn't like kids. God knows what Jean said to the authorities for them to agree to it, perhaps that we were distantly related, I don't know. She knew we couldn't have another after you — everyone did, bloody wives. You tell one and you tell them all. I didn't know that then, of course. Emma's always needed a bit more looking after than you did. She was always so vulnerable. You were always so strong, even when you were little. Do you remember that boy you liked — what was his name? Luke — that was it. You went with him to the pictures when you were thirteen. Emma wouldn't come out of her room all afternoon. She was so lost without you, she made you stop seeing him. Isn't that right?'

I do remember that. I had liked Luke for years — since we started secondary school. In Year 9 he'd asked me to go and see *Demolition Man* — it was a fifteen certificate, so I was going to tell my dad we were going to watch *Hocus Pocus*.

'Can you believe it?' I said to Emma on our walk home from school. 'After all these years. I thought he'd never guess that I liked him.'

Emma didn't reply.

Luke was due to pick me up at one o'clock the following Saturday. When that day came, Emma never got out of bed.

'Are you sure you should go?' Mum said as she and I stood on the landing outside Emma's bedroom door. 'You can't leave that poor girl on her own.'

'I'm not leaving her on her own,' I said. 'You and Dad are here.'

'What's all this commotion?' said Dad, coming up the stairs. 'I'm trying to read the paper in peace.' He joined Mum and me; all three of us standing too close together on the small landing.

'Mum won't let me go to the pictures,' I said. 'After I told Luke I was going. And you both promised.' I folded my arms, pouting.

'Of course you can go and see the film.' He looked at Mum. 'Why are you saying she can't go?'

'I should've known you'd take Stephanie's side. You always do. You're thick as thieves, the pair of you.' Mum folded her arms too. She nodded to Emma's door; there was a name sign on it that was pink with silver stars. 'Remember what that poor girl went through.'

Dad narrowed his eyes at Mum. They stood there for ages, just staring at each other.

'She's going,' he said. 'And that's final.'

Mum had simply shrugged. The doorbell had sounded and I ran down the stairs, relieved to get away from the drama.

I feel a speck of rain on my face. Mum is staring into the pitch black at the end of the garden. I need a drink. I can't believe she's bringing up all of this now. My mind's working hard just to keep up with what she's saying.

'You know,' she says, still looking into the darkness. 'Dad always took your side. Every time. It was like he wanted nothing to hurt you.' She takes a sip of her wine. 'I suppose he loved you more than he did me.'

I roll my eyes, knowing she can't see me. 'That's not true, Mum. Dad adored you. You know that.'

'Sometimes it's hard to remember things like that,' she says. She turns on the plastic chair to face me. 'I thought you'd be a quiet child. But you were always angry at me; I couldn't do anything right. If I said the sky was blue you would have argued that it was green.'

'I don't remember being like that. Why would you think I'd be quiet?'

'I don't know.'

Perhaps she thought I'd take after Dad. Or she might be annoyed that I'm more like her than we both wanted to admit. How can she say I was always angry at her when I was only a child?

She could be right. Sometimes I can look at her — as I'm doing now — and it's like I don't know her at all; behind her eyes lies a stranger.

'Maybe it's because I compared you with Emma,' says Mum. 'She was so reserved, needed so much more looking after. After what she'd been through with that terrible woman.'

'Emma's not as weak as you think,' I say.

'And to answer your question,' she says, ignoring what I just said. 'Jean is *not* the type of person to go on a bounty hunt to find her daughter and steal her child. She's known all these years where her daughter was and never once has she come to say hello, or even sent her a birthday card.'

Mum's thoughts are all over the place — it takes me a few seconds to catch up.

'But how do you know that she knows where Emma is?'

The plastic chair tumbles down as Mum gets up.

'Because I've written to her every year since she left her.'

36

Maggie

I don't think I can face David on my own, but I've been ringing Jim all afternoon and there's no answer. Mobile. He's got a mobile phone — he wrote the number on a card.

It rings ten times before his answering machine sounds. I dial again. And again. On the third attempt, a woman answers. She sighs before speaking.

'Hello, this is Jim's phone.'

'Hello? It's Maggie. Is Jim there?'

'Ah, Maggie. Jim told me all about you. I'm afraid Jim's been poorly. I'm at the hospital.'

'Poorly? He never mentioned it.'

I perch on the arm of the settee next to the phone table.

'Well, that's Jim for you.'

'I'll ring for a taxi — I'll be there in half an hour.'

I wait for her to say not to bother, that he'll be out in a few hours, but she doesn't. I hang up the phone quickly. I didn't ask who I was speaking to. It must have been one of the nurses. But then, if it was, how did she know about me? It must be his back. And he can witter on to anyone about anything.

I put on my coat and wait by the front door.

The house is so quiet I can hear the ringing in my ears.

★ ★ ★

The hospital isn't big, but I've no idea where I'm going. I stand at the end of the queue for reception. Why hadn't Jim told me he was ill? I've been so self-centred. He's always there to listen to my problems, I'm always going on about them. I'll make it up to him. I'll cook him his tea every week: my homemade steak pie with mash. He'll love that — it was Ron's favourite.

There's a tap on my shoulder.

'Excuse me. Are you Maggie?'

It's a woman — in her fifties I presume. Her hair is short, styled nicely with a lot of hairspray; it doesn't move when her head does. Her earrings coordinate with her necklace, and I bet the nail varnish on her hands matches that on her toes.

'Yes. How did you know?'

She smiles. Her eyes are red. She looks the type to wear mascara, but there's none on her lashes. My heart starts thumping hard and it's getting harder to breathe.

'Jim said you always wore a navy raincoat — and a matching hat. Whatever the weather.'

'He did?'

She nods.

I don't want to be here. I think I'd better leave before she tells me something I don't want to hear. She takes hold of my elbow and guides me to the nearest bench.

'What ward is Jim on?' I say quickly. 'Did I tell you he never mentioned he was ill? I didn't know. I feel terrible for not knowing.'

She sits me down and puts a hand over mine. Why is she being so nice to me? I've never met her before in my life.

'I'm so very sorry, Maggie. Jim died this morning. He suffered from cancer of the kidney, but he had a heart attack last night.'

'Oh,' is all I can say.

I take hold of this stranger's hand. I am still wearing my gloves. Around me, there are people: patients, relatives, doctors. It's like I'm on another planet — a witness looking in through the window.

Jim's not dead. We had so much to do.

I hear the ringing in my ears again; it's so loud. A man in a wheelchair goes past, dragging an IV drip to the side of him.

He can't have died without telling me.

What am I going to do without him?

The woman next to me hands me a tissue. It's only then that I realise the tears are pouring down my face.

'No. No, I can't believe he's just gone. I can't.' I press the tissue against my face. I turn to look at her — she's crying too. 'I'm sorry. I don't know you — have I met you before? I'm sorry if I have.'

She shakes her head.

'We only got back in contact recently. I'm Anna. I'm Jim's son's ex-wife.' She smiles. 'I know — it's a bit of a mouthful. He sent me an email. He said he never saw his grandchildren through Tom — we've three boys, you see, eight, ten and thirteen. We arranged a get-together.' She takes her hand from mine and wipes her face. 'It was meant to be next week.'

'I'm sorry, Anna.'

This can't be happening. Everything's coming at me at once. I can't handle all of this without Jim.

She sits up straight and takes a deep breath.

'Do you want to see him?' she says.

'I . . . I don't know.'

'You don't have to. There'll be time before the funeral.' She takes out a piece of paper from her pocket. 'He wrote a list of songs he wants. He's paid for it all.'

My mouth drops open. 'I wish he'd told me.'

'You were probably the only person he could be well with — someone who wasn't always talking about his illness.'

She dabs her nose with a tissue.

'Can I give you a lift anywhere?' she says, standing up. 'I can drop you off at home?'

I stand too. 'Yes, please. That's very kind of you.'

All this time I've been missing my family, and Jim was searching for his. It's just too awful to comprehend. The poor, poor man.

I feel numb, like I'm on autopilot. If I can get through this now, then I can have a good cry when I get home. I can't have an emotional breakdown in front of a virtual stranger.

★ ★ ★

226

'I'm popping to Jim's later,' she says, as we pull up outside my house, 'to feed his bird. Would you like to come with me?'

'Are you sure you don't mind?'

'Of course I don't. I know how close you two were. I had only chatted with him a few times on the phone and he talked about you all the time. He said you were his best friend.'

Oh God. I can't be in this car right now.

I get out quickly. 'I'll see you tonight then.'

I rush down my front path, and get inside the front door. I close it and lean against it. My whole body is trembling.

A tear falls down my face — for Jim and for myself. I haven't got anyone else left. What am I going to do without him?

★ ★ ★

I'm ashamed to say that I have never been to Jim's flat. I had wrongly assumed that he still lived in the same house he had when Sylvia was alive. The apartment block is just five minutes' walk from my house and I feel terrible that I never visited him.

I managed to pull myself together when Anna called for me at six. I had spent the afternoon sitting at the kitchen table in silence, not wanting to eat or drink. I can't believe he's gone. I think I'm still in shock.

I follow Anna through the double doors, trying to keep up with her. I imagine she's one of those people who's always in a rush, always busy. She pushes the button to the lift several times; I'm surprised when the doors open. I don't think I've ever been to a block of flats where the lift has worked.

'It's so nice here,' she says as the doors close. 'Quite modern. Though of course it's for people of retirement age only, so it's well-kept.'

'Hmm.' I think Anna might be a bit of a snob, but I don't say anything.

Jim's place is on the third floor, number thirty-four. The corridors are carpeted and there are framed pictures on the walls. It's like a hotel.

I don't know what I expected, but Jim's flat is immaculate. There's a small hallway that leads to his living room, which has a settee and an elegant armchair next to the gas fire. Alongside it is an occasional table; on it a folded newspaper on the crossword page — his reading glasses on top of it next to a pen with its lid on the wrong end.

Under the table is a pile of puzzle books and what look like photo albums. If I were alone, I'd go straight to them, sit down and look at the pictures. Anna has gone into Jim's bedroom, through a door off the living room. It would be wrong for me to go in there.

There's a pine sideboard under the window with pictures in frames on top. There's a carriage clock — I pick it up to look at the engraving: *To Jim Arkwright. For forty-five years' service at Ellwood's Electrical.* Forty-five years — I can't believe it. Ron had taken early retirement after Zoe went missing. I didn't know Jim had stayed at Ellwood's that long. I place the clock down gently and pick up the photo with Jim and his wife on their wedding day. Such a handsome couple — so happy. Where do they go, moments like that? They just vanish in an instant.

'This one or this one?' Anna's holding up two suits.

'Is this for his funeral? Already?'

I sit down on the nearest seat to me. How could she be so practical at a time like this?

'Sorry, Maggie. I know it's a bit soon, but I have to head back to Scotland tonight. This is the last chance I'll get to collect his suit before the funeral.'

I nod slowly. She has other family, children to get back to, whereas this is Jim's life, my life. I suppose it's better that Anna is organising it — I'd have been useless. He probably knew that all along.

'The one on the right,' I say. 'It was his favourite. He bought it on Savile Row in the nineties.'

'Good choice. Nice and smart.' She smiles a sad smile.

'What's going to happen to all of his things?'

She drapes the suit on the back of the settee, and takes the other to hang up.

'He wanted it to go to charity. The good stuff.'

She reaches into her pocket, and hands me an envelope. 'This is for you. I'm sorry I forgot to give it to you earlier.'

I take it from her, and put it in my bag. I want to read it alone.

'I was wondering, Anna. Would it be okay if I had a look through his photo albums, before you give them to your children? It's just that — '

'Of course it's okay, Maggie. Hang on, I'll get them for you.'

She collects the books from next to his chair — I'm surprised she knew they were there.

'Actually, I have a favour to ask you. Sometime after the funeral, could you possibly help me go through Jim's belongings? I know it might be painful . . . '

'Of course I will.' I take a look around Jim's flat and all of his memories in photos and pictures. 'It would be an honour.'

37

Catherine isn't happy with me. She never seems to be happy with me. It's not my fault I'm here — it was her idea. That's what I heard Michael say anyway.

We left the barbecue early because she said I had a tummy ache, even though I didn't. She drove really slowly back to their house. She said she was being careful in case anyone stopped the car. I didn't tell her that George drove really fast and no one ever stopped us, because nothing I say is useful.

I've been sent to the bedroom to think about what I've done. I am trying really hard to think of what I've done, but I can't remember. When she asks, I'll just say I'm sorry.

It's my favourite place by the window anyway. It's been sunny every day since I got here — I wish I could go outside more.

There's a person in the garden opposite. It's a woman. I lean on the windowsill and press my nose against the window. She has the same hair as Mummy. I try really hard for my eyes to see better. She doesn't have the same clothes as Mummy, but I don't have the same clothes as in England either. It's Mummy — I'm sure it is.

I knock on the window, but she's too far away.

I try to unhook the lever on the window, but it's got a lock on it — I can't find the key.

I knock harder, but I'm scared the window will break.

'Mummy!' I'm not loud enough. I cup my hands around my mouth — they do that on the telly. 'Mummy!'

She still can't hear me.

'What the hell is going on?'

Oh no, it's Catherine. She's still holding the handle of the bedroom door, but her face looks angrier than I've ever seen anyone.

'Why are you shouting? Are you trying to get me into trouble?'

I shake my head.

'Why were you shouting *mummy*?'

I point outside. 'My mummy's over there.'

Catherine frowns and sit down on my bed. She narrows her eyes to look better, like I did. I can't stop my body shaking. I think I need a wee, but I daren't move.

'You silly little girl. That's not your mummy, is it? How on earth could that be your mummy? It's the woman who lives opposite.' She stands up, but she's still staring at me. She grabs hold of my hand and tugs me off the bed. 'What have I told you about talking about your mummy? I'm your mother now and you'd better get used to it.'

She pulls me out of the bedroom and down the stairs.

'This'll teach you a lesson.' She opens the cupboard under the stairs and pushes me into it. 'You're not coming out until you're sorry. No more talking about mummy. She's dead to you, do you hear?'

I nod my head, and blink really fast so my

tears don't come out.

She closes the door and I'm in darkness.

What have I done that was so bad? Why didn't she just let me say I was sorry?

I slide down the wall until I'm sitting on the floor. I bring my knees close to my chest. I can't believe my mummy's dead. I put my arms around my head and cry the hardest I've ever cried.

38

Stephanie

I've been thinking about it ever since she told me last night: how has Mum been writing to Jean all these years and not mentioned it to Emma and me? Mum had gone back inside the house with her bottle of wine before I could ask if Jean had ever replied. I can't believe she wrote to Jean every year. It's so unlike Mum to have spared a thought for someone she deemed unworthy. Did she feel guilty that she took Emma away from her biological mother? Why did no one talk about it after Emma came to live with us? There was nothing for Emma to be ashamed of.

There are so many questions I've thought of since; when will I have that opportunity to talk to Mum again? She knows I'd never ask her in front of Emma.

I've caught Mum looking at me throughout the day, like she can't quite be sure that she spoke to me outside in the garden last night. I wanted to grab her by the shoulders, shake her and shout *just tell me the truth*. But that would never do, would it?

'What were you and Mum talking about last night?'

Emma's washing dishes, her back to me. It's the first time I've seen her doing anything remotely domestic. It's also the only chance we've had to speak alone. Mum has been hovering between us all day, as though she's afraid I'm going to say something to Emma.

I get up, grab a tea towel and stand next to her. It's dark outside. Another day has gone without Grace here. I glance quickly at Emma. Matt has barely spoken to her since she revealed she was being stalked by a man from work. She hasn't mentioned it since.

'Nothing important,' I reply at last.

'I can't believe Mum's smoking again,' says Emma.

'What? Since when has Mum ever smoked properly?'

'You're joking, right? She was always having a crafty ciggie at the back door.'

'Sometimes I think you grew up in a different house to the one I did.'

Emma hands me a dripping plate. 'I probably did.'

I try to dry the plate with the sodden tea towel. *You shouldn't dry the dishes straight after washing them — you'll soak the pot cloth.* Was it Mum who used to say that? I don't think it was.

'The police called while you were on the phone to Jamie. They want us to give them our birth certificates.'

'What? Why?'

She shrugs. 'I don't know, do I? I guess it's what they do.'

'They wouldn't ask for things like that. They have access to all that from the station — they have official documents online. Didn't you ask them why?'

'Obviously not. I've got more important things to think about.'

'But why would they ask us to get them? If they've got something to say, why don't they just come out and say it?'

'Say what? Jesus, I don't know, Steph. It's just what they said.'

'It doesn't sound right. Where's Nadia?'

She shrugs again. Why isn't she bothered about this?

'Did you give them yours?'

'No. They only asked an hour ago. And anyway — I've no idea where mine is. I'll have to go down to births and records to get another copy.'

'You're not doing that — it's ridiculous. I'll ring them in the morning, sort this out.'

'But you've got yours, haven't you? If it helps them find Grace, then we have to do as they say.'

'Somewhere. Of course I have. Why would that help them find — '

'Shall we take a drive out to yours? I could do with getting out of this house.'

'I really don't think — '

'Please, Steph. Matt's driving me mad. He's not spoken to me since he found out about Andrew. I'd rather he shouted at me than ignore me. Please.'

I grab my keys from the table.

Andrew. So that's his name.

* * *

Emma's rubbing her temples. We've been in the car for five minutes and she hasn't said a word.

I've stopped asking questions about the birth certificates. I'm beginning to doubt if the police asked for them in the first place — that perhaps it's Emma's elaborate excuse for getting out of the house.

'I wish you'd told me about Andrew,' I say, breaking the silence. 'I could've helped you — come with you to report him to the police. Matt wouldn't have had to know.'

'Whatever. You can never keep anything from Matt.'

'What? Why would you say that? Of course I can.'

'What about that time I said I might be getting a promotion, that I might set up a bank account to save up a surprise holiday fund? And what about — '

'You didn't say that was a secret. You said it as though everyone knew.'

'I said not to tell him. I said it was a surprise. Why would everyone know if it was a fucking surprise?'

'I . . . I didn't realise. I'm really sorry, Em.'

She tilts her head up, her eyes to the roof of the car. 'Oh, whatever. I couldn't care less.'

'What?' I press my foot on the brake and pull over.

'You're stopping? How dramatic of you — dramatic as ever.'

'Emma? What's wrong? I'm not being dramatic; I'm trying to talk to you.'

'Aahhh!' Emma's punching the seat next to her legs, shouting at the top of her voice.

She brings her hands up to her hair and grabs

each side of her head.

'I think I'm going insane. This isn't happening.' She pulls her hair with her hands. 'I don't know if I can even feel this.' She slaps one side of her face. 'Am I really here, Steph? I can't feel anything.'

I turn and grab both of her hands, wrestling with her.

'Emma. Emma!'

Finally, her hands are still.

'You are real, you are here. And I'm so sorry you're going through this.' I pull her hands towards me and wrap my arms around her. 'This is the worst nightmare. I'm so sorry.'

She's crying the hardest I've seen her cry. I rock her gently from side to side.

Please, God. If you're there. Make them find Grace. I don't know what Emma will do if they don't.

★   ★   ★

When we pull up onto my drive, Emma is staring straight ahead. My house looks almost sinister without the lights on.

'Do you want to wait there, Em?' I open my car door. 'Emma?'

She shakes her head back into the present. 'What? No . . . I'll come.' She looks through the windscreen, narrowing her eyes. 'What's that in the window?'

I look to where she's looking. 'I can't see anything.'

'I thought I saw something. It was probably a

shadow — or a reflection.'

I'm suddenly nervous of going inside my own house. It looks like a stranger's house; my skin covers in goose bumps. Why am I so afraid?

I'm relieved as Emma gets out. I walk round the car and link my arm through hers.

'We should be noisy going in,' I say. 'That'll scare them off . . . or at least it'll warn them we're coming so they can hide.'

I can't believe I'm contemplating going inside when Emma's seen something through the window.

'There's probably no one there.'

'Probably? What did the shadow look like?'

'I don't know. A man.'

'How are you being so calm about this? It might be that stalker, Andrew. Do you think we should call the police?'

'It'll be fine. Look — the lock hasn't been damaged. I'll just check round the back.'

'Emma — '

She's running towards the back gate. When did she get so brave? I'm frozen to the spot. If I count to ten and she's still not back, then I'll go round the back. One, two, three —

She's back. 'Emma, thank God. I was worried about you.'

'Jesus, Steph. Why have you gone all weird?'

'Er — because there might be some weirdo out there.'

She just looks at me, taking the key from my hand. She opens the door and pulls me inside.

'Let's turn all the lights on,' she says. 'Light always makes you feel better, remember? Do you want to check upstairs?'

'In a minute.'

My house is freezing. The heating hasn't been on for days and it feels as though the bones of it are stone cold. Dishes are still in the kitchen sink — our breakfast bowls from last Monday are still on the table.

All our important papers are in the cupboard under the stairs, but the light hasn't worked for weeks.

'Can you do me a favour, Em? There's a blue box file in the understairs cupboard — would you be able to get it out for me? You know I'm claustrophobic.'

She's rubbing her hands together, trying to get warm.

'There's no one in there, you know.'

'I know . . . I'll come with you.'

'It's fine, Steph. I'll get it.'

I watch her from the door — she's not bothered at all.

'Why aren't you scared, Emma? What about that stalker?'

'He won't come after you.' She pulls out the file and closes the door, turning to face me. 'Because, technically, he's not my stalker. I've been seeing him for three months.'

39

It was five minutes before Michael got home that Catherine opened the door. She was kneeling on the floor in front of me.

'I'm so sorry. Will you forgive me? I don't know my own mind sometimes.'

I don't know how long I was in there — an hour, or it might have been three, because it was dark outside when I was let out. Michael usually gets back when the day has finished. Catherine put me in there to forget about my mummy, but she was all I thought about.

Catherine's made me a hot chocolate and we're in the posh living room — they have two. One has loads of toys, and the other doesn't. It's the tidiest room out of all the houses I've been in. Granny likes to keep hers tidy, but hers is small — a living room and a kitchen — that's all there is downstairs.

Michael's upstairs getting changed out of his uniform. He looks smart in it, but I've never seen a uniform like that before. I thought he was a soldier, but he told me yesterday that he wasn't — I can't remember what he does, but it's with planes.

'Is that nice? Would you like marshmallows in it?'

I shake my head.

She moves from her chair to sit next to me on the sofa. 'You won't tell Michael about our little game, will you? He'll be ever so upset — he really wants to be your daddy.'

I already have a daddy, but I think Catherine knows that. She seems to know everything. She knows what I'm thinking too. I have to stop thinking about Daddy in case she locks me up again. Think of the hot chocolate.

'Is Michael her daddy too?' I'm looking at the photo of the blonde-haired girl. There's only one of her today. 'Where are the other pictures of her?'

'I've put them away for safe-keeping.'

'Okay.'

'You look just like her, don't you?'

She has the same hair as me, but she has blue eyes, mine are brown. Cow eyes, my gramps says, but I can't think about him.

'Is that a school picture?' I say.

'Yes.' She stands up and walks over to it. She turns it round to face the wall. 'I think we'd better get some photos taken of you — would you like that? In fact, I still have her uniform upstairs.'

She almost runs out of the room, and up the stairs. I don't want to wear that girl's clothes — I don't know her. I look down at the checked pinafore I'm wearing. Maybe I'm already wearing her clothes.

'All right, kidder?' Michael's wearing jeans and a t-shirt. He looks less like a proper grown-up in his normal clothes. 'I was thinking . . . would you like to go out of camp tomorrow? We could go to the water park. Would you like that?'

I nod, even though I don't know what a water

park is. I don't know how they could make swings out of water.

'I'll get Catherine to get you a bathing suit. I'm sure she would.' He sits down on the chair Catherine was sitting on a minute ago. He leans towards me. 'I know she seems pretty scary, but she means well.'

'Ta da!' Catherine's back and she's holding up a uniform. Her smile goes away when she sees Michael.

'What the hell are you doing, Catherine?'

He gets up quickly and takes her out of the room.

I wish I could hear what they're talking about.

I shuffle to the end of the sofa. Michael's whispers aren't as quiet as Catherine's.

' . . . can't bring her back, she's gone.'

Catherine's crying again.

'Now, now,' Michael's saying. 'We'll sort this out. If you'd just let me call someone, we can get her back home to her parents.'

'No!' Catherine's not trying to whisper any more. 'I swear, Michael. If you do that, not only will I tell the police that it was all your doing, I will fucking kill myself. Do you hear?'

'Stop being so dramatic, Catherine. We can tell them it's a misunderstanding.'

'A misunderstanding? You think they'll believe that? We'd have to tell them about George — about what he did, that he lifted her off the street. And I took her out this afternoon — to Mary's. What do you think they'll say when they hear about who this girl really is? Eh?'

'He took her off the street? Oh God, Catherine.'

243

She sighs. 'What's done is done. We just have to make the best of it.'

'How can you be so flippant about it?'

'Do I look like I'm being flippant?'

Someone's opening the patio door.

'I thought you'd given up,' says Michael.

I can smell it. Sometimes Mummy used to go outside and have a cigarette when she thought no one was looking. No, I mustn't remember things like that — Catherine will know.

Michael said *parents*. It must mean Mummy isn't dead.

The patio door slams shut. Their voices are getting closer. I shuffle as fast as I can to the other side of the sofa, look down at my empty cup and pretend to stir the gloop at the bottom with my fingers.

Michael pops his head round the door.

'I'm just nipping out. Do you want me to bring you some sweets back?'

'No, thank you.'

He looks surprised, but I'm not hungry. The hot chocolate has made me feel sick.

'I'm really tired,' I say. 'Is it okay if I go to bed?'

'Er . . . yes. I'll just get Catherine.'

I wish he could put me to bed.

They're whispering again.

When she comes back in the room, it's like she hasn't been crying. She's smiling.

'You poor little lamb, of course you can go to bed. Would you like a bath first?'

'No, thank you.'

'Come on then.'

She holds out her hand to me. I put my cup on the carpet, and take her hand.

40

Stephanie

I needed to sit down after she told me. She met Andrew at work and he's older than her, more mature; he made her feel safe. Matt was distant towards her: there in body, but not in mind — all the bloody clichés I had associated with Neil's affair with that woman from work. The truth is that she was selfish, bored. I can barely look at her as she sits at the kitchen table opposite me.

'So how long has it been going on?' I say.

'I told you. About three months — not long. Though he's been flirting with me since I started there.'

I glance at her. She's resting her forehead on her hand, her eyes fixed on the table.

'For *two years* he's been coming on to you, and you haven't mentioned anything to me?'

'There wasn't anything to talk about. It was just a typical office flirtation.'

I wince, feeling like she's punched me in the stomach. She looks up at me.

'Oh God, Steph. I'm sorry. I hadn't thought about Neil and that woman. Not until now. Oh shit. I'm so sorry.' She sniffs, and dabs her nose with a tissue. 'To be honest — I thought you fancied Matt. I tried to ignore it in the hope it went away. I knew how vulnerable you were after Neil left — I didn't want to embarrass you by mentioning it. I knew you wouldn't have done anything about it.'

My face burns. I didn't do anything about it, but Matt had tried to kiss me only a few days ago.

'Perhaps I did like him,' I say. 'But it was only a silly crush, harmless. I never would do anything about it. I'm seeing someone now.'

She looks up at me. I don't mention that Karl and I have only had a few dates.

'Really?'

'Early days,' I say. 'Anyway. This isn't about me — it's about you. When did you end it with Andrew?'

She takes a deep breath in and exhales, slowly.

'Last Monday. Exactly a week before Grace was taken.' She bites the skin around her thumb again; it must hurt to the touch now; she's been picking at it so much.

'What made you start seeing him in the first place? I don't understand why you'd risk everything.'

She leans back in the chair and looks to the ceiling.

'Andrew actually listened to me, you know? If I was quiet, he'd be the only one to notice. It started as working lunches — not that we talked about work much. He was single, well, divorced. He had so much time for me. Then we started meeting up at night, when I told Matt I was working late. Matt and I . . . let's just say it hasn't been great recently — perhaps it hasn't been great for years. We were so young when we got together — he was the only man I ever slept

247

with. Remember I was only eighteen; not a mature eighteen at that, not emotionally anyway. Sometimes I feel so distant from him — like he doesn't know the real me.'

'Then why don't you tell him about you, that — '

'I don't want to talk about it to anyone.'

'But what about — '

'Don't go there, Steph. Not right now.' She sits forward and places her arms on the table. 'Since Christmas, Matt has been working so many late nights, and when he comes home, it seems all he can talk about is Grace: how she's doing at school, what he's got planned for them at the weekend. It's like I don't matter. They're so close — him and Grace. It's like I'm the odd one out sometimes. They go to that chess club every week. I've tried hard to learn it so I can join in, but I don't get it. And now he's teaching her to play the bloody guitar. I don't see my place any more. I used to be the one who did everything for her. But she's getting so independent, it's like she doesn't need me. And Matt hasn't touched me for months, not like that anyway.' She sighs.

'Andrew was the one who made me feel alive again. Oh, God. What kind of person do I sound like?' She puts her hands over her face. 'I've brought all of this on myself. Andrew was so angry when I said I wouldn't see him any more.'

'Do you think he's capable of doing something like that . . . of kidnapping a child?'

Emma shrugs as though her body can't be bothered. She stares at the kitchen table, her eyes moving from side to side. She sits up quickly.

'The texts,' she says, reaching into her handbag on the floor. 'He sent me some nasty messages before Grace went missing.' She pulls out her phone — the second one she had in the car the other day — and hands it to me. 'The security code is 0105.'

I tap in the code and bring up the messages: they're all from the same person. I click on one.

I know you don't mean it, Em. We have something special here xx.

The next three say the same sort of thing, but when it gets to Wednesday the tone of them changes: *I can't believe you're ignoring me. I'll tell everyone in the office about this. And I have pictures. I'm sure your husband would be very interested to see them.*

The final message from Andrew is the most sinister:

So you won't even look at me, let alone talk to me. You're mine, Emma. I'll make sure you never forget that.

'Shit, Emma. Why have you kept these to yourself? I could have helped you.'

'But you would've told Matt.'

'Not with something like this. Has he texted you since Grace went missing?'

'No, he's been ringing me — on my work phone and on the landline — you wrote his number down on the notepad the other day. He's left me several messages, but I've only listened to one. He told me he was sorry — and that he didn't mean to be so nasty. He asked if he could help find Grace. What a stupid thing to say. Can you imagine? 'Hey, Matt. Meet Andrew. He's the one I've been shagging behind your back. But don't worry, he's offered to help look for our missing daughter.''

'Have you told the police about Andrew?' I say. 'He could've taken her. All this time you've had these messages and you've said nothing!' I look into her eyes. Anger rises up to my chest, my neck, like it's strangling me. I want to grab her by the shoulders and shake her.

'Of course I've told the police.' Tears are pouring down her face; her hands grip the sides of her head as though she's digging her nails into her scalp. 'I told them not to tell Matt, for now. I told them how Andrew threatened to get back at me when I finished with him. I *finished* with him, Steph. I came to my senses, if you will. So, yes, I've shown the police, they've got copies of the messages. He probably wouldn't hurt her. He was just upset with me because I ended things.'

'He *probably* wouldn't? What the hell? That man in the photo — the man with Grace from the CCTV — he came to your workplace.'

'I know . . . I thought Andrew might have asked him to take her. I haven't been thinking straight.'

'Oh, did you now? You're a fucking detective now, eh? And you didn't bother to tell the rest of us.'

She covers her face with her hands. 'Stop being so horrible to me. She's my child! Don't you think I'm suffering enough without you shouting and swearing at me?'

250

I turn away from her and open my kitchen cupboards; I'm sure there's some brandy in here somewhere. Where the hell is it? All I find is a whisky miniature from two Christmases ago. I open it, and drink it till it burns my throat. Shit.

I lean against the kitchen counter; I still can't look at her. Lies. She's been lying to me for months.

'Have the police questioned him?' I say, turning slowly round.

'I don't know. I haven't heard anything.'

'Haven't you asked Nadia?'

'When am I going to have a chance to ask? Matt's with me the whole time.'

I grab her by the wrist and lead her to the door.

'Come on. If you're not going to ask her, then I will.'

She stops still. 'What was that?' She's looking towards the hallway.

'Wait here.'

I run down the hall, up the stairs. The whisky and adrenaline are masquerading as courage. I turn on the hall light. I check in Jamie's room: nothing. Under his bed, in his wardrobe: nothing. The bathroom's empty — so is my bedroom. I lean against my doorway, out of breath from the short run up the stairs and the panic.

The spare room.

Had the door been closed when I left here? I never close that door, never needed to.

The floorboard creaks as I near the room. It's only small — enough for one single bed and a

251

wardrobe. If there's anyone in there, there's nowhere to hide.

I push the door gently. I hold my breath.

Silence.

I slam it open and flick on the light.

I quickly open the wardrobe doors and jump back.

Nothing.

I open the drawers under the bed. They're empty.

I almost burst into laughter at how silly I'm being. Of course there's no one in my house.

'Nothing up here,' I shout.

But as I turn round, something catches my eye.

The curtain is blowing with the wind. I'm sure I hadn't left the window open.

★ ★ ★

Emma's nearly hysterical when we pull up outside her house.

'What if Matt hears you ask?'

I get out of the car and walk around to her side. There are at least ten more tea lights along their fence, flickering in the darkness, some in jam jars to keep the flame burning.

'You keep him talking,' I say. 'Come on.'

When we walk into the house, it's as eerily quiet as mine was. Before we left, I quickly closed my spare room window and ran out of there.

I make a mental note to mention it to Nadia later.

'Where is everyone?' I whisper to Emma.

'Mum left ages ago.'

She knows I don't mean Mum. I should have noticed that Nadia's car wasn't parked outside. I open the door to the living room to find Matt asleep on the sofa.

'We'll just have to ask Nadia tomorrow then,' says Emma.

I close the lounge door and already Emma is halfway up the stairs.

'I won't forget, you know.' I'm talking to her back.

She stops and turns, her finger on her lips.

'Shh. You might wake him. I'm going to try and get some sleep.'

I sit on the bottom of the stairs. It's ten thirty. It seems silly to go back home now. I don't even want to go back there after tonight. My skin prickles with the idea that someone might have been in my house.

I rest my head against the banister. My mind is racing with too many things: that Andrew can't be that dangerous — Emma doesn't seem to be overly worried about him; that Jamie gets to school safely tomorrow; and that Grace is still alive.

I don't think I'm going to sleep tonight.

41

Maggie

I've been feeling dazed since yesterday, and so desperately sad — I didn't think things could get any worse. I'm sitting at the kitchen table and I keep expecting to hear Jim's tap tap on the window, but the only sound is the ticking of the clock.

David is due here at nine thirty. The same time he always used to come round — it's as though time has gone backwards, but my God how things have changed. He confirmed that he was coming last night, but still wouldn't tell me anything over the phone. Nine fifteen. My stomach is sick with nerves.

I read Jim's letter the first time last night and have re-read it twice since. I unfold the light blue paper. His handwriting is so neat, I've never seen it before, which sounds strange after the years we've known each other.

Dear Maggie,

If you're reading this, it means that I've gone before I wanted to. I'm sure you understand why I didn't tell you. I didn't want to be a burden to you, what with all the other sadness you have in your life.

I'm writing this after taking you to the library. I've every faith that one day you will be reunited with Zoe, and I hope to God it happens sooner rather than later. You deserve to be happy, Mags. As I told you, I was looking for someone myself. I don't know if Sylvia ever mentioned to you that our son, Tom, went to live in Australia after he left his wife and three boys in England (though don't get me started on that one — as you know yourself: you can't control your children). I always thought they would make contact at some point, but months turn into years, and I received my diagnosis, so I thought I'd take fate into my own hands.

You must have met Anna by now. She's a bit high-maintenance, isn't she? But she seems a decent enough sort. I'm hoping to meet the boys next week, so fingers crossed I make it that long. I feel all right in my head, but my body is telling me otherwise.

I'll not keep you longer than necessary. To be honest it's good to have your undivided attention without you interrupting me all the time. It's so much easier writing this than it is talking to your face (you'd have hit me with the tea towel by now, no doubt about it).

Thank you for being such a dear, dear friend to me. Life could have been lonely without Sylvia, but you gave me a reason to get up in the morning.

I wish you all the very best, Maggie.

Until we meet again.

Jim.

I fold away the letter.

The house feels so empty. I can't feel Sarah here any more. It's as though everyone really has abandoned me. Even the sickness about Grace Harper seems to have healed. I haven't checked the news this morning — in fact I haven't since I heard Jim died. Just saying those words in my head it doesn't feel real. Perhaps if I tell someone, if I hear myself say it out loud, it will seem more tangible.

One of Jim's albums is open in front of me. Black and white and coloured photos of his children — he was obviously the one who took the pictures as there are only three or four of him scattered through the two albums. They looked such a happy family. Towards the end is a photo of three boys that is more recent than the others — Anna and Tom's children, I expect. I'm glad he got to see a current picture of them.

Nine twenty. I wonder if David will be on time. He was never early. I'll get the cups ready and pre-boil the kettle so we don't have to wait. Shortbread, he always liked shortbread.

At exactly nine thirty, there's a knock at the door. I glance at myself in the hall mirror. He's going to think I'm so old.

I open the door, and David's standing there.

He's wearing trousers with pockets up the legs, and the type of raincoat that I see hikers in the village wear. I hope he hasn't walked all the way here. His face looks the same, but thinner. His hair is still light, but there's less of it.

'Maggie. Long time, no see.'

256

I've always hated that expression. 'David. Come in, come in.'

I want to ask him straight away what he's doing here, but perhaps that's rude.

'How long has it been?' I say. 'Twenty-five years?'

He follows me into the living room. 'Twenty-eight.'

I gesture for him to sit down on the settee; I sit in Ron's chair by the fire. 'Has it been that long? I must have stopped counting.' I try to smile, but I'm not sure how I feel about him. 'I know it was years ago, David, but I was ever so disappointed you didn't come and talk to me at Sarah's funeral. I was lucky to have Jim with me, but I've thought about it a lot over the years.'

'I kept my distance because I'd failed in my search for Zoe. I blamed myself for what happened to Sarah . . . what she did to herself. It was because I couldn't find our daughter. Since then, I've regretted not coming to the wake afterwards, paying my respects to you — especially as you'd lost Ron as well that same year. But I was in such a bad place myself — I didn't want you feeling sorry for me . . . I know you would've done. I couldn't believe Sarah was dead. I'd lost everything.'

I want to reach out to him. 'It wasn't your fault about anything, love. Of course it wasn't. The blame lies with whoever took Zoe, you must realise that now. You should have come with me to the funeral, been in the same car. I would have welcomed you. I thought you didn't care. There was only distant family there apart from me. And then I heard afterwards that you'd moved on . . . your new family.'

He looks down at his hands. 'There's no new family. I didn't move on at all. And I *did* care, Maggie.' He says it so quietly. 'I was heartbroken when Sarah left me. I couldn't see how ill I was then, when I had everything I wish for now: a wife, a daughter. Depression, the doctors call it now. I wouldn't have thought that at the time — I thought I was dying — the tiredness, the anxiety, no appetite. I thought I had cancer or something.'

'I wasn't there for you. I should have helped.'

He shakes his head. 'I wouldn't have taken help. When Zoe went missing, all I knew was that I had to search for her — that once I found her then everything would be okay.'

'I'll get us some tea.'

He was obsessed with finding Zoe. He travelled across Europe for so long. Was it his illness driving him, or was it a father's inherent need to find his daughter? I called mine the sickness; was this the same? Do I suffer from depression? It's hard to tell when I've felt sadness for such a long time.

Tea, strong with three — at least that's how he used to drink it anyway.

'Do you still take sugar, David?' I shout.

No reply.

'David?'

Perhaps he's going deaf. He looks as though he's getting on a bit. I put two sugars in it anyway and carry it through. He's staring at his mobile phone — his eyes slightly wider, his

258

mouth open. I set the cups down on the table.

'Are you all right?'

He blinks a few times. 'I . . . I . . . ' He puts his phone in his coat pocket.

'Do you want to take your coat off? You look as though you're not stopping.'

'I've got some news, Maggie. It's why I came here.' His voice is shaking.

'If it's bad news I don't want to know. I've had enough of bad news.'

He picks up his tea and drinks half of it.

'What are you doing? It's boiling hot!'

He wipes his mouth with the back of his hand. 'It's Zoe. I've found her.'

I stare at him, not saying anything — to give him a chance to say he's joking or that he said the wrong words out loud.

But he doesn't.

He's looking at me, smiling. There's a spark to his eyes that wasn't there years ago. I thought there was something different about him; I should've noticed it when I opened the door.

He's found Zoe.

The words I've been waiting to hear for thirty years.

'You've found her?' I stand; the cup I was holding falls to the floor. 'Where is she? Is she in the car with you?' I rush to the window. 'Did you come by car? Where did you find her? Is she all right?'

'Sit down, Maggie.'

If he's found Zoe, then why isn't she here? Why is he telling me to sit?

I don't think I can breathe.

'Oh, David. Don't tell me she's dead. Please don't tell me that, I couldn't bear it.'

'She's not dead. Please, sit down.'

I do as I'm told. I clasp my hands together to try and stop them shaking.

'I'll start at the beginning — is that all right?'

I nod.

I want to know right now, but this man has been searching for years — the least I can do is hear his story.

42

Another long journey. Everything is so far away here. Germany must be really big. Catherine has packed three suitcases for herself as *Michael will join us soon*. He'll have to drive back once he's taken us to the water park. Poor Michael.

'What colour's my new swimming costume?' I say, leaning forward in my seat.

Catherine looks at Michael, then turns round to me.

'We're not going swimming, love. Remember? I told you, we're going on an adventure.'

Not another one. I thought going to the water park *was* an adventure, but grown-ups think driving for hours is an adventure.

'Where are we going?'

I'm getting braver. If I don't mention Mummy, Daddy, Granny or Gramps for a few days, then I can ask what I want and she won't get mad.

'Well.' She's still facing me. 'We're heading south . . . it's a pretty long way, but we can stop off somewhere. Then, in three days' time we have a plane booked — isn't that exciting?'

I nod. I remember who I can't think about. I try to put them all in a box in my head.

'Is it a holiday?'

'It is, darling. It is.'

I smile at her, because it's better to do that. If I shout, she shouts three times as loud.

'Remember what I told you this morning?' she says. 'About that little game?'

I nod. Of course I remember, it wasn't that long ago.

She put lots of pieces of paper in a glass bowl. There must have been hundreds of little pink squares.

'Go on, pick one,' she said.

'What are they?'

'Names. I think you need to pick a new one — so you can start afresh.'

'Oh.'

'It's not that I don't like your name, it's just that I think it would be good for you, that's all. I thought it would be fun if *you* picked it. Do you not think that's fun?'

'Yes, it's fun.'

I reached into the bowl and wriggled my fingers in the little pieces of paper. They felt so light. I picked the one that wouldn't go away, that kept sticking to my fingers. I handed it over to her.

She looked so excited as she opened the piece of paper — her whole face changed, like she could be a nice person if she tried hard.

'I can't wait to see what it is, can you?'

'No.' Her smile made me smile.

'There it is. Do you want to know your new name?'

I nodded. I wished she'd hurry up.

'Stephanie! Do you like that?'

'I suppose I do.'

'Oh, you suppose, do you?'

When she said that I thought she was mad at

what I'd said, but she smiled.

'Come on, Stephanie,' she said, getting up from the floor. 'Oh, it really suits you, don't you think?'

'Yes.'

Catherine has opened the car window and the wind is blowing in my face. It makes the tears on my face cold. I need to stop crying all the time — soon she's going to notice.

Stephanie.

My name is Stephanie.

I don't think anyone is going to call me Zoe ever again.

43

Maggie

David has been talking for an hour. After he left Kent, he went to Jersey. He'd heard rumours in Dover that a girl had been seen there; one who didn't look like the rest of the family. He spent months there, he even got a job behind a bar. He only left when he'd spoken to nearly everyone on the island after hearing vague mentions of Germany. It was always a friend of a friend who'd told him.

Years later he was still in Germany after travelling to different regions. There were mentions of RAF bases, but no one knew anything or anyone in person — again it was all speculation and rumour.

'The thing was, Maggie,' he says now, 'the same name kept coming up again and again. This was over years. It'd been nearly twenty years since Zoe had been taken and I realised I'd heard his name too many times: Jürgen, Jorge, Yorgos. I had to do something about it.'

'Hang on, David. Twenty years? I thought you'd moved to Hull by 1999 — when Sarah died? Did your girlfriend not mind you travelling so much?'

'Ah.' His phone starts buzzing. He reaches over to his coat pocket and takes out his mobile phone, pressing a button to stop it vibrating.

'Like I said to you before, there was no new family. I told everyone all of that so you wouldn't worry about me any more . . . so you'd think I'd stopped looking for Zoe. I told a few of the villagers here — the ones with blabber mouths — that I'd moved to Hull to start again. You know what they're like round here — love a good gossip. I knew it would get back to you. I couldn't bear the idea of letting you and Ron down. He said he was proud of me. I thought I'd be a disappointment to him if I didn't find her.'

My hand goes to my mouth. 'Oh, David. All these years . . . I thought you'd forgotten us, that you'd moved on. And all this time I could've been helping you. I've been rattling round in this house for such a long time.'

He looks down at his hands. 'There are lots of things I regret, Maggie, but I have to start forgiving myself.'

'You've nothing to forgive yourself for. You haven't stopped searching for your daughter.' I pour him another cup of tea. 'Go on, love. You've been waiting years to tell me this story.'

'I'd heard about this man, from the people that came to the bars I worked in — ex-pats, you see — there are loads of English people scattered around the world. But the world is slightly smaller when they have such close communities around Europe — at least one of them knows someone else in another country. I'd heard that this man had been in Cyprus. Apparently, he'd been bragging for years about what he'd done. So I headed over there.

'I'd been there for so many years, working in the same bar so people would know where to find me if they had any information. I'd become almost famous for being the man looking for Zoe. I even had her picture up in the bar.

'But one night, a month or so ago — late, about eleven — a man walked in. The place was beginning to wind down as it was out of season — the only customers were residents. Anyway, he looked worse for wear, but the first words he said were, *I hear you've been looking for me.* I just stared at him. He was older than I expected — in his late sixties maybe. Even before he told me his name, I knew it was him. There was this tiredness behind his eyes. He held his hand out to me, but I didn't shake it. How could I? He just shrugged and pulled out a stool at the bar. *Are you going to get me a drink? I think this is going to be a long night.*'

'And you got him a drink? Who was he? What had he done?'

'He was the man who took Zoe.'

'What's his name?'

'George. His name's George.'

'Oh.'

'He used to do favours for people — he worked in the NAAFI on the base in Germany — though many jobs he took on were gardening, getting English food items, things like that . . . it was the eighties — there was a market for all sorts of stuff. It must have been the money that tempted him to do something so awful — that and the booze he was so fond of.'

It hasn't sunk in. It's too much information.

266

I get up and walk to the window. Is Zoe hiding somewhere outside, waiting for the big reveal? I see nothing, not even John having a smoke next door.

'What else did this George tell you?'

'He said a woman had offered him ten thousand pounds, thirty thousand Deutsch marks — to find her a girl. A five-year-old girl who looked like a photo she had. He said her name was Catherine, and that her little girl, Stephanie, had died a year before. Desperate was the word he used to describe her. George was brought up in Preston, so he came back to the town he was most familiar with. He watched her for days.'

I don't need him to finish. 'And Zoe looked like this girl. She was a replacement daughter for this Catherine woman.'

'That's right. She would've had my sympathy if she hadn't done what she'd done. Who does that? Replace one child in your affections with another? It's like two children have gone, not just one.'

'Why didn't this George go to the police — it was on the news, in the papers?'

'He wouldn't go to the police, would he? He'd taken a child off the street. And it wasn't in the papers much over in Germany. He delivered my little girl to their door.' He takes a deep breath. 'He took Zoe to them in a suitcase. He had made her crouch down into a ball, and he said she had done it without asking questions. My poor little girl.'

A single tear runs down his cheek. He's had

weeks to take this information in, yet he speaks as though he's just heard it.

'Why has he told the truth now?'

David wipes his face with his arm.

'He blew all the money he got from them on drink. I don't know what he's been living off since, but he's dying, Maggie — said he's got only months to live. He said it must've been a sign that he saw my poster of Zoe just after his diagnosis. Perhaps he thinks it's divine retribution that he told me — as if saying it out loud was enough to make up for what he'd done. Believe me, I wanted to kill him after he told me all of this. But that would have made me the same kind of person he was, wouldn't it? I told him I'd go straight to the police when he left. He just shrugged and said, *I know how to disappear. I've done it for thirty years.*' David shakes his head slowly. 'You know, Maggie. I'm just so happy that's she's alive. My gut feeling . . . intuition . . . whatever you want to call it, wasn't wrong. I've felt my little girl here.' He puts a hand to his chest.

I'm shaking. I need to sit down. I feel so angry. I take the photo of Zoe from the mantelpiece and hug her tightly. 'Oh my poor, poor girl. You were alive all this time, my love.' I hold the photo in front of me, and stroke her beautiful face.

'Where's Zoe now?' I say, sinking into a chair.

'You're not going to believe this.'

'David, after what you've just told me, I'll believe anything.'

'Have you heard about that missing girl?'

'Grace Harper? As a matter of fact, I have. To

be honest, I've been a bit obsessed with the case.'

'Grace is Zoe's niece.'

'What?'

'Yes.'

'But how can that be? It's too much of a coincidence.'

'It's no coincidence at all. Before I came here today, I went to the police and told them everything I know. I asked for Detective Jackson, but of course he retired years ago.'

'What did you tell them?'

'That I know who took Grace Harper.' David gets up. He kneels at my feet and takes hold of my hand. 'It was Scott, Maggie.'

'No.' I move his hand away from mine. 'No.' I get up from the chair. David catches the photo frame before it reaches the floor.

I'm still in my slippers, but I'm out of the front door. This isn't happening, it can't be. He knew how it broke us when Zoe was taken — how could he do this to another family? I have to find him, tell him to take Grace home where she belongs.

'Maggie!'

David's coming after me, but I don't want to talk to him. I need to find Scott.

'Maggie, wait!'

I want to hide from him and put my hands over my ears so I can't hear any more of his news. My stupid knees. I'm in agony. I want to sprint away from here, blow away on the breeze.

'Maggie! Why are you running away?'

He touches my shoulder and stands in front of me, bending over to catch his breath. I keep walking, but he walks backwards to keep up with me.

'I'm tired,' I tell him. 'I'm tired of everything. When you told me that Zoe was still alive, it felt like my heart had softened a little bit. But . . . you told me there was no bad news. Why did you trick me like that?'

'I wasn't tricking you, Maggie. I'd never do that to you. I just . . . ' He stops to catch his breath again. 'I don't know. I just wanted you to know that Grace Harper would be all right too. Scott's not a murderer . . . he's just a little misguided.'

'A little — Did you see what he did to Ron?'

'It was a long time ago. He's changed.'

It dawns on me, what he's saying. I stop walking. 'Have you been in contact with Scott? Is that how you know all of this?'

He nods.

'I can't believe you're standing in front of me telling me all of this. Did it not occur to you to keep me updated when it happened, with all this news of Zoe? It would have been the little bit of hope that I'd been waiting for, for all of these God-awful years.'

My head is spinning. The sound of the cars, the children in the playground, a buzzing noise — I can't think. I —

'Maggie — '

David catches me. I hadn't realised I was falling. I need to sit down.

'Let's get you home.'

I try to wrestle him away, but my balance is off.

'I don't want to go home.'

His arm reaches the other side of me so he's supporting me by both of my elbows. He walks me over to a concrete bench.

I take several slow, deep breaths.

The ringing in my ears is beginning to lessen.

The bell sounds in the schoolyard — end of playtime.

'Do you remember Jim?' I say. 'Ron's friend from the pub.'

'Jim . . . Jim.' He nods. 'Yes. Good old Jim. How's he doing?'

'He died yesterday. He became a bit of a pal to me these past few years.'

'Oh, Maggie. I'm so sorry.'

David looks straight ahead as he puts a hand on mine.

'So am I.'

We sit a few minutes in silence. I lean back against the cold concrete and let the moment wash over me, feeling the sun on my face. The warmth spreads down my neck, down my legs.

Zoe's alive.

I sit up quickly.

'What you said about Grace . . . that Scott has her . . . it's not Zoe's daughter, is it?'

'No. Like I said, Grace is Zoe's sister's child.'

'I knew it was Zoe in the paper. She was pictured next to Grace Harper's mother during the press conference. I cut out her picture — from last week's *Gazette*. I bought loads of copies and placed them around that picture of Sarah. I thought I was imagining things.'

'You weren't. She's the image of Sarah.'

I take a deep breath before my next question. 'Have you seen her?'

He shakes his head. 'I wanted to speak to you first. To see if you wanted to come with me. I haven't thought about how this is going to work yet, but I think we need to go there.'

I can't help it. I bury my head in my hands and cry as though I were five years old. I can't stop. My whole body cries with me. This is the reason I'm still alive; why I've had to say goodbye to so many people I love. I thought I'd been left behind, but I was placed here, waiting for Zoe to come back. I wasn't abandoned. *Thank you, God. Thank you.*

44

Stephanie

I needed to get out of the house again. I've only walked to the shop, but the fresh air is helping to refresh me. I must have only had a few hours' sleep last night. Mum arrived at ten thirty this morning, but she joined Matt in a drink when he opened a bottle of wine at eleven. It seems her time of respectable drinking has gone out of the window. I've told them they shouldn't be drinking; we need to keep a clear head in case we get some news. It falls on deaf ears. It's like they expect the worst.

I walk back slowly, taking double the time it usually takes. Before I reach the front door, it opens. It's Nadia.

'A photograph has come through the letter-box.'

'What? When?'

I've only been gone thirty minutes.

'About five minutes ago, I think — Matt noticed it. Did you see anyone on the street while you were out?'

I shake my head. 'No . . . I don't know . . . I wasn't really paying attention.'

Inside, Mum's cradling another drink in her hands — it looks like vodka now.

'Have you seen the photo?' I ask.

She nods. I can't read her expression.

Matt's been staring at me since I walked in the room. He takes me by the hand and into the kitchen. I turn to see if Emma noticed, but she's looking at the photograph.

'It's that picture,' he whispers.

'What picture?'

'The one we used on that reunion website.'

'But I thought we took it down.'

'Of course we took it down. Why are you acting so stupid? Obviously they downloaded it before that. Fucking hell.'

He turns his back on me and leans forward against the sink. He twists the cold tap on and splashes water on his face.

'But that can't be how he found her, can it?'

'We put our kids on the internet.' He grabs a tea towel and dries his face. 'Why the hell did we do that? Your mum's always going on about not sharing things on the internet — *you never know who's watching*, she said. She was right.'

'Are you sure it's the same one?'

'For God's sake, Steph, *Yes*. And it has a message on the back: *Not so happy families now, are we?*'

Oh shit.

Andrew.

It must be him.

I turn away from Matt and out of the kitchen.

'Nadia. Can I have a word?'

She narrows her eyes for the briefest of moments. 'Sure.'

I walk into the hall and out of the front door, hoping that she's following.

On the doorstep, she folds her arms. 'What is it, Stephanie?'

She's always so formal with me.

'This Andrew. I think he might be the one who's taken Grace. It all makes sense — the message about happy families, that it's payback time. It's because Emma dumped him, you see. She told you that, didn't she? That he was bitter about it all. You must have seen the texts . . . the things he was saying to her. He was threatening her.'

Nadia sighs. 'Yes, she told us all of this. We've had this man in for questioning, but he's been released without charge.'

'What? Why didn't you let us know? I thought you were meant to keep us up to date with everything.'

'It's not our only line of enquiry. We have other leads. We can't tell you everything we know — it'd get your hopes up . . . it'd be a rollercoaster. Do you understand that?'

I nod. I feel utterly stupid. Thinking in my head that I knew it all — that I knew everything there was to know. What an idiot.

'Why did you ask us for our birth certificates?'

'It's another line of enquiry.'

Shit. I thought Emma had made it up as an excuse to get us out of the house.

'About our family? But surely you've got access to the certificates and all the official documents — you've got access to everything.'

'I can't say much more until we have a clearer picture.'

The front door opens.

It's Mum. I don't think she's as sober as I first thought.

'Mum, you shouldn't be drinking. Do you know what time it is? It's half past eleven in the morning.'

'I think I know what this photo is about,' she says, swaying slightly. 'Your dad, Stephanie. I think he made an enemy. Do you remember?'

'What? Do I remember what? What am I supposed to remember?'

Mum and Nadia are both looking at me.

'It's nothing,' says Mum, waving her hand. 'It's the drink talking. I'm making it up. But he *could* have made an enemy. If I told everyone about what we did. Oh Jesus, what am I saying? I never drink this early . . . and the pills. If your father knew I was back on the pills . . . he always hated them. They make me talk about crazy things. Ignore what I'm saying, Nadia.'

Nadia? Why is she bothered about what Nadia's thinking?

'What's going on?' I say, looking from one to the other. 'What the hell are you talking about, Mum?'

Nadia puts her hands around my shoulders. 'Let's get you inside.'

Everyone's quiet when we go back into the sitting room. Mum collapses onto the sofa next to Matt.

'What did you mean, Mum?' I say. 'About Dad?'

I can't believe Dad would make any enemies. He was the kindest, gentlest man.

'What's going on? What's happened?' says Emma.

'Nothing, love,' says Mum, taking another gulp of whatever spirit's in her glass.

'It wasn't nothing,' I say. 'Mum said that Dad made an enemy. And whoever this person is has taken Grace.'

'What?' Emma kneels at Mum's feet. 'Is this true, Mum? What did Dad do that was so bad?'

'He didn't do anything,' says Mum. 'Will you stop going on about it. I wish I'd never said anything. Maybe he had an enemy, maybe he didn't. I can't remember what's real any more.' She leans forward, patting Emma on the top of her arm. 'I'm just trying to help . . . wracking my brain thinking about who's behind all of this.'

Matt gets up. 'Nadia, is there something you're not telling us?'

Nadia's leaning against the doorway. As usual her expression is unreadable. I thought she was meant to be here for us, to be on our side. Why have I been so naïve? Don't the police always suspect the people closest to the victim?

'We've received a tip-off that we're looking into.'

'What is it?' says Matt. 'Did someone recognise the man in the picture?'

'Something like that. This is just one of several lines of enquiry we're looking into.'

She keeps coming out with the same old lines. I can't bear it.

'Can someone get me another drink?'

'I think you've had enough, Mum,' I say.

'I'll get it,' says Matt.

It's true that when you spend enough time in someone's company they lose their shine.

'Did you know,' says Mum, her words are slurred. She must have taken more than one of her pills and mixed it with the alcohol. 'I once knew this little girl, who had the same name as you.' She's pointing at me. 'Such a loving child — used to follow me everywhere, and I followed her right back. She loved daisies. We used to make them into chains. *Don't pick the dandelions*, she'd say, *they'll make you wet the bed*. She learned that at school — the short time she was at school at least. She loved the colour blue — I decorated the whole of her bedroom blue. I had to paint it myself of course. It was just her and me for years. Your dad didn't know her like I did — it was always work, work, work, with him. And then . . . and then . . . '

Mum's face crumples.

Matt comes back from the kitchen with her tumbler full. For fuck's sake, she doesn't need any more. She's away with the fairies. Why is she talking about dandelions? She's finally lost it.

'Here you go, Milly.'

She grabs it and doesn't say thank you. 'All the names on the pieces of paper were *Stephanie*. Do you remember? You picked it out.'

'I don't know what you're talking about,' I say. She's not even looking at me.

'Can I ask you a question, Matthew?' says Nadia.

Matt looks confused; I think Mum's not the only one who's been on the vodka.

'Why do you call her Milly?'

'Eh?'

278

'Your mother-in-law. Why do you call her Milly?'

Matt falls, rather than sits, in the armchair. He smiles. I don't think it's funny. I want to go over and slap his face, and tell him that he shouldn't be laughing.

'You answered your own question.' He sits there smugly. I want to pour that drink over his head. 'Mother in law. M — I — L . . . Milly. It suits her better than Catherine, I think.'

'I see,' says Nadia, but she's not smiling.

I think Catherine suits Mum just right. Distant, no fun, no compassion, no nicknames. She always calls me Stephanie, not Steph. Is that how she thinks I am too?

Nadia's mobile rings and, as usual, she takes it outside.

I have never seen Mum this drunk. Would she talk about Jean in front of Emma in this state? I daren't be the one to mention it. It's too cruel; Emma's going through enough.

'So it's not your little stalker then, Emma?' says Matt.

'It's not a fucking joke,' she says.

Her cheeks are red and her eyes appear half their size.

'This is our daughter's life we are talking about.'

'Don't you think I know that?' He leans forward as though attempting to get up, but stops trying. 'This is the worst kind of torture anyone could ever deal with. Not knowing where my little girl is. Out there in the shithole of the world with fuck knows who and they're doing

279

God-knows-what to her.'

Emma winces.

'But what am I meant to do?' he says. 'They won't let me go out there and look for her. They've searched the house three times — taken up our floorboards, for fuck's sake. Imagine them thinking that we'd done something . . . What the fuck am I meant to do?'

Emma grabs his glass just in time as he puts his head in his hands and sobs. She looks around at me, at Mum, then places the glass on the floor. She puts her arms around his head and cries with him.

It's getting cloudy outside, but no one is turning the lights on — are we all going to end up in darkness? After a few minutes of watching Emma and Matt together, Mum wriggles herself so she's perched on the end of the sofa.

'I can't bear this,' she says.

'For fuck's sake, Mum, can you not let them have a bloody moment together.'

She wobbles her head around until her eyes meet mine.

'Did you just swear at me?'

'Yes.'

She raises her eyebrows as though she doesn't really care.

'I wasn't talking about them two. I was talking about everything.'

As she says *everything* she waves her arms around, splashing drops of vodka over me.

'Mum!'

She places her drink down on the carpet, and slides off the sofa so she's on her knees, using them to move towards me. She takes hold of my arm.

'I'm so sorry, love. I'm so sorry. I thought I was doing the right thing. He said that we were the better option for you. I said to look in the deprived areas.'

'You're not making any sense. It's me: Stephanie.'

'Maybe it's not you who I need to apologise to,' she says.

'Are you listening to this, Emma?' I say. 'She's getting us mixed up. Do you remember when you were a kid?'

Emma breaks away from Matt, her face wet and her eyes red.

'Stop it, Stephanie,' says Mum. 'There's no need for Emma to hear this.'

Mum's putting her hand on my face, she's trying to cover my mouth, but I bat it away with my arm.

'Get off her, Mum.' It's Emma. She's always on my side when it's between Mum and me. 'What the hell is going on?'

Emma still won't swear in front of Mum. Always the better daughter than I was — not because she tried, because she didn't need to.

Mum lets Emma hold her hands, as though she's defeated.

'Tell her,' I say. 'Tell her about when she came here.'

Mum looks up at me and shakes her head. 'Don't do this, Stephanie.'

'What?' I shift myself around so I'm no longer

next to her. '*Me* do this? It's you who's done this, not me.'

'Done what?' Emma's almost shouting now.

If Nadia hadn't heard the conversation before, she has now.

'Tell her!' I say.

'Emma isn't who this is all about.' Mum's waving her arms around again.

'I shouldn't have to be the one to tell her,' I say. 'Please. Do this for me.'

Her face seems to crease as though she's trying to stop herself from crying. Finally, she nods. She looks at me, but there's an expression in her eyes — what is it? It's not hate. Is it compassion?

Nadia kneels between Mum and me. 'Everything all right here?'

'Everything's fine.' I say. 'Mum was just about to tell Emma something. About her mother.'

'Stephanie, I've told you. Please don't do this right now,' says Mum.

'Are you kidding me? This woman could have taken Grace. I'd say it's the right time to talk about this, wouldn't you?'

'Stephanie.' Nadia stands up. 'Now really isn't the best time for this.' She keeps looking at the clock, as though she's expecting someone and they're late.

Mum narrows her eyes at her. 'I'd better call a taxi. I need to get some sleep.'

'If you could hang on for a minute,' says Nadia.

'Why?' Mum gets up and picks her bag up from the side of the sofa. Nadia steps towards

282

her, grabbing her by the wrists as Mum stumbles to the door.

'Mum?' I follow her.

Her hands are shaking; her eyes are locked on Nadia's. I watch them, my heart pounding. I look to Emma. Her eyes are wide, looking at everyone in the room; she doesn't know what's going on either.

'I don't understand,' says Emma.

'Can you let me tell her?' Mum says to Nadia.

There are tears running down Emma's face. What was I thinking? She's going through enough — she doesn't need to hear this now.

'I'm not sure you'll have time,' says Nadia.

A blue flashing light illuminates the room.

'Oh God.' Mum drops to her knees. 'I can't do this, not on my own. Why did you have to leave me, Michael?'

I kneel down beside her. 'Why are you so scared, Mum? It's okay. They said Grace might be found.'

'They're going to arrest me.'

'What? Course they're not, you've done nothing wrong.'

She covers her face with her hands.

'I have. I've done something so unforgivable. No one is going to speak to me ever again.'

I stand up.

'Nadia, what's she talking about?'

Nadia opens her mouth to speak, but there's a bang on the front door. She rushes to it.

There's a trample of feet — three uniformed police officers file into the hallway.

'Have you found her? Please tell me she's

okay.' Emma speaks, but she's ignored. How the hell can they ignore her?

Hines barges past the uniforms.

'Not yet, Emma, but we think we might know where she's being held. We received information earlier today that confirmed most of what we already know, but has given more specific details.'

He stands back to let the officers through.

'I'm afraid this investigation has uncovered a series of events.' He turns his back on Mum and faces Emma and me. 'It's your mum.' He looks to us both. 'Do you have any idea what I'm talking about?'

'Catherine Atkinson' — a policeman has hold of my mother's hands — 'I'm arresting you for the abduction of Zoe Pearson. You do not have to say anything, but anything you do say may be . . .'

'Zoe? Who the hell is Zoe?' says Emma, almost screaming.

They're putting handcuffs on Mum.

'You can't do that.' I'm trying to get their hands off Mum's wrists. 'What are you doing?'

She looks up at me — her face wet with tears and mascara.

'I'm so sorry,' she says, almost at a whisper as she's escorted out of the house.

I rush to follow her. 'Wait!' But Nadia takes hold of my arm. I shake it off. 'What's this got to do with Mum? Who's this Zoe?'

'I think you should sit down.'

Nadia's looking at me.

Emma's on the floor, leaning against the

armchair, clasping her knees and rocking back
and forth.

'Do you know what they're talking about?'

She shakes her head. 'I thought you were all
talking about me.'

Nadia guides me to the sofa and sits me down.

I need to get out of this house. I've been here
too long. This room's closing in on me. I need to
see Jamie. He always grounds me; he's my reason
for breathing. Nadia's going to tell me something
and I don't want to hear it. Why isn't it Emma
sitting here instead of me? Isn't it her mum, not
mine, that's in trouble?

'Do you know about Emma's mum?' I say to
Nadia, hoping that my words are quiet enough.

Nadia nods.

How can she know that?

I look down at my hands. Of course she
knows. She knows all there is to know about my
family. Since Grace disappeared they have dug
deep into everything.

Nadia's hand reaches over to mine. It's a
strange feeling. Nadia has never held my hand
before — she's usually so formal. She seems
more uncomfortable with it than I am.

'Do you want me to organise a counsellor for
you?' she says.

'For me?' I stand up. 'Has something
happened to Jamie?'

'No, no.'

'Then what? Why would you need a counsellor
for me? Emma and Matt are here, and their
daughter's missing — why would *I* need a
counsellor?'

She puts her other hand on mine. I want to wrestle free of her.

'Steph,' she says. She's never once called me Steph. 'I'm just going to say this how I've been told. So bear with me. Okay?'

'Okay.'

'After we'd put the photo up of the man who was with Grace, we had a tip-off that it was in fact a relative of yours who had taken her. You will not know this relative because — ' Nadia takes a deep breath. 'Because you were abducted when you were five years old. You are Zoe Pearson, and you were taken from a street in Preston as you were getting sweets from a shop. You were taken to Germany to a family in the forces eleven months after they had lost their own child, a girl called Stephanie.'

There's buzzing in my ears. My knees are sinking. My head hits the floor.

45

I've had to tie her up after she tried to get out of the room yesterday. Who knew that such a little girl would have such a feisty spirit? It's always the quiet ones, isn't it? I listen at the door before going inside. She's asleep, or pretending to be, so I leave her to it. She wasn't interested in the kids' videos I'd got from the charity shop. I only had the old telly with a video player — it doesn't even receive a proper signal now everything has gone bloody digital. I'd thought she'd be grateful that she had something to watch, but she's been sleeping most of the time. Must be used to better things.

My contact delivered everything to the right people, but he went off-plan when he broke into Zoe's house. I don't know what he thought he'd find there. Just as well she didn't catch him, would've scared her shitless. I'll get someone to have a word with him. Dickhead. He's a fucking liability.

I sit on the edge of my bed and look out of the window. It could be my imagination, but I'm sure more people than usual are looking at the house. I wish I had a television now. Need to keep tabs on what they know. The radio just plays shit music, there's never enough news.

There's a kid playing football in the street. Is it the weekend? I haven't kept track of the days. What the hell is wrong with me? Is it school holidays? Sometimes I wonder at which cross-roads I gave up my choice to have a family — meet a nice girl, have a few kids. It would have suited me, I think. *Circumstances can trick us into thinking we're powerless, but remember: we can control our own circumstances.* No — that wasn't in my readings — I think Tommy Deeks told me that.

In quiet times, I wonder when everything went so wrong. Was it me? My counsellor would go on and on that my brain was affected by the amount of weed I smoked. She'd obviously just been on another course or something.

'That can't be right,' I said. 'I feel exactly the same as I always have.'

'But that's your subjective opinion.'

'Of course it is. It's the only opinion I have.'

She hadn't liked that of course — someone being cleverer than she was. And what did she know anyway? Always going on about my childhood as though it would reveal some hidden message as to why I behaved the way I did.

Being darkened in their understanding, excluded from the life of God because of the ignorance that is in them, because of the hardness of their heart.

I had a happy childhood. I used to go fishing with Dad, when he still liked me. We'd set off at four or five in the morning, some ridiculous time like that. I didn't mind it then. Mum would have packed us some butties the night before and Dad would make us a giant flask of tea. Actually, it was probably a normal-sized flask, it just seemed giant then. It was my job to carry the radio and the maggots. Wriggly little bastards. They freaked me out even then. We'd sit all day together, side by side, hardly saying a word. But they were good days.

I got in with the wrong crowd — that's what they call it, isn't it? I just called them my mates. They weren't a bad lot. But I never went out fishing again after that. That wasn't what changed me.

No.

What changed me was that Zoe was stolen. And that bitch will soon realise who she's dealing with.

Whoever makes a practice of sinning is of the devil, for the devil has been sinning from the beginning. The reason the Son of God appeared was to destroy the works of the devil.

The sound of my mobile phone makes me jump.

A sales text. For fuck's sake.

I've phoned him about ten times now and he's not replying.

Why did he give me a name and not expect me to do anything about it?

46

Maggie

We've several hours' drive ahead of us. I haven't been out of Lancashire for years. David says Lincoln is nearly three hours away. It's strange to think that Zoe has been living there all this time and I've never even visited there. I grabbed a few things and left, happy to be out of that house for the first time in a long while.

'Do you think they'll be on the news yet?' I say to David.

I don't think I've ever been in a car with him before. He drives so fast, and the motorways are busy; enormous lorries take up most of the left lane. Everyone's in a hurry.

'They might not have found them yet,' he says. 'Scott only gave me a vague description of where he was keeping her.'

David's mobile sounds again. It's attached to the dashboard with some contraption. I can't see who's calling, but it's probably Scott. Part of me longs to listen to his voice. I want to hear him say that he's sorry, to be the little boy who looked up to his dad, or the teenager who used to take his niece to the park. I want him to be who he was before everything went wrong: the day Zoe was taken.

'Can't you just answer him?' I say.

David keeps his eyes on the motorway.

'The police said not to. He might realise I've told them.' He glances at me. 'I'm crap at lying, Maggie. He'd know it in my voice.'

I nearly jump when the phone beeps.

'He's left a voicemail,' David says.

'Aren't you going to play it?'

'Do you want to hear it?'

'I don't know.' I look out of the window. There's a little girl in the passenger seat of the car travelling next to us. She breathes onto the window and paints a happy face with her finger. I can't un-hear Scott's message once it's been played. 'Okay.'

'Are you sure?'

I nod. 'Yes.'

He pushes a button.

'David? Why the fuck aren't you taking my calls? You've told them, haven't you? What did I tell you about this? I'm going to have to move her now, aren't I? I can't promise her safety now, can I? You fucking idiot.'

'Shit.' David hits the steering wheel.

My heart is pounding again. Was that really my son? He sounded like a thug. Oh God, please don't let him hurt Grace.

David puts on his indicator and pulls into the left lane. The next services are a mile away. He puts his foot down on the accelerator.

'Shit, shit, shit.'

He grabs his mobile phone and hands it to me.

'Can you find Detective Hines? I need to talk to him now.'

I look at the thing in my hands. I daren't tell

him I've never used one before. He glances at me, and shouts, 'Call Detective Hines!'

'I'm trying, David.'

'Sorry, Maggie, I'm talking to the phone.' I can hear the sound of ringing at the other end. 'Press the speaker button.'

I do as he says.

'Hines.'

'Detective Hines, this is David Pearson. I've just had a message from Scott Taylor. He thinks I've told you — he's going to move her.'

'Right. Thank you, David.'

Four beeps. He's hung up.

David breaks hard as he nears the services car park. He parks away from the other cars.

'I'm going to have to ring Scott.'

'Are you sure? What if he does something stupid?'

He looks at me. 'He's already done something stupid.'

I hand him the phone, and he gets out of the car. I get out too; I need to listen to this.

'Can you put him on speakerphone?'

He shakes his head, putting the phone to his head. 'He'll be able to tell . . . the sound of the motorway will be too loud.' He walks back and forth along the length of the car. 'Come on, come on . . . Scott? Can you hear me? . . . It's David. What are you doing? I missed your call because I was driving . . . No, I haven't told them . . . I went to see someone . . . ' David sighs, takes the phone away from his mouth. 'Do you want me to tell him you're here?'

I nod.

'I went to see your mum, to tell her I found Zoe . . . yes, yes, okay, that *we've* found Zoe.'

David rolls his eyes at me. It'll be Scott's own version of the truth, what he's told himself to justify his actions.

David holds the phone towards me.

'He wants to talk to you. You don't have to if you don't want to.'

What's the worst he could say to me? I've imagined the worst from him anyway, that he'd tell me I'm the scum of the earth for telling the police on him. David hands me the phone. I take a deep breath and look to the sky before I put it to my ear.

'Scott, it's me. It's Mum.'

'Oh, Maggie.' He sounds like he's crying. 'I got your letter. Did you get the flowers? I'm so sorry for what I did to Dad, you have to believe me. I've made it better, see. I got their attention — now they know what it feels like.'

He sounds so different, so old. His voice is so much coarser. I try to stay calm, but I'm shaking.

'But we could have just written to Zoe.' I've got to make him believe I'm on his side — I don't want him getting angry. I know what he's capable of. 'You didn't have to take that poor little girl.'

'Write to her? What good would that have done? Catherine Atkinson would have just made up another set of lies, don't you see that? Did David tell you what she did? Put Zoe in a suitcase. Catherine's managed to keep up her act for decades. She'll have been expecting a letter, had her lies all ready. No, it had to be done this way, you see. Did David tell you that he's been looking for her for all of these years?'

He talks so fast. My mind's all over the place. It takes me a few moments to register that he's waiting for an answer.

'Yes, he told me.'

It's freezing, and the noise of the motorway is too distracting. I get back into the car.

'What's all the noise? Where are you?'

I look out of the window.

'On the M6. In Staffordshire, I think — the services. Where are you? Are we far?'

He laughs. Then silence.

Has he hung up?

'Ah, you had me there, Maggie. I was nearly going to say where I was then. You understand why I can't tell you though, right? It's nearly over. I just have to get rid of the girl. Then we can be a family again, yeah?'

'Scott, what are you going to do with Grace? She's all right, isn't she?'

He sniffs. 'Of course she's all right. I'm not an animal, am I?'

It's not right to be scared of your own son, is it? But I remember the look in his eyes when he was standing over his father all those years ago. He *was* like an animal — he couldn't control himself. Ron thought he'd only been hit once, but Scott had hit him again, and again. That's what the doctors told us. Ron had three cracked ribs and a broken jaw. Thank God he blacked out before he felt the rest.

'Of course you're not, love.' I try to hide the

fear from my voice. 'Where's Grace now?'

He sniffs again, twice. 'She's upstairs, in the bedroom.'

I'm panicking — I have to cover the mouthpiece in case he can hear my breathing. I take two deep breaths. Breathe, breathe.

'Are you still there?' he says.

'Yes, I'm here.'

'I have to go. I think the police are coming. If they find her here with me, I'll be sent down again.'

'What makes you think they're coming?'

'I can feel it. I think David's grassed me up.'

''Course he hasn't, love.'

Love is the last thing I want to call him, but I have to keep him talking. If I keep him on the phone, then he won't do anything to that little girl. I don't even know what he's capable of any more.

'I've got to go.'

'No, Scott. Don't hang up. We've got so much to talk — '

And he's gone.

David gets into the car.

'What's he going to do to that little girl?' I say to him. 'You've been in contact with him — what will he do? What's he been saying to you? Did you know he'd do this?'

He starts up the engine. The tyres screech as we pull out of the car park.

'Of course I bloody didn't!' He glances at me. 'Sorry, Maggie.' He thumps the steering wheel again. 'I shouldn't have told him their names. I thought he'd want to know about Zoe. I didn't think he'd do anything as crazy as this.'

He puts his foot down to rejoin the motorway. I grip on to the sides of the seat.

'Let's hope the police find them before he has a chance to do anything to her,' I say.

David glances at me. 'You think he will?'

I look out of the window. It's pouring with rain.

'I've no idea.'

47

'Come on, we've got to be quick.'

She tries to get up, but she can't. Ah fuck, the ankles — I forgot about them.

Her legs shake as I untie them from the chair.

'Calm down, I'm not going to hurt you. Not if you're a good girl.'

She's free, but she still doesn't get off the chair. I grab her arm and drag her off. Her trousers are soaking wet. So is the chair.

'Why didn't you tell me you needed a piss, eh?'

Fucking kids.

She makes a noise through the tape, but I can't understand what she's staying.

'Sorry, kid. The tape has to stay. We're on the move.'

How the hell am I going to do this?

I carry her in a fireman's lift down the stairs — she stinks of piss.

Bin bag, that'd do it.

I just hope to fuck I bought some.

I put her on the sofa.

'Now just stay there. I'm just going to look in the kitchen. I can still hear you, you know.'

Under the sink — that's where Maggie used to keep them. I must have put them there too, old habits and that. I can't believe she's with David. After all these years. We're all going to be reunited. I tear one of the bags off, and shake it out. Think I'm going to need to . . . top and tail her — that's what they used to call it. I tear another bag off and sling them over my shoulder.

'What the . . . Get away from that window. What do you think you're doing?'

She's making noises too, banging on the window. The little shit. She's going to get me into trouble.

A slap should do it.

It makes a louder sound than I thought it would. She doesn't move from the floor.

Shit.

Got to keep moving.

Bin bag over the head, another to cover the legs. Tape, I need tape.

I chance a look out of the window.

Nothing. Yet.

Tape, tape. Where the fuck is the tape? When did I have it last?

Fuck. It's in the car.

I put my baseball cap on and pull the visor over my eyes. Nosy bastards round here. I open the front door. Just act normal. That's it. Just a few more steps till I get to the car.

The tape's in the glove compartment.

I shut the car door again. There's no one out here. I can't look around too much — it'll look suspicious.

I close the front door and lean against it. How the hell am I going to get her into the boot? There's no one outside now, but there might be in a minute.

My holdall. It's big enough for that kid — she's only skinny.

I race up the stairs.

I'm too old for all this shit.

It's in the cupboard it's always in. Good, good. It's all coming together.

Downstairs, I open the bag as wide as I can get it. She doesn't move as I pick her up. I daren't check her pulse.

Fuck.

I should've asked for money . . . could've got away from here, started again.

But they needed to be taught a lesson, bunch of smug rich bastards. My sister died because of them — they deserve everything they get.

I zip up the bag. There's room to spare in there.

I grab a couple of jumpers off the airer and stuff them in the outside pockets around her.

Shit. Poor kid. She didn't ask for any of this.

Can't think about that.

I hoist the strap onto my shoulder. It's not that heavy.

I lower the cap visor again and stand behind the front door.

Deep breath. Come on, you can do this.

I close the door behind me. It's clear outside. Thank fuck it's not the school holidays; there's no one about. One foot in front of the other, that's it.

There's all kinds of crap in the boot. I have to put the bag on the ground to clear a space.

What's that?

A car.

Sounds like it's going at a fair speed. I grab the bag and shove it in, slamming the boot shut.

I take my time reversing. Shit always happens when I rush. Got to calm down. I've nearly done this. Twenty miles an hour's the speed limit on this road — when the hell did they start changing it to that?

Nice and steady, don't go over the limit and they can't stop me. That's what it used to be like anyway, they've probably changed it all now. No one's got any rights these days.

I'm at the junction when I see blue lights in the rear-view mirror; they're reflected in house windows. I see the lights before the cars. As I turn right, they stop outside my house.

Too slow, you pig bastards.

48

Stephanie

Nadia is comforting Emma; Matt is pacing up and down. I feel like I'm not here. I'm lying on the sofa with a headache so painful it's like my brain's about to explode.

The detective left quickly after he got a phone call. Something to do with them moving Grace. They seem to know where she is — at least that's what they said to Emma.

'We've got an address from a photo appeal,' he said. 'On the local news. A team is setting off as we speak.'

Emma wrapped her arms around herself. 'Thank God.'

Then his phone went.

'Right. Thank you, David,' was all he said before he ran out of the house, the uniforms following him.

It's all a blur. Did what happened before really take place? Did Mum get arrested or am I confused? I can't remember. Zoe Pearson. The name isn't even familiar to me. Surely if I'd been someone else I'd remember. They've made a mistake. I look like my dad — that's what everyone used to say. Or were they being polite? *Did* I look like my dad?

I pick up my bag. There must be a picture of him somewhere. We were so close. I check all the

301

sections of my purse, but no, there's no photo. I dig deeper to the bottom, but all there is is a handful of crumbs.

'What if he hurts her?' says Emma.

For a moment I forgot where I am and why.

'Who's got her, do you know?' It's Nadia I'm asking, but they both look up.

Nadia gets up and walks over to me. She has that look of sympathy that she's used twice on me now. She crouches at my feet.

'Would you like me to organise for someone trained to talk to you about it? Only, it's someone from your past . . . someone you haven't seen since you were little.'

She's talking in riddles again, like they did before Mum left.

'Just tell me, Nadia.'

'It's your uncle who has Grace. Your father, David Pearson — the person Detective Hines just spoke to on the telephone — has been searching for you for a very long time. He asked your uncle, Scott Taylor, for his help in locating you — God knows why he asked *him*, he's been inside more times than . . . anyway, he found you, and Emma. He's been watching you two for a while — had a flat up in Horncastle. I imagine he wanted to get back at your mum, and get your attention.'

'Right . . . right.'

I stand up; I don't know why. The room is spinning and my stomach is turning. I won't make the bathroom. I run through the kitchen and out the back door, and vomit into the drain.

★ ★ ★

302

'I can't take any more of this,' says Matt.

He pulls on his trainers and puts on his coat. 'Where are they?'

Nadia shakes her head. 'I don't know.'

'What do you mean, you don't know? I thought you had an address.'

'He's not there.'

'What? Have you got her father's mobile number then?'

He nodded at me when he said *her* — looking at me as though I were dirt, as though daggers went from his eyes into my chest. I didn't think he'd registered anything the police had said to me, but obviously he had. He's taken it all in quicker than I have. I can't think about it.

Emma looks up at him. 'What did you just say?'

'You heard me.'

She stands up in front of him.

'Don't talk to my sister like that.'

He narrows his eyes at her. 'She's not even your sister.'

'How dare you? Why would you even say something like that? We don't know the full story yet.'

'Oh, I dare all right. It's her fault Grace was taken. If it hadn't been for her, Grace would still be here with us.'

'It wasn't her fault. Did you not hear what they said to her? That she was taken as a kid. She was only five years old — three years younger than Grace is.' She turns round to face me. 'To think, all this time, Mum took a child. She left a mother, like me, waiting for years and years

303

without knowing where her daughter was.' She rushes over to me, knocking me sideways as she grabs me in a hug, sobbing. 'It's horrific.'

I put my arm around her and smooth down her hair.

'It's okay, Em. They'll find Grace — they're nearly there.'

It takes a few moments for her to raise her head. The skin around her eyes is red and swollen. She looks so young.

'I'm crying for you as well,' she says.

'Let's get Grace home before we think about anything to do with me.'

She nods and wipes her face with the cuff of her cardigan.

'Do you think she's all right?'

I nod. 'Of course she's all right.'

But I'm lying. I really don't know if she will be. I pull Emma closer so she can't see my face.

49

I thought there'd be some banging coming from the boot of the car, but there's nothing. She must be asleep. She'll need it — she's not slept properly in days.

Maggie's on her way. She's finally going to see Zoe again. I'm not a total waste of space. I wonder if she'll have me back at home for a bit, just till I get back on my feet. I've been trying to get on my feet for years. Never happened. Black cloud over my fucking head everywhere I go. But it will get better. This was my mission in life, I can see that now.

I just need to figure out what to do with this kid.

Shall I just dump her?

Or ask for money? She might as well be of some use to me. But, it never goes right if you ask for money, does it? That's what they want you to believe on the telly. They never get away with it, do they? But I'm a lot smarter than those wasters.

I need to think.

I'm on a dual carriageway — I can't just stop anywhere.

There's a parking sign for five hundred yards away. That'll do.

I pull in and there's a sodding camper van already there. An old couple, folding away their camping chairs and putting away their picnic. A

305

camper van. Now why didn't I think of that? Could have been on the move all this time, maybe I'd have ended up in Scotland. They'd never have found us. Ah, fuck it, I'm here now.

They keep looking at me; I imagine they want me to say hello.

I nod and smile at them.

Yeah, yeah, you couple of boring camping bastards. Off you go. I reach over to the passenger seat for a newspaper that's been there for months — I've read the same headline a thousand times.

It takes them ages to get in their van.

There's a sound from the boot.

Great. Brilliant timing, kid.

Fuck, the couple have left something on the ground. It looks like a map. Ignore it, you two, come on, just leave.

They start the engine and their indicator light comes on.

Bang, bang from the boot.

'Shut the fuck up, kid,' I shout. 'I really mean it this time.'

The banging stops. She's finally learning.

My hands are sweating as the camper pulls out of the lay-by. I breathe out — I must have been holding my breath. What the fuck am I doing? I should be retired by now, living in Spain with my own bar.

The canal. I'll drive down there. I've got no gun, no knife, but if they threaten me, at least I can push the car into the water.

I love it when a plan comes together.

50

Maggie

We're nearly at Lincoln. David's driving so fast I'm surprised we haven't been pulled over by the police.

'What are we going to do when we get there?' I say to him. 'Do you even know where we're going?'

'I'm heading to Emma Harper's house — the girl Zoe grew up with. They must be there. The detective wouldn't tell me, but I'm guessing it's there.'

'Are we just going to turn up? How do you know where she lives?'

'Her address was online. And to be honest, I haven't thought that far ahead. I just have to see if Zoe's okay.'

'I'm sorry,' I say, after a few minutes.

'What are you sorry for?'

'That you came so far out of your way to come and get me. You could have seen her already.'

'You're her grandmother, Maggie. I couldn't let you hear it on the news. Those reporters will get hold of the story soon enough. It's like they do their own investigating these days.'

'Like you did, you mean?' I smile at him.

'If I didn't, then we wouldn't be on our way to see her, would we?'

Neither of us say it, but if he hadn't searched,

307

then little Grace Harper wouldn't have been taken.

'I couldn't have known what Scott was going to do,' he says.

'I know, love.'

We've been driving without the radio on since we began the journey, not wanting to hear if anything bad happens.

'I've been thinking about what you've said,' I say, 'about Zoe being taken abroad. How did they get her into another country with no passport?'

'It was 1986. Kids didn't need a passport of their own. They just listed them on their parents'. George said he stole a passport that listed an eight-year-old girl on it — though God knows how border control could've thought Zoe looked three years older than she was.'

His mobile phone rings again — he presses the speakerphone button.

'David Pearson?' It's a woman's voice. 'I'm DS Rachel Berry, working on the Grace Harper case with DI Hines. Do you know where Scott might have taken Grace?'

'He's moved her?'

'Yes.'

David mutters under his breath.

'I don't know. Like I said before, I've only been in contact with him in the last few months.'

'Right.'

She doesn't sound convinced about something. I hope she doesn't think David has anything to do with it.

'Can I help at all?' I shout. 'I'm Scott's mother.'

'Er . . . hang on one second.'

'This is Detective Hines, is this Mrs Taylor? We've been trying to get hold of you.'

'I'm with David. We're on our way down.'

'Er . . . Okay. Have you any idea where Scott may go to — a place he used to like as a child?'

'I don't know — we're not from round here. We're from Preston.'

He sighs. I'm too slow for him, too old.

'Try to think. Do you think he'd take her out of the country, on the ferry, perhaps?'

'No, he wasn't the adventurous type. I don't know.' I'm starting to panic. I'm no use at all. 'He used to go fishing with his dad, when he was little. That's all I can think of.'

'Okay — thank you.'

Four beeps again.

'People don't say goodbye these days, do they?'

David shakes his head, but he's not really listening to me.

'Whatever Scott thinks about these people,' he says, 'Grace Harper has grown up believing Zoe — or Stephanie, which she goes by now — is her auntie. And that's what Zoe — Steph — Jesus, I don't know what name I should be calling her. But . . . anyway . . . my daughter accepts Grace as her niece. They're related, blood or not. I can't believe what Scott has — ' He looks at me. 'Sorry.'

'You're only saying what I'm thinking.'

'What if . . . '

'What?'

'What if Zoe were to speak to him?' says

309

David. 'Surely he'd talk to her. She's the reason he's done all of this.'

'Will he answer his phone?'

'I don't know, but it might be worth a try. I'll call Hines back.'

51

Stephanie

Hines passes me the headset of the landline.

'I don't think I can do this,' I say.

'I'm not going to force you, but it's the best chance we've had so far in talking to him. You might be able to reason with him.'

He hands me a card with a list of names on it.

'But I don't know him.'

'It doesn't matter. He knows you.'

I nod, and the detective presses the numbers on the phone. He answers after three rings.

'Who's that?'

I swallow. I can't speak.

Emma mouths *please;* her hands are in a praying position.

'Hello? It's Steph — ' The detective nudges me and points to the card. 'It's Zoe.'

'Who?'

'Zoe.'

'Hang on. I can stop in a sec.'

Oh God. This is the man who took Grace, the man who still has her, who might have hurt her. I try to swallow the nausea I'm feeling.

'Zoe? Is that really you? I can't believe it! After all these years. I've been watching you these past few weeks, you know, but I've not dared speak to you. Not without David knowing. I had to do right by him, you see.'

I look down at the note card. *David Pearson: Zoe Pearson's father. Scott Taylor: Zoe Pearson's uncle.*

'I . . . I . . .'

I don't know what to say. This man is related to me, yet I feel nothing towards him but hatred. It's as though someone has erased my memory and people are trying to fill in the gaps with things that can't be true.

The detective rotates his index finger. I turn the card over.

'Where are you now?' I say.

He takes a breath — it sounds phlegmy — like he's about to spit it out.

He does.

Bile rises to the back of my throat.

'Are they with you?' he says.

'Who?' My voice is a whisper.

'The police.'

The detective nods.

'Yes, they're here. They just want Grace back. Shall I come to you? So we can finally meet properly.'

The detective gives me the thumbs up, but I don't think this man will fall for it. He's got this far — he's not stupid.

'Now, now, now,' he says. 'You must know I can't tell you that.'

'Is Grace all right? You haven't hurt her, have you?'

'Zoe! How can you ask me that? I'm your uncle, for God's sake. As if I'd ever hurt a child. I used to take you to the park — do you remember that?'

'I . . . I don't know. I can't remember anything about you.'

His voice doesn't sound familiar at all, but he has a northern accent; whenever I've heard it in the past, it's made me feel safe, warm. It's not making me feel that way now.

'Those bastards didn't hurt you, did they?'

He's talking about Mum and Dad, like they're criminals. If this is all true though, then I suppose they are.

'No, they didn't.'

DS Berry is on another mobile phone. She puts her thumbs up to the detective. They both rush outside.

'You are really Zoe, aren't you?'

'They keep telling me I am.'

'How long have we been on the phone? Shit — '

He's gone.

I'm still staring at the phone when Nadia takes it from me.

'You did really well, Stephanie. We managed to locate him.'

'What? Is that what I just did?'

She nods, smiling.

I don't know how I feel. I've just spoken to someone who's meant to be related to me by blood, yet I've helped the police find him. My hands are shaking; everything's shaking. It's like my legs are about to collapse from under me. Emma grabs me in a hug.

'I'm so proud of you.' She pulls away, and holds the top of my arms. 'It can't have been easy, but you did brilliantly.'

313

'I didn't actually know what I was doing.'

I sit on the arm of the chair.

'Too right she should have done it,' says Matt. 'It's a member of *her* family that took Grace.'

'Shut up, Matt. You're not thinking straight. This hasn't got anything to do with Steph — she's still the same person, isn't she?' Emma doesn't take her eyes from mine. 'Now we need to pray that Grace's okay.' She turns to Nadia. 'Can we go to where they think she is? She will be with him, won't she?' She returns her eyes to me. 'I mean; you don't think he's done anything to her . . . killed her . . . left her?'

Her gaze won't move from mine.

'I really hope not,' I say.

A single tear runs down her cheek. She nods slowly.

'Can we?' Emma turns back to Nadia.

'I'll see if I can get an update. I won't be a minute.'

'I've got this feeling,' says Emma, once Nadia is outside, 'that she's all right. Does that sound silly?'

'No, it doesn't.'

'Do you feel it too?'

I wish she'd stop asking me questions like this; I hate lying to her.

'Yes. I feel it too.'

She smiles at me. 'I love you, Steph.'

'I love you too, Em.'

She hugs me again, and I wrap my arms around her tightly.

'Enough of all of this,' says Matt. 'You're making me feel sick. My little girl's out there,

314

and you two are hugging like it's all happy families.'

'I wish he'd shut the fuck up,' Emma whispers in my ear.

'It's okay,' I whisper back. 'I don't blame him.'

I pull away from Emma's embrace.

'I'm sorry, Matt.'

I'm not sure why I should be sorry, but it's what he wants to hear.

He doesn't look at me, but says, 'Okay.'

'They think they've found him,' says Nadia, like she's out of breath. 'By the canal.'

'Where by the canal?' says Matt.

'I'm sorry — that's all they said. I've probably already told you too much.'

'You haven't told us enough.'

Matt grabs his car keys from the mantelpiece.

'Wait!' says Nadia, blocking his exit from the sitting room. 'I'll drive. We will go together. But promise me you'll do as I say, and not get out of the car unless I say so.'

'Yes, yes.'

'Matthew. Promise me.'

He stands back slightly. 'Okay. Fine.'

'Right. Let's go.'

52

Schoolboy error. I should've known from all those telly shows that they'd try to trace the call. I didn't think that would ever happen to me — I've never been that important before. Wait till I tell Maggie that I've spoken to Zoe. I've seen her, of course, but it's not the same as connecting, voice to voice. I feel bad that I lied to her, about not hurting a child. I've never hit a female in my life, let alone a child. Possessed, that's what Maggie used to call me when I was using. *You're possessed by the devil, child.* Perhaps some of that has lingered in me — something I've no control over. I wasn't even a child then, but I was always her youngest. Not any more though, eh? I've been older than Sarah for thirteen years. Can't think about her.

It'll take them at least five minutes to get here. Shame really, the view is so nice. Sometimes when I see a sight like this, a sort of clarity fills my mind. Memories, I guess. Thoughts of what I could have been.

Can't dwell on that soppy shit.

I thought she'd have banged again, seeing as we've been still for at least ten minutes now, but nothing.

Shit.

I daren't look.

I need to get out of here. Leave the car, leave everything.

I put on my cap and grab the keys from the ignition. I'm not going to make it easy for those bastards. As I open the door, I realise how far away from any fucking path I've parked. What the hell was I thinking? I'm on the embankment. There's a couple walking their dog. They've stopped right behind the car.

'Are you all right?' one of them says. I think it's a bloke, but I'm not sure.

'Car trouble. Bloody satnav.'

They seem to relax a little.

'I know what you mean,' says the other one. 'We ended up in a pig farm in Derbyshire last year, didn't we, Sebastian?'

Sebastian nods.

'I'll just get my bearings,' I say, 'then I'll be off.'

Now that's code for get the fuck out of my face, you pair of twats.

We look at each other for a few moments before they take the hint. I sit on the boot and try not to stare after them too obviously. Need to get them out of sight, but they're not walking fast enough.

Sirens — more than one. It sounds like they've got a convoy.

I don't know what I thought would happen now. Shit.

Walk away. I could just casually walk away.

The canal path runs in the opposite direction to the dog walkers, but it will lead me to the high street. I grab another hat from my pocket: a flat cap. I look just like my dad in it. I stick my hands in my pockets, and just walk away.

317

53

Stephanie

Nadia has put her police lights on as we travel at speed through the city — they reflect in the shop windows. Emma's clutching Grace's teddy and blanket ready to give to her.

'They found a blue Volvo by the edge of the canal,' says Nadia, translating the garbled message from the police radio.

'Is she in it?' asks Emma. 'Have they got him?'

'I don't know. We're nearly there.' She turns round and glances at Emma. 'Remember what I said — do *not* get out of the car. We don't want to antagonise him and make him do something stupid.'

Emma nods, but if we do see Grace, she and Matt will be straight out of this car. The locks on the doors are down. Would Nadia lock us in?

I lean my head on the window, feeling the hot sun on the top of my head. I feel sick at the idea of what we're going to find. Scott, the man on the phone, sounded unhinged, confused. I don't know who I imagined took Grace, but I could never have thought it would be a member of a family I didn't know I had. No, I can't think about that now. If I think about everything, I'll lose my mind. I have to keep it together for Emma.

'Okay,' says Nadia, but I think she's talking on

the radio. 'Emma, Matt. A team has approached the car, but there's no sign of Scott Taylor.'

Emma leans forward, grabbing the headrest of the seat in front of her.

'That means we can go there too, doesn't it?'

'Let me have a word with the detective when we get there.'

We turn down into an entrance of a park, trees on either side. We're driving down what looks like a pathway, but Nadia has put her lights on again. It's not really necessary as there are four or five police cars ahead, parked on the grass. We stop behind one of them.

Nadia turns off the engine.

'Now you stay here. I know you want to rush out and see what's happening, but we can't have you wandering round, no matter how quiet everything seems. Do you understand?'

We all nod.

Matt can barely keep still — I don't think he's going to stay in here.

Nadia narrows her eyes at him.

'I'm going to lock the doors, okay? For your own safety. We don't know whether this man is armed or not. All right.'

'For fuck's sake!' Matt bangs the car door with his arm. 'That's not even legal. This is a joke. My daughter could be over there, and we're sitting here having a chat. Jesus! I can't fucking bear it. And you expect me to wait?'

'I'll be five minutes, tops. I promise.'

Nadia doesn't wait to argue with him, and gets out quickly, locking the doors with a push of the button on her key.

We've only been sitting here a few minutes and an ambulance is behind us. It drives past the police cars and onto the grass.

'Oh my God,' says Emma. 'Is that for Grace?'

Matt tries to open the car door, pulling it with both hands. 'This isn't right. I'm going to complain — this is illegal. We need to be out there!'

'Why is the ambulance going that slow?' says Emma.

'We're near the canal,' I say. 'They have to be careful — cars aren't meant to go near there.'

'I need to get out.' Emma is shaking, holding the teddy so tightly, the skin around her knuckles is white.

I bang on the window. 'It's okay. Nadia's coming.'

She's running towards the car. I can't read her face. Is it good news?

She opens the door.

'I'm so sorry about that . . . the ambulance.' She's trying to catch her breath. 'We've found Grace.'

★ ★ ★

We're running alongside Nadia. There's a blue car near the canal. From here it looks like the boot's open.

'Is she all right?' I ask her, but she doesn't seem to hear me.

Surely she wouldn't let us go and see something terrible, surely it's not that Grace's dead and we're about to see her body. They

320

wouldn't do that to us, to Emma and Matt.

The detective's talking to one of the ambulance crew. He frowns when he sees us.

'Nadia, do they know what they're about to see?'

Nadia bends over slightly to catch her breath again. 'Not yet, sir.'

He shakes his head and walks towards us. Emma grabs hold of my arm.

'They wouldn't do this to us if she were dead, would they, Steph? They wouldn't let us see her like that.'

I can't answer her because I don't know.

'We found her,' he says, finally.

Matt doesn't listen any longer, he rushes to the ambulance.

'Wait, Matthew,' says the detective, but it's useless, Matt wouldn't listen.

The detective steps closer to Emma. 'There's still a pulse.'

Emma's knees wobble before they sink to the ground. I wasn't in time to catch her. I grab under her arms and pull her with me towards the paramedics.

I stand at the doors as Emma crawls onto the steps of the ambulance.

'She's going.'

I don't know which of the two paramedics shouted that. They are both standing either side of a stretcher and all I can see are little legs being shoved around as they try to shock her back into life.

54

Maggie

'Shall we switch on the radio?' I say, reaching over to the car stereo. 'So we can hear what's happening.'

'It's not like Sky News, Maggie,' he says. 'We can't just switch it on and they tell us what's going on.'

I pull my hand back and rub my thighs; I can't bear it. 'But where are we?'

'Lincoln town centre.'

It looks just like Preston city centre: loads of nondescript buildings punctuated with high-street shops. Here, though, the cathedral seems to tower over everything else, like a guardian watching over us.

'But it's so quiet here, how are we meant to tell where Scott is?'

David sighs. He's fed up of me already, I can tell.

He stops suddenly.

'We're on double yellows, David.' I look outside, checking for police. 'They might tell us off.'

When I look back round, David's hands are covering his head.

'I don't know. I don't know what to do any more.'

He's breathing in and out through his nose,

like he's hyperventilating.

I think he might be crying.

'I'm sorry, David.' I put my hand out to him, but he bats it away. 'Shall I ring the detective, and ask where they are?'

He shakes his head under his hands. 'They aren't going to tell us where they are. We aren't important to them. You do know that, don't you? No one gives a shit about us.' He leans back and looks up to the ceiling of the car. 'It's my fault all of this happened. If I hadn't asked Scott for help, then . . . ' He slams a hand on the steering wheel. 'Jesus. I'm probably going to be arrested for this.'

'You won't get arrested, David. You did nothing wrong. You were looking for your daughter. Who'd have thought it would have come to this?'

He looks up, shaking his head.

'Now I know she's alive, that should be enough. I should just leave her to her life. I've already done too much.' His hands grip the steering wheel. He lowers his head. 'But she's my little girl. Five years old she was. She doesn't even know me.'

He groans, is that the word for it? No, he makes a sound that is pain. A sound that travels straight to the middle of my chest. For just a second, I feel what he feels. It's what he's felt for years.

What is it like to not know?

My child, my Sarah, I know how she died.

'You can't stop now, David. I won't let you.'

I look up to get our bearings.

323

'Do you have a map? I've never been here before.'

We're stopped fifty metres from a junction. Ahead of us, on the other side of the road, is a bus stop.

He looks just like Ron, that man. He's wearing a flat cap; Ron always wore a flat cap. Without taking my eyes off him, I grab David's arm.

'Look,' I say.

Slowly, David lifts his head and finds where I'm looking.

He reaches for his phone.

'Hold on a second, David.' I grab his wrist.

'But he might run — he could disappear again.'

Scott's sitting on the plastic seat of the shelter. He briefly lifts up his cap to wipe his forehead. He puts a hand in his pocket and brings out a packet — tobacco probably. I hope he doesn't still smoke that other vile stuff. Although that was just the start of it — relatively tame compared with what he got into after that.

I won't be able to look at him for much longer. I need to capture everything to memory. He's still as skinny as he used to be — there's not even a middle-age spread that Ron had. Scott's as thin as he was at twenty-one. What else has happened in his life to bring him to this? My boy. If circumstances had been different, he might have had a family, a decent job. We could've had a relationship. He and I have been ruined. His breakdown might be more apparent, more brutal — we're suffering in different ways, but he's still part of me.

'I'm calling Hines now, Maggie.'

I nod slowly.

I can't make out David's words to the detective as I look at Scott.

I used to watch him for ages when he was little, before he noticed me looking. He'd smile then, basking in the attention. When I gazed at him as a teenager though, he'd say, *Stop staring, Mum. You're giving me the creeps.* Always so melodramatic.

He takes his rolled cigarette and puts it to his lips. I can barely see his eyes under the cap, but the hand holding his lighter hovers in mid-air. Has he caught me looking at him?

Slowly, he stands.

My heart's pounding.

Without thinking, I've opened the car door.

'Where are you going?' says David. 'You'll make him run. He's . . . '

I can't hear his words any more.

I'm walking slowly towards my son. He's standing on the edge of the kerb. I'm on the opposite side. He looks left and right. He's coming towards me. Should I try to run away? Would he hurt me?

I'm shaking.

David's shouting something, but it's just noise.

Scott's standing in front of me.

'Mum.'

It's the first time in thirty years that he hasn't called me Maggie.

There are wrinkles around his eyes, grey stubble on his face. To me, he's aged in an instant.

'I'm so tired, Mum.'

He throws the unlit cigarette to the ground and folds his arms. Instinctively, I reach out and rub the tops of his arms.

'You're shivering.'

He takes off his cap and holds it in both hands.

'I thought I was doing something right,' he says. 'I don't know how it went so wrong.'

This was the man I expected to see in the dock of the court twenty-seven years ago, after hurting his own father — remorseful, aware. But now, after everything that's happened, I'm not sure if he's upset at what he's done to Grace, or if he's sorry for himself.

'Where's the little girl, Scott? Where's Grace?'

His eyes briefly flicker with recognition at the mention of the girl's name.

'In the car . . . I . . . '

He looks confused.

'Have you hurt her?'

I'm not sure I want to hear the answer. Surely he wouldn't hurt a child?

'I don't know, Mum. I . . . '

I take a step back.

'Oh, son. What have you done?'

He takes a step away from me, too. He's frowning.

'I don't know . . . '

There are police sirens in the distance.

David's abandoned the car — both doors are open. 'Maggie, get back in the car. He's dangerous.'

'You wouldn't hurt me, would you, son?' The

sirens are getting closer. 'Do the right thing, love. Wait here — hand yourself in.'

He puts the cap on his head and tips it over his eyes.

'I'm sorry, Mum.'

He turns round and runs in the opposite direction.

55

I thought I'd hate her when I saw her again. But I didn't. She seemed so old. I knew she wouldn't look the same, but God, she's aged. Every time I've thought about her — I've seen her expression as she stood over Dad.

No. I can't think about that now.

Breathe, breathe. My lungs feel like they're giving up on me, they're burning with the cold air. I can't run for much longer. People are staring at me — they always look at the running person when sirens are sounding. No one's trying to stop me — they're stepping away from me, like they're scared of me, like I'm a leper.

I see them — two cars, five hundred metres away. I turn down an alley. Either side are back yards of terraced houses. The uneven cobbles make my steps unsteady.

A panda car blocks the exit I'm heading for. I turn round; another one, barricading the opposite entrance. Shit. I can't make it easy for them. I'll never be a free man again.

There's a blue wooden gate to my left — it looks rotten round the hinges. I give it just one kick before it opens. It's not even locked. I bolt it behind me and lean against it.

Did the police see me come into this yard? I need to think. I've trapped myself in here. What a fucking idiot.

I look up at the house. It's like the terraced

house we grew up in. Red bricks, shed out the back, green gutters. There are two faces at the bedroom window — a boy and a girl. The little boy's resting his chin on his hands. He waves at me with his fingers. I put a finger to my lips. 'Shh.'

There are footsteps in the alleyway behind me: five, or maybe six coppers. My breathing's too loud; the bastards are going to hear me. I look up again to the children. The boy copies me, putting a finger on his lips, but the girl turns round. There's someone behind them. A woman. She pushes her children away from the window and narrows her eyes at me as it slowly dawns on her what's happening.

I should be running, but I can't take my eyes away from the bedroom window; my feet are welded to the floor. I'm in their back yard. I want to tell them I won't harm them, but that wouldn't be true, would it? No matter what my intentions are now. It's like I can't help myself; the monster takes over me.

She's banging on the window so bloody hard I'm surprised she hasn't made a hole in it. Now she's pointing at me. Great. The cops will know exactly where I am.

I sink slowly to the floor, the rotten wood rough against my back. The door rattles, pulling me back and forth with it; they're trying to get in.

I ought to move. I could check the back door of the house, go through to the front. Come on, Scott, get the fuck up.

I crawl on my hands and knees, the gravel giving my legs tiny electric shocks of pain.

I get to the door and hold my hands up to the handle. I'm just inches away when the gate bursts open. I don't turn round. I close my eyes. The gravel crunches with heavy footsteps. Two, or maybe three pairs of hands pull me up from the ground.

The handcuffs are hard and cold around my wrists. Pain tears through them as the bastards push me around by my elbow.

'Scott Taylor, I'm arresting you for the kidnap and attempted murder of Grace Harper . . . '

'Attempted murder?' They're pulling me through the gate. 'You mean she's still alive?'

We reach the panda at the end of the alley.

'Shut up, you piece of shit,' says one of them.

She presses my head down and I'm bundled into the car.

★ ★ ★

The ceilings are usually the same in places like this: white peeling paint and grey plaster underneath. They didn't clear this one out before I came in though; there's still a picture of someone's wife or girlfriend or whoever it is on the ceiling. Unless the bloke in here before left it 'cos he was sick of the sight of her. Or he died. Whatever.

The bolt drags across from outside and the door slams open against the wall.

Always in a bad mood, these coppers.

A uniform holds the door open for a woman in a suit. They dress like men these days.

'Get up,' she says. 'Come with me.'

330

'Aye, aye, Captain,' I say, but she doesn't laugh. Miserable cow.

I try not to look at her backside as I follow; there are two blokes next to me — they're watching me a bit too closely for my liking. One of them grabs my arm as the woman — a detective probably — opens a side door. He almost throws me inside.

'Easy, tiger,' I say, brushing the scent of pig off my arm.

I reckon they train them not to react. Back in the good old days, they would've thought nothing of giving me a slap in the face for not answering a question within three seconds.

The woman pulls out a chair next to a fat bloke with the smallest round glasses. He looks like Piggy from *Lord of the Flies*. I remember watching the video at school.

'I'm Detective Rachel Berry,' she says, still standing. 'I'm about to interview you in connection with the kidnap and attempted murder of Grace Harper.' She gestures to the man sitting. 'This is Mr Anthony Rawlinson, who's been assigned to represent you. I'll give you a moment with your solicitor before I begin questioning.'

'No need,' I say to her, but she's gone.

'All right, fella,' I say, holding my hand out to him. He takes my hand — his is cold and sweaty. 'I don't think I've had the pleasure before, Anthony.' I know how to speak to these *fellows*. Most briefs I get are posh bastards, trying to ease their conscience working for Legal Aid, representing the poor unfortunates like myself who

331

find themselves in a spot of bother.

Anthony reads my sheet. Fuck knows what they've got on there.

'Just answer *no comment*,' he says.

'You what? That never helps, does it?'

'It certainly won't make things worse.'

'I'll see how I get on.'

'I advise you to answer *no comment*.'

He's like a bloody robot. He's not trying that hard to convince me; he's not even looking at me. He doesn't give a flying fuck what happens.

He's still reading the sheet when Rachel Berry comes back in and sits opposite me. A breeze of her scent wafts over my face. Don't recognise that perfume. Musky. I haven't been close to a woman for ages; they usually look at me like they're worried they'll catch something just by sitting next to me.

She flicks a switch on the machine next to the wall.

I watch her as she introduces everyone to the tape. They have cameras everywhere now too, one on either side of the room.

'Scott Taylor,' she says. 'You were captured on CCTV with Grace Harper, on Monday 26 September.' She pushes the picture towards me.

I told you, cameras everywhere. I glance at the picture.

'Course it's me,' I say. 'You're not going to show me a picture of some other bloke, are you?' I smile at my brief next to me, but he's just staring at the picture of the kid and me. Bet he can't believe his luck today.

'Can you tell me how you managed to kidnap

Grace Harper from the street unnoticed?'

'I'll take that as a compliment.'

Rachel rolls her eyes. There are little beads of sweat above her top lip. I wonder what it'd be like to lick them off. Salty or sweet? She could do with getting a haircut though — her hair's a bit straggly at the bottom. Sarah wouldn't be seen dead with hair like that. No way. My sister was at the hairdresser's nearly every bloody week. Or month. I can't remember.

She taps a pen on the table.

Tap, tap, tap, tap, tap.

I want to slam my hand on hers to stop the sound.

But I don't.

I'm being good now. She seems all right.

I move my chair closer to the table, dragging it harder on the floor than I have to. She winces at the sound. Two can play at that game. It worked. She stopped tapping.

'I'd been watching them,' I say. 'Do you know that some mothers let their kids walk home on their own? Am I allowed to smoke in here?'

She shakes her head.

'It was worth asking. Never know if they're going to change the rules back again. Would've been nice to have a smoke while I told you my version of events. *If we say we have no sin, we deceive ourselves, and the truth is not in us.*'

'Why do you keep talking like that?' she says. 'Quoting from the Bible.'

I sit up in my chair. 'I don't keep doing it.'

'You do.' She doesn't break eye contact with me. 'It says here,' she holds up a piece of paper, 'that you were reciting biblical verses all the way to the police station.'

'Bollocks was I. It's just something I learned inside,' I say. 'Anyway . . . isn't that what we're meant to do when we're banged up? Follow the righteous path?'

She tilts her head to one side. 'You mean you learned the skill of trying to appear insane, when in fact you are perfectly fine and knew exactly what you were doing.'

'I don't know what you're talking about.'

'I think you know full well what I'm talking about.'

She sighs, and looks again at the sheet of paper in front of her.

'So you were watching the children,' she says.

'You make it sound like I'm a kiddy fiddler. I'm no fucking nonce. I hope you write that down.'

She glances at the digital recorder and rolls her eyes again. Like I'm some kind of bloody imbecile.

I shift in my chair. The plastic's digging into the back of my legs. They make them uncomfortable on purpose.

'Bet *you* wouldn't let your kids walk the streets on their own, would you?' I say to her. 'Not in this day an' age. Can you believe that? I mean — how old were they? Six, seven?'

'Eight,' says Rachel.

Doesn't say more than she has to, this one.

'I saw her mother watching them as well,' I say. 'Too busy spying on her kid to even notice I was looking at them too. I knew she couldn't keep that up; one day she was going to let her go on her own. She only lived up the road from the school. Quite a challenge, I tell you.'

Rachel has that look on her face — like I smell of shit or something.

'Stuck-up bitch,' I say.

'Excuse me?' says Rachel.

'Emma — that was the mother's name. I learned that when I went into her workplace. Didn't even look at me. Thinks she's better than everyone else. But you can get close to people when they're not expecting you. There's a lot more dads outside the school gates these days, did you know that?'

Rachel ignores me; she's writing something in her notepad.

'There was a dog outside the library,' I say. 'Nearly every day it was there, poor little sod. I did it a favour, really. I mean, what's the point of having a dog if you're just going to tie it up outside a bloody building all afternoon?'

The two coppers look at each other. Yeah, I get it. They're bored — they've got better things to do. But I haven't. I don't speak to people much.

'Anyway,' I say. 'I grabbed the lead like I owned it. No one gave a shit. Walked it to the sweet shop on the corner. Could see the girls were still in there. The tallest of them — don't know her name — well . . . she always comes out first . . . likes to open her sweets as soon as she can and get them in her face. I used to be like that — though we never got sweets every day like they did.' Rachel hovers her pen over the table. She'd better not start bloody tapping it again. 'I made the dog run away — had to kick its backside to get it going, like.'

Rachel frowns. 'Why?'

'*Hey*, I shouted to the taller girl. *Help me, my dog!* And the kid's off down the road, chasing after it. Grace Harper didn't notice a thing — even though she was standing at the crisp box near the door of the newsagent's. Everyone outside was looking at this dog — going crazy it was. It went into the road and people looked worried it was going to get run over.

'I just went into the shop and grabbed her. Light as a feather she was. Had to put my hand over her mouth, but she didn't try to shout — probably because she didn't know what was happening. My car was just round the corner. I put her in the boot and I drove off.'

I like to think it was by design rather than luck that no one noticed, but fortune favours the brave, as they say.

I lean back in my chair. A nice ciggie and a cup of tea would be perfect right now.

Rachel's lip curls up at the corner. She thinks she's got me now, doesn't she? The copper next to her rolls his eyes. They probably think I don't notice these little things. They think I'm stupid, but I'm not. Why do people think that if you confess, you're an idiot? To get caught in the first place is careless, but what happens when you're tired of running? Sometimes, there's nowhere else to run.

'So what happened next, Scott?' she says. 'What happened after you got Grace Harper into your car and drove away? Why did you walk

336

through town when anyone could've seen you with her?'

I look up to the ceiling again. It's different in here now. They must've given it a facelift. It was nearly thirty years ago, when I was brought into the cells for the first time. I woke up on a bastard-hard bed — couldn't remember how I got there. Thought I'd been pissed up or high on the street and left to sleep it off.

They kept asking and asking and asking me what happened. Didn't believe me when I said I couldn't remember. Twenty-four I was. I'd done all sorts that night: vodka, coke, E.

'I'll repeat the question,' says Rachel. 'What happened after you kidnapped Grace Harper and placed her into your vehicle?'

Back then, I told them I couldn't remember anything about my dad. I'd never hurt my dad, why would they say that? They read his injuries out to me from a piece of paper — told me what I'd meant to have done to him.

'Are you saying *no comment*, Scott?' Rachel won't shut up. She's not letting me think.

I couldn't have done all that. When my dad described it in court, I was floored. He couldn't look at me. He believed it. So did Mum.

I used to babysit for Zoe. Sarah and David would go to the pub quiz every Tuesday night. They'd pay for my bus fare there and back to their house, and bunged me a tenner when they got home. Zoe was four years old then — she'd just started school.

'You wouldn't mind reading her a story, would you, Scottie?' Sarah said when I arrived. She always called me Scottie when she wanted something. 'Zoe's been looking forward to it — she says you're her favourite uncle.'

I shrugged off my jacket and hung it on the banister at the end of the stairs.

'I'm her only uncle,' I said.

'So that means you're my favouritest, my best and my *only* uncle in the whole world.' Little Zoe was standing at the top of the stairs in her pyjamas, her hair still wet from her bath.

I stood at the bottom, looking up to her, and bowed like a butler.

'Well, my dear, darling, and *only* niece,' I said. 'The honour must be mine.' I ran up the stairs as Sarah and David shouted goodbye and clambered out of the front door. 'So will it be *The Very Hungry Caterpillar*,' I said, chasing her into her bedroom, 'or the very scary *Twits?*'

She got into bed and pulled the covers up to her chin, giggling.

'*The Twits,*' she shouted. 'They are *gruesome!*'

I could be silly with Zoe — she didn't judge me; she liked me as I was.

'Scott!' DS Berry slams a folder onto the table.

When Zoe was taken, the atmosphere of our house changed. Her and Sarah had been living with me, Mum and Dad. For a few weeks, the house was full of life. Then the darkness came.

'When do you think Zoe will be back?' I asked Mum after a month of her being missing.

She pulled the dressing gown tight around her middle, looking smaller than she'd ever looked; it

338

was like she was shrinking.

She frowned at me. 'Can't you see your sister's upset?'

It was like no one wanted to talk to me any more.

Now, I look up from the floor and into Rachel Berry's eyes.

'*And if anyone will not receive you or listen to your words, shake off the dust from your feet when you leave that house.* Nobody notices me, you see, Rachel. I'm almost invisible.'

'Scott!' She's shouting at me again. Why does she keep doing that? 'What happened when you took Grace Harper to your house?'

'I'd never hurt a child,' I say. 'Not on purpose.'

The solicitor next to me clears his throat.

'No comment.' If I were to die right now, no one would care. 'Is she going to be okay?'

'What?' Rachel's eyebrows are scrunched up near her hairline. 'The girl?'

'Yes. Is Grace Harper going to live?'

She doesn't answer me. She glances at the copper guarding the door. They know something and they're not telling me.

She's right, I suppose. I don't deserve to know. I'm nothing. Everything I touch turns to shit. They should just put me down.

56

Maggie

I see this room in this bed and breakfast even when I close my eyes: the blue curtains that go all the way to the floor, the teak dressing table and matching bedside cabinet on which I put the photograph of Sarah and Zoe. The portable television in the corner that looks as though it's been here since the place was built. I've looked at every inch of it. Eight days we've been staying here, but it feels so much longer. She still won't see us. All we could do was pass the address of this place to the police and wait.

David was wrong about the police — they did care about us. David presented them with all the information he'd collected. He still had that green folder, plus about twenty more.

'I'll need to take a statement from you both,' the detective said to us — Hines was his name. Poor man looked as though he hadn't slept in a week. I knew that feeling.

It took hours for David to tell them what he knew. Years of searching different countries. I'm glad they wrote it all down.

'I didn't think they'd take me seriously,' David said afterwards. 'I'm just a dad looking for his daughter.'

'You're more than that,' I said. 'You found her. The police never did that, did they?'

As we were about to leave the station, I went to the desk.

'Do you have an address for Detective Jackson?' I said. 'He worked for Lancashire constabulary.'

The policewoman behind the counter looked blank for a moment.

'He's retired,' I said.

She shook her head.

'We don't have any records here for retired police officers,' she said. 'But if you contact Lancashire police they might be able to help you.'

I reckon she only said that to get rid of me. She wouldn't have known about Zoe. Not until now, at least.

'We'll find Detective Jackson, Maggie,' said David. 'We'll let him know.'

Catherine Atkinson was charged with Zoe's kidnap and is currently in a remand centre awaiting trial. I saw her photo in the newspaper. If I saw her on the street, I wouldn't even give her a second glance. She looks ordinary, like me. But her eyes look cold — though I might just see her that way. She was the woman who brought Zoe up. I can't imagine her caring for my granddaughter, being kind to her. It's just a picture though. I suppose you can't see what's behind a person's eyes in a photograph.

There's a knock at the door. It's nine thirty, so it'll be David. Never too early, never too late.

I swing my legs off the bed, put on my shoes, pick up my handbag, and walk to the door. Another day of waiting in reception, looking out of the window for any sign of her.

I open the door.

'Can I come in?' says David.

'Shouldn't we get downstairs? Today might be the day.'

I stand aside to let him in anyway. He pulls out the chair at the dressing table and perches on the end of it.

'Shall I make you a cup of tea?'

He nods.

'Have you heard any news? About the little girl?'

I wait by the bathroom door, holding the kettle.

He shakes his head.

'Then what is it?'

He covers his face with his hands. The sobs take over his shoulders; he can barely breathe.

'Oh, David.' I place the kettle down and sit on the edge of the bed.

'Why won't she see me, Maggie? I'm her dad.'

He drops his hands from his face, which is wet from tears.

'She needs time to come to terms with it. It must have come as a terrible shock. Imagine finding out your whole life was based on a lie. Imagine finding out that who you thought of as Mum had actually abducted you as a child.'

He takes out a tissue and wipes his eyes. He leans back in the chair.

'I had this dream for so many years,' he says, 'that when I found her, we'd run into each other's arms, like they do in films, or *Surprise*

Surprise.' He looks up at me and laughs through his tears. 'I know — torturing myself watching programmes like that — but they gave me hope, that we'd have a happy ending, you know?'

I can't stop the tears falling from my eyes; I can't be the strong one any more.

'I know, love. I never let myself dream we'd find her, but when you came to me that day, and told me that you'd found her — that one day I could have some sort of family again — I *did* dare to dream. I pictured what life would be like with her in it again, to have someone to care about, to talk to. But . . . '

David put his hands over mine.

'Things never turn out the way you plan them, do they?'

'No, love. No, they don't.'

He pats my hands before he stands up.

'I'll just wash my face, then we'll go downstairs.'

I don't want to be the first to say it, but we can't stay here forever. David's the one who's been searching all these years.

'Maggie?' He's standing at the doorway of the bathroom. 'I think this should be the last day we wait. It's Jim's funeral the day after tomorrow, remember. I'll leave a forwarding address with the landlady.' He dabs his face with a towel. 'I know it might be a big ask but — '

'You can stay at mine for as much time as you need. As long as you don't mind sleeping on the settee.'

He nods and gives me the saddest of smiles.

'Thanks, Maggie.'

★ ★ ★

We're sitting at the table by the window where we can see the main road, the newsagent's and the corner shop. The first day we sat here, we thought she would turn up at any minute. We wore our smart clothes: David wore his suit, and I bought a navy-blue dress from the charity shop in town. Every car that came past we looked at.

'Do you know what car she drives?' I asked David.

'No.'

It's amazing how little we know about her. I brought the photograph from the newspaper on that first day, so I would know exactly what she looked like. Now, after all these days of waiting, her image is ingrained in my mind. I would know her from across the street.

Mrs Abbott, the owner of the bed and breakfast, places a pot of tea on the table.

'No joy today?'

David lowers his paper and shakes his head. He's been reading everything he can find about her, and what happened to Grace. I, on the other hand, can't bear to read anything about it. The television is on in the corner, with subtitles in case the ambient noise gets too loud, but I dread seeing his face on the screen again.

He was on every hour when we first arrived here. They actually televised what appeared to be his mugshot. How did they manage to get their hands on that? The news didn't give away many other details about Grace — only that she was found by the canal in the boot of a car. What must that child have gone through, and at the hands of my own son? I can hardly bear to think about it.

David folds his paper and places it on the table.

'I think we should leave after this cup of tea, if that's okay with you?'

It feels as though we're giving up, but how long would we be here until Zoe wants to see us? It could be weeks, months, never at all. I can't bear to think about never seeing her after all of this. But this is David's decision, I must respect that. If it wasn't for him, we would never have found her. At least she's alive. That alone should keep me going, shouldn't it?

'Yes, that's all right. I suppose we could always come back if we hear from her.'

'I wonder where she is right now.' He looks out of the window. It's a view we've become accustomed to. 'Perhaps she's at the hospital. Maybe we should give it our last shot to see if we can find her, to see if she wants — '

'No, David. She's been through enough. All these people have decided things for her; they've changed and controlled her life. Catherine took her off the street; Scott kidnapped her niece. We have to leave her to make up her own mind about whether she wants to see us or not, we must give her that.'

He dabs his face with a serviette.

'You're right, Maggie. I know you're right. It's just so hard.' We drink the rest of our tea in silence.

As I pack my things into my weekend bag, I feel as though I'm abandoning her. What if I never get to see her? Do I forget we ever found her? I couldn't do that. I have to have hope.

'Sarah, love, if you're listening,' I say to the empty room. 'Tell Zoe we love her, will you?'

I look about the place before I leave and take a picture of it with my mind's eye. We came so close to her. I drag the bag off the bed and shut the door behind me.

57

Stephanie

I've been in rooms like this before. Cold, bland rooms contrived to convey serenity. The walls are painted beige, off-white, and there are crap countryside pastel drawings on the walls. We're on the ground floor, obviously, so as not to give the 'clients' an option for a final exit out of the window. Her certificates line the walls: *Maria Lewis, Diploma in Counselling and Psychology.* There are at least three, like she needs reminding.

'So,' she says, leaning back with her arms folded.

This is only my second session. I don't know what she wants me to say.

'Have you had any flashbacks at all?' She looks at her notepad. 'Have you thought about travelling by boat to see if it triggers any dormant memories?'

'No, of course I haven't. What would I want to do that for?'

Maria's already asked me if I remember the journey from England to Germany, but I don't. She asked if I remember being locked in a suitcase in the boot of a car, but I told her that was Grace, not me. She said I must have suffered a significant trauma in order to forget, but I think she's just making it up as she goes along.

'So what *do* you remember?'

I shrug.

There isn't much online about Zoe Pearson's — my — disappearance. There weren't as many newspapers back then. There were a few that copied old content onto their websites, but no coverage to the extent of Grace's case.

I saw Sarah's — my mother's — face in one of the photos — they didn't have many. If you go on the internet and search crimes in the eighties, you hardly ever find many pictures. But I knew her as soon as I laid eyes on her.

I look out of the window. Emma's waiting in the car outside, like she did for my last session. Why didn't they offer *her* counselling? She's been through a lot too. I wonder what she's listening to on the radio.

' 'Ninety-Nine Red Balloons',' I say.

'Excuse me?'

'You asked me what I remember. It's that song — the German one. I told Emma once that she used to sing it all the time. But yesterday, she told me that she'd got it from me — that I was the one who taught it her. It's funny the things we forget, isn't it?'

She raises her eyebrows.

'Yeah okay,' I say, before she does, 'apart from the big stuff.'

'Have you thought about hypnosis?'

'No.' I fold my arms. 'I don't want to remember.'

'What about your life before Catherine and Michael? Do you want to try to access those memories?'

I shake my head. 'There's a reason why my brain has chosen not to show me these things. And I don't want to know — what if it's something bad?'

'This is all up to you. You can change your mind whenever you like — it's your journey.'

Oh for God's sake. Why does she have to spoil it by spouting crap like that? I don't have to remember everything in order to move on. What's wrong with dealing with things as they arise instead of purposely dredging things up? Happiness is overrated anyway. It would be so exhausting to pretend to be cheerful every day.

She glances at her notepad again; she must have a list of questions written on it.

'How do you feel about Grace's abductor?'

'I don't feel anything about him.'

She purses her lips. She can't force me to say things, to think about things I don't want to. We sit looking at each other. I don't want to speak to her any more. This is all a waste of time. I wish someone would wipe the memories of the past few weeks — can she do that? No, of course she can't. This is what I've been left with, to pick up the lie-of-a-life of the person I thought I was.

Emma gave me the contact details of Maggie Taylor and David Pearson: my grandmother and father; people I'm biologically related to, but wouldn't recognise if I passed them on the street. They're staying in a B&B in the city — or rather they were. They've probably gone home by now. I don't know what to say to them yet. It's too big, too important — I can't just pick up the telephone or turn up at their door.

'Have you looked at your birth certificate yet?' she asks me.

I shake my head.

I look at the clock: only five minutes left. If I just sit here in silence, then it will nearly be over. I close my eyes in the hope she won't talk to me any more.

I scrolled through thousands of archived newspapers, looking everywhere to find out what Catherine's birth daughter — the first Stephanie — died from. In the end, I found a copy of her death certificate from the General Register Office. Even though she died in Germany, it was on an RAF base. *Accidental death due to road collision.* She was only four and a half years old. Poor little girl — she's the one who's been forgotten.

Did Catherine and Michael ever talk about her? I wonder if they talked about *my* birth parents — or if they simply buried it so they didn't have to think about it. If I search Mum's — Catherine's — house, I'm sure I would find a photograph of that poor child hidden away somewhere. I don't think I lived up to the memory of that little girl; I was always a disappointment to Catherine. I still can't imagine what she was thinking — to replace one child with another. And Michael. Why did he go along with it all? He seemed so decent, so loving, so honest.

I will never know why. And that's why it's so frustrating. At some point in the future I'm going to have to ask Catherine. And hope that she tells me the truth.

'How is Jamie?'

'What?'

'You were daydreaming again.'

She can't help herself. She needs to fill the silence. Perhaps she should get some counselling for that. I open my eyes.

'He's fine. There's no reason why he shouldn't be fine, is there?'

No matter what his father says. Neil thinks I'm going crazy, and it's his excuse to have his son all the time. But Joanna doesn't actually want to have Jamie all the time, the self-involved person that she is.

But I can't tell Maria that. She's not interested in petty things; she wants to know about the big stuff. Like how I've been left feeling so empty that I don't know how I'll ever feel normal again; that everyone has read about me in the newspaper and they pity me when they look at me. I want to escape and start again, but someone already did that for me, didn't they? Catherine decided she wanted another child and that child was me. I'd understand if she'd treated me with love and compassion, but she didn't. I'm named after her dead child, and I don't know what to do about that. I am Stephanie; I've made that name my own.

The tears fall down my face, thinking about what I have, what could have been, but I don't really know the answer to that because my real mum is dead. I'll never know.

I have Jamie and he is my everything. But I don't think I'll get over the sadness that I feel.

58

Maggie

'I Watch the Sunrise' is the first hymn. The chords of the church organ echo through every inch of the place. I haven't heard the song for a while; I let the harmony wash over me. The ladies in the choir left at the back are singing beautifully. I whisper the words, trying hard not to take in the meaning of them. I can't fall apart.

I thought the next funeral I'd go to would be my own. When I visited Ron at the funeral home, I expected him to look fast asleep. Everyone said it would be like watching him sleeping, but it wasn't. He looked as though the life had been sucked right out of him: an empty shell. His skin was cold, so cold, like a statue. It only had a hint of him — or someone that could be related to him, but the essence of who he was had vanished.

I vowed never to visit another after that.

Until Sarah.

When I found her on her bed, I thought *she* was sleeping. I might have even smiled at her; she looked so peaceful — without the furrowed brow she always had when awake. That changed in an instant when I saw the vodka and the pills next to her.

I visited her every day at the funeral home, so she wasn't alone. I didn't have time to visit Jim before today, but in a way, I'm glad of it.

'I'll be seeing you, Maggie,' were the last words he said to me. He was walking towards my front gate and he didn't turn around as he said goodbye. I suppose the living always look for a sign after a person's died — a hint of a final farewell that would be ignored had you seen them the following day.

'Jim was a popular man,' says the priest now the song's finished. 'He would do anything for anybody.'

I wonder if someone told the vicar to say that or if he already knew? He was right about what he said though. People throw that phrase around a lot, but Jim put others first all the time.

It's hard to picture him in that wooden box at the front. It's a thought I banish from my head, otherwise the tears wouldn't stop. There's a large photo of him next to the coffin. He's holding up a cup of tea, as if saying *cheers* to us all. Next to it is the picture of him and Sylvia at their wedding. Perhaps they're together now.

'All Things Bright and Beautiful' begins to play, and the rain starts hammering against the stained-glass windows. I almost want to laugh; it's like he's playing a joke on us. I've known him for over fifty years, but for sixteen of those, he was my best friend. I reach into my pocket and bury my face into the tissue as I cry. I don't care who sees me.

★ ★ ★

The church hall has a row of tables at the back, laid with sandwiches, cakes and sausage rolls.

Jim had written down all the details of what he wanted: the food, the music, his coffin, and the words to be carved on the headstone underneath Sylvia's. Typical Jim: he didn't want to be a burden to anyone. I hope he knew how many people loved him, the light he brought into their lives. I keep thinking about it, but I wouldn't have coped over these years had it not been for him. Only months had passed between Ron and Sarah dying, and Jim had been at my door on the day of her funeral.

All the familiar faces are here to see him off: Mrs Sharples from the newsagent's; Sandra and her poor husband, Peter; and Sheila, the harlot from the library (though at least she had the sense to wear black, and a skirt to the knee). The older you get, the fewer the people who come to your funeral. There were hundreds at Sarah's — her friends from school, from work — near enough the whole village. Everyone talked about the sadness of it all. You don't hear uncontrollable weeping or the words *gone too soon* when you attend an old person's funeral.

Anna's brought her three boys — Jim's grandsons — all lovely in their matching suits. The youngest was holding his mother's mobile phone in the church; I expect it kept him quiet. I'm sure Jim wouldn't have minded, though there were a couple of busybodies who tutted at them — they call themselves Christians too. I had worried that the boys might have been a bit young for a funeral when Anna told me they were coming, but they've been a credit to her.

'Ah, Maggie.' Anna walks towards me with

such confidence; it helps that she's tall. Unlike me, the only short one in the family. I could never be called graceful. 'Come and meet my boys.'

She takes hold of my hand and guides me towards her sons, sitting in a row on plastic chairs, eating cake from paper plates.

'Hello there, young men,' I say. 'Don't you look smart?'

The eldest nods, and says, 'Yes.'

I'd crouch in front of them if my knees and I were thirty years younger.

'How are you bearing up?' I ask them. 'Upsetting, funerals, aren't they?'

The middle one shrugs. 'Mum says Grandad had a good innings. I remember him from when I was three.'

'Eliot!' scolds Anna. 'Sorry, Maggie.'

'It's all right, love,' I say, smiling at her. 'I'd forgotten how honest little ones are — and not afraid to speak the truth, like us old folk.'

The eldest looks at Eliot. 'You don't remember Grandad. I'm the only one who remembers him 'cos I was five when we last saw him. He gave me a pound for sweets.'

'No, he didn't.'

'Yeah, he did.'

The little one holds up his plate. 'Can I have another cake, Mummy?'

Anna takes his plate.

'I'll leave you to it,' I say.

I'd forgotten how exhausting little ones are, too. No wonder Anna looks so harassed all the time.

Sheila from the library's sitting in the corner, dabbing her eyes. I'm sure she'd have worn a widow's lace if she could. I'd say hello to her, but she probably wouldn't know who I was. Only had eyes for Jim, that one. And any other male that came into the library, no doubt.

I push open the church hall doors.

There are a few people I've never seen before, smoking outside, chatting. There's always relief when a funeral has finished. The worst bit's over with. For now.

The rain has stopped, but the clouds are still heavy in the sky. It's only a short walk to the gates of the cemetery. Jim will be buried here, along with Sarah and Ron. Now, when I visit them, I can bring something for Jim too. I know more people dead than alive.

Ron's ashses are buried near the yew tree in the middle, which is probably older than the lot of us put together. Someone's tied a wind chime to one of the branches; the sound of it tinkles in the air.

The honeysuckle I placed in his vase the other week has withered and died. I grab it and cast it aside.

'I'll bring you some nice flowers next week,' I say aloud.

I pat the top of his headstone, and walk the familiar path to Sarah's.

Most of the air in the red balloon tied next to her grave has gone from it. I pull it apart to release the last few breaths, roll it into a ball and put it into my pocket.

'We've found her, love,' I say. 'David found

356

her. I don't think I can believe it.' A gust of wind catches the chime, and I smile. 'That sounds like the ice cream van you used to follow.' A car horn sounds in the distance. Everyday life going on as normal.

I look up to the clouds — they've all but covered the sun. Zoe . . . Stephanie is out there, under the same sky — living and breathing. It breaks my heart that I haven't seen her yet.

'I'll bring Zoe to you, Sarah. One day. I promise.'

59

Stephanie

Emma has a retro radio station on in the car, but I switch it off.

'How was it today?'

I lean back in the seat.

'Same as last week. What am I supposed to say to that woman? As if talking about it will change anything.'

She looks in her mirror and indicates to set off.

'But talking about it might change how you feel about it. I hope it works for Grace when she comes out of hospital — they've arranged talking therapy for her as well.' She glances at me with a small smile before pulling into the road. 'You can always talk to me, you know, if you don't want to go back there.'

I turn my head to look out of the passenger window.

'You don't want to hear all of my shit — you've been through enough.'

'We all have. But Grace is making a good recovery.'

'Physically maybe.' I turn to Emma. 'Shit, sorry, Em. You're right. Grace will be fine.'

'It's what I have to believe, Steph. I have to be grateful that she doesn't remember being in that boot or being slapped around by that maniac.'

'If it's any comfort, I don't remember when it happened to me. I know it's not the same. They say he didn't hit me or anything . . . '

She reaches over her hand and takes mine in it.

'I'm so sorry, Steph.'

I blink so I don't release the tears; surely they've run out by now. I feel as though I've been crying for weeks. I need to think about other people. I look at Emma while she's driving. Her brow has been in a slight frown ever since Grace was found — it's like she's constantly thinking about what happened to her little girl.

Grace told DS Berry that she remembered only fragments of what happened to her. She said that Scott had tied her to a chair and put children's cartoons on for her to watch, but forgot to feed her, didn't take her to the toilet. It was heartbreaking listening to Emma relate it all back to me. She raised Grace in such a loving environment, unlike her own with Jean. It haunts Emma to know that her little girl has suffered, like she did as a child.

'Will you ever look for your real mother, Jean?' I say. 'To see if she's still alive?'

Her frown deepens. The night Grace was found was the first time Emma had ever mentioned her real mother. She'd been standing by the window in the hospital room, looking through the blinds, her arms folded.

'I still have a picture of her,' she'd said. 'It was in the rucksack that I packed when I left. In my own little mind, I thought if I didn't bring that photo with me, then I'd forget what she looked

359

like. Even then I knew I might never see her again. She was that sort of person — the type who could compartmentalise her life.'

'So you *do* remember her?' I'd asked gently.

She'd pulled up a chair next to mine.

'I've never had trouble remembering Jean, Steph. In some strange way, I loved her. She was my mother — it was the only home I'd ever known. But at the same time, I wanted to forget about her. The horrible things she would do — make fun of me in front of her friends. Once, she cut my fringe so short, until it was only about a centimetre long. She thought it was hilarious, so did her drunken friends. I wore a hat to school for nearly a month after. The first day I did, the teacher made me take it off. Everyone in class laughed at me, but I took it, I didn't cry. The teacher, Miss Davison was her name, she was lovely — she said I could put it back on again. I wanted to ask if I could come home with her, but I never did. I knew what the answer would've been.'

'Oh, Emma. I didn't know. Mum . . . Catherine . . . never said anything like that. She said that Jean had left you without food for days.'

'It was three weeks.'

My hand went to my mouth, and she nodded slowly.

'I know. It felt longer. But I got into a routine. I was last year of primary school, so not as young as Grace. I got myself to school every day, had free dinners. I knew how to survive, how to save food so I wouldn't run out too soon . . . hide money I found down the sofa dropped by her

360

friends. To think none of them helped me. Shocking when you think about it — the horrible situations people witness, and then justify their inability to change it by leaving it to someone else to deal with.

'It wasn't the first time she'd left me. But it had never been as long as that before. After two weeks, it was the school holidays. No school meals. And then Catherine . . . She was like my guardian angel, which sounds crazy now, but she seemed to appear from nowhere. She didn't, obviously. Someone must have told her about me — she used to volunteer for that homelessness charity. Do you remember?'

I shook my head. Emma might as well have been talking about a completely different Catherine to the one I grew up with. No surprise there.

'Well,' she continued, 'I remember a man and a woman coming to visit me at your house — they must've been from an adoption agency or something because after a while I had a new surname — the same as yours.' She put a hand on mine and squeezed it. 'But hey — I'm here, I survived. Though, I suppose that's why I was a bit of a limpet when we were teenagers. And now all of this. We're a right pair of fuck-ups, aren't we?'

I can't remember if we laughed or cried at that.

Emma drives into the hospital car park and pulls up the handbrake.

'I don't know, Steph. I don't even hate Jean any more. I know that I should. I suppose you

361

hate Mum, for what she did. It's so hard, all of this. Catherine was the person who rescued me, but she was the person who took you from a family that loved you.'

I don't want to ask Emma if she's visited Catherine; she probably has. I don't want to hear what that woman has to say. Emma might not hate Jean, but what I feel for Catherine goes beyond hate — I loathe her. I can't even tolerate thinking about her.

I turn to the back seat and reach for the teddy for Grace.

Emma laughs. 'Like she hasn't got enough.'

'I know, but this one is so cute.'

'That's what you said about the other three.'

When we get to Grace's room, Matt's at her bedside.

'Should I wait out here?' I say to Emma.

He's barely acknowledged me since Grace was found. He hasn't apologised for shouting at me, but then, I wouldn't know what's been going through his mind after Grace went missing. He must have been thinking irrationally to think it had anything to do with me.

'Let me have a word with him,' she says.

They've been doing bedside shifts so one of them has been with her twenty-four hours a day; as far as I know, they've hardly spoken to each other. I peek through the window into the hospital room. Matt's stretching. He must have been sitting there for hours.

My heart pounds as he walks towards the door. I turn so I'm facing the corridor, my back against the window. I see him from the corner of my eye. He lingers for a few seconds, then walks away. I look at his back as he heads towards the lift. He stops. I look away quickly as he turns around and walks back. He stops only a few feet away from me.

'Grace's been asking for you,' he says.

'Thanks.'

He gestures to the row of three seats on the opposite side of the corridor.

'Will you sit with me for a minute?'

'I . . . '

'Don't worry, I'm not going to have a go at you again.'

He sits down. I sit at the opposite end to him.

'I've been staying at my mum's for a few days,' he says.

'Have you? Emma never said anything.'

'No, well, I suppose you've got bigger things to talk about. Anyway, I told my mum what I said to you . . . I thought she'd back me up, you know, say that I was right to say those things, but she was horrified with me. She said how could I say those things to someone who has just found out her life was based on lies, that her real mum had died. I hadn't really thought about it from your perspective. I just thought about Grace, and that man and — '

'It's all right.'

'No, it's not, Steph. Stop being so understanding. I can't believe you're not raging. If it were me, I'd be up at that remand centre punching her in the face.'

I try not to smile, but it leaks out anyway.

'I have thought about that. For those first few

days I was probably in shock, then I was furious. To be honest, I can't think about her without it burning up inside me, and I haven't stopped crying for weeks.'

'Emma says you've been seeing a shrink.'

'Yeah.'

'Does it help?'

'I think it's too early to tell. I might need help for years.'

'Well, yeah, I've always thought that about you.'

'Very funny.'

'Anyway, I am sorry for what I said to you. I just wanted you to know that.'

I nod. 'Okay.'

He gets up from the chair, and glances through the window of Grace's room.

'Emma told me everything that happened between her and Andrew,' he says. 'Three months.' He folds his arms. 'I never even guessed she was having an affair. I suppose it made us even.'

'What do you mean?'

'That I had feelings for you. I shouldn't have, I know — there's no need to look at me like that. I'm sorry I tried to kiss you that night.' He puts his arms out wide. 'Why am I saying all of this to you? It's like you see straight through me.' He puts a hand through his hair. 'What I'm trying to say — badly — is that I'm sorry.'

'Thank you.'

'You don't have to say you forgive me or anything.'

'Okay.'

'But if, you know, you ever feel like saying you forgive me, then that's fine.'

'I'll let you know.'

He shakes his head, a slight grin on his face.

'I'll see you soon then, Steph.' And he walks away.

Emma peers her head round the side of the door.

'Ahem. Auntie Steph, we have a patient in here who has been promised yet another teddy bear.'

I pick up the toy and walk into the room. Grace is sitting up and there's colour in her cheeks. There are pens and paper on the table across her bed. Her eyes light up as she sees me. I can't believe she looks so well after what she's been through. I thought we'd never see her again.

'A pink elephant!' she says. 'I love it, Auntie Steph.'

'I thought you might,' I say, grabbing her in a hug. Every time I hold her, I don't want to let go.

'When can Jamie come and visit?' she says into my shoulder. 'I haven't seen him for ages.'

'I can bring him tomorrow if you like.' I stand up and stroke her hair.

She nods her head, and hands me a picture.

'What's this?' I say.

'It's a cake drawing of course,' says Grace. 'Mummy says we're going to start our own bake club every Sunday. You can come too, if you want?'

'That sounds brilliant, Grace. Tell you what

— I'll let you and Mummy practise first, and then I can be your official taster.'

She tilts her head to one side.

'Okay,' she says. 'You and Daddy can be testers. And Jamie. You can all score me and Mummy.' She leans forward and whispers, 'Don't tell Mummy, but I already know how to bake a cake. We made one at school last term.'

She puts a finger to her mouth. I do the same.

'Have you thought any more about contacting your father?' says Emma quietly, pouring water into Grace's beaker. 'I saw that woman this morning — the one who owns the B&B that he and your grandmother were staying at.'

'Really? What did she say? What were they like?'

'She said they waited in reception every morning until late at night, every day for over a week.'

'Did they? I thought they'd have gone back up north.'

Emma frowns at me. 'Why would you think that? They've spent so long looking for you, they wouldn't just leave you the same day they came.'

I feel a pain in my chest when I think of them both waiting for me, hoping I would come and find them.

'It was all too much, Em. Everything was too much.'

'I know. You were in shock. You hardly spoke to anyone for days.'

She reaches into her handbag, pulls out a card and hands it to me.

'This is Maggie's address. I know you have it

already, but I wrote it down again for you, just in case.'

I feel the smooth card in my hand. I've been scared to even think about them properly. It was easier to think about Sarah, my mother, because she was dead. Dead people can't disappoint you — you can make them into whatever you want.

I looked her up on the internet. That's how I found out about the smaller details of my life. My life before Catherine and Michael. I read that I was loved, but my parents had been fuck-ups. My mother was an alcoholic and she left my father because he lost his job — or it might have been the other way round: that my mother was an alcoholic and my dad left her, then lost his job. It's hard to tell from newspapers in the eighties — there were lots of half-truths and guesswork. It was red-tops or posh-tops — the latter seldom reported my absence. There were a few journalists who kept the story going, on the big anniversaries of my abduction. The saddest headline of them all was of Sarah's death. *Tragic Mum's Suicide*. I wish I hadn't read the comments section of that newspaper. Half of them felt sorry for her, but said, *It's probably for the best that she died, at least she's not suffering not knowing where her daughter is*. And some were trolls who hated her: *She must have had something to with her daughter's disappearance — maybe she sold her, she was jobless and they lived in a rented house*. So easy for them to judge behind the anonymity of a computer screen. There was only one way I could learn the truth.

'Are you going to write to them?' says Emma.
'Are you sure you wouldn't mind?'
'Because Maggie is that man's mother?'
I nod.
'I thought I might, but I don't. From what I've read in the news, they had no contact since he was arrested for beating up his father. That poor, poor woman. What a life.' She dabs the tears that have collected at the corners of her eyes. 'So you'll write?'

I run my fingers over the writing.
'Yes,' I say. 'I think I will.'

60

Maggie

Another one came through the post yesterday: a letter from Scott, asking me to visit him in prison on remand. Why would he think I'd want to see him after everything he's done? Not after what he did to that poor child.

I pull my covers over me. It's after nine, but I still don't want to get out of bed. This house doesn't feel like my home any more — it's tainted by everything. I miss Jim, and his constant chatter; he was always so cheerful.

But Zoe's still alive. I still have to repeat it to myself to keep it real.

It's been nearly a month and still she won't see me. I feel like my heart can't break any more. I should just go to sleep and never wake up, but then I've felt that for years, why should today feel any different?

There's a knock on my door.

'Maggie, can I come in?'

David backs into my bedroom, and turns round holding my tray: boiled egg, a round of toast and a pot of tea.

'It's a letter,' he says.

But I don't get my hopes up.

'It's from Zo — Stephanie. She's put her name on the back of the envelope. It's addressed to both of us.'

369

I sit up properly. My heart beats faster; my hands start to shake.

'I should get dressed before we read it. This is a special occasion.'

David places the tray on the end of the bed. The china cup rattles on the saucer, he's shaking that much.

'Go on then.'

'Really?' I whip away the bed cover.

'I'll go downstairs and give you five minutes. Be quick, Maggie.'

I open my wardrobe and my favourite dress is there. I hope it doesn't smell of mothballs, I've been waiting for a special occasion like this to wear it. I grab the skirt and sniff it. It's a little musty, but nothing a quick spray of cologne won't fix.

It still fits. In fact, it's a little baggy. I grab my powder from the dressing table and give my face a quick press, a little dab of lipstick. I run the comb through my hair and I'm done.

'I'll come downstairs, David,' I shout.

I leave the bedroom and the breakfast on its tray.

'I've put the kettle on again.' He's sitting at the table — holding the letter in both hands.

I sit next to him. 'Oh.' I put my hand on his. 'You don't think it'll be bad news, do you?'

'It would've been on the news if Grace hadn't made it.'

'No . . . I mean bad news in that she never wants to hear from us or see us.'

'But we haven't contacted her, have we? She must have got this address from the bed and breakfast. It's not like we've been plaguing her with letters and phone calls. You said she had to make up her own mind, didn't you?'

I nod. 'Go on then, open it.'

David's hands shake a little as he gently prises the envelope apart.

'Do you want me to read it out, or do you want to read it yourself?'

'I'll read it myself. You read it first.'

I say that, but I really want to grab it out of his hands just to feel the same paper she's written on. I watch his face as he reads. He rests his hand under his chin, his eyes fill with tears.

He folds the note and hands it to me.

'It's only short, but . . . I'll let you read for yourself.'

I keep looking at him as I take the letter, not wanting to spoil it by peeking. I hold it in both hands and open it quickly.

Dear David and Margaret,

I'm sorry to be using your first names, but I'm sure you will understand. To say that the events of the past few weeks have been a shock is a bit of an understatement.

I have been thinking of you both constantly, as I have Sarah, my mother. It is so desperately sad that she passed away, and I am trying to come to terms with that, and other things around the circumstances that led to our separation.

I would very much like to meet you. Would this be all right? Please can you confirm this would be okay? I've put my

email address at the top of this letter.
  Stephanie.

'Oh, my darling girl. She writes so well, doesn't she?' I dab my eyes with the back of my hand. 'She's coming, David. She's actually coming home.' I move the letter away from me in case I ruin it with tears.

David gets up from his chair and puts his arms around me, and we cry together. For the first time in so many years, they are tears of pure joy.

'Right,' I say, wiping my face again. 'There is so much to do. I have to get this place looking the best it's looked for years. I might even bake a cake.'

I stand up and get my notepad from the kitchen drawer.

'Don't tire yourself, Maggie. We could always buy one.'

I turn and see a cheeky grin on his face. I grab the tea towel from the surface; I throw it and it lands on his head.

'That told me,' he says, his voice muffled by the cotton.

I bend over and laugh, until my tummy hurts.

★　★　★

I'd truly forgotten what it was like to experience happiness. Now, I feel like a different person. I've barely slept a wink. I doubt David has either as I heard him boil the kettle at least three times in the night. You couldn't tell from looking at him now, though. He's put on a suit and his eyes are sparkling. He's been dressed since five o'clock this morning and they're not due until midday.

It's half past eleven now and he hasn't moved from the window. I wondered whether to put out all the photographs of Sarah, but it might be too overwhelming for her. Instead, I've laid a tablecloth and put out a nice selection of sandwiches and cakes that I got from the village. Since I got her letter I've not stopped smiling. I even popped in to see Mrs Sharples yesterday morning.

'Morning, Maggie,' she'd said, barely looking up from the magazine behind the counter.

'Morning, Rose,' I said.

Her head shot up at that. I thought it might. It's too long to keep a grudge, especially when she didn't know I held one against her. After all, it's not her fault that this was the shop Zoe was going to when she went missing. It doesn't even look the same as it did then.

'I haven't seen you for weeks,' she said. 'Haven't you been wanting the papers?'

'David's been staying a while. You remember him? Zoe's dad?'

She nodded. 'Of course.'

'He's got a laptop computer. I've been reading the news online.'

I looked to the left and automatically picked up a paper.

'That's super, Maggie.'

I laid the paper on the counter.

'Still,' I said, looking at it. 'Old habits die hard. Staring at that computer for too long gives me a headache.' I reached into my purse for the money. 'Did you hear my news?'

She nodded. 'I'm really happy for you, Maggie.'

'She's coming to see me tomorrow, for lunch. She's bringing her son — my great-grandson — can you believe it? I have got family after all.'

I didn't know if Mrs Sharples remembered about Scott, but she didn't mention it.

'And she's bringing her sister, Emma. Do you have any of those biscuits, with the jam in and hole in the middle?' I know Jamie's thirteen and far too old for party rings, but everyone likes a nice biscuit, don't they?'

Mrs Sharples walked from the counter and picked up the red packet of biscuits.

I looked down to my right instinctively and realised I'd left my trolley at home.

'Oh dear. I've forgotten my shopper.'

'No matter,' she said. 'I've got these new paper bags. Much softer on the hands.'

She placed the groceries inside and handed them to me.

'Good luck,' she shouted after me as I left.

I said far too much to her. I couldn't help myself, my mouth just wouldn't stop. She'll probably tell the whole village.

I don't care one jot.

David peeks through the net curtains again. 'God, I'm so nervous. Are you nervous?'

'A little bit.'

I'm really nervous, but I want him to think I'm calm. If he thinks we're both nervous, he might have a breakdown.

'Deep breaths, David. Deep breaths.'

He nods as he paces around. He goes to the mirror in the hall.

'How do I look? Is this all right? I don't look too weird in this suit, do I?'

'David, you look fine. She's not going to care what you're wearing.'

'Course she will. If she's anything like Sarah, she'll care. Hated anyone looking common, she did.'

I chuckle at the memory. *Dad*, she said to Ron. *You are not going to parents' evening in a jumper with holes in. Mum! Make him change it — I don't want him showing me up.* Sarah was only nine at the time; she hid it better when she was grown up.

'Let's go to the window to wait,' I say, pushing him back into the living room. 'I don't want to miss a single minute of her.'

61

Stephanie

The satnav says we're thirty minutes away from
Maggie's house. We've stopped off at least eight
times since we left; my nerves have been so bad
that my stomach is empty. Jamie has been quiet
for most of the journey, in the back with his
headphones on.

'Do you want to call Grace again before we
get there?' I say to Emma.

'It's okay. Matt said she was going for a sleep.
I'll phone her later.'

'Is it weird having him back at the house?'

'Not really. I was barely there myself — only
going back to sleep and shower. I practically
lived at the hospital.' She glances at me. 'Are you
trying to take your mind off things?'

'Perhaps.' I smile as I look out of the window.
'It's prettier than I thought up north.'

'It's so bizarre to think that you lived here for
the first five years of your life, isn't it?'

I got their letter three days after I sent mine.
The notepaper was pastel blue and the
handwriting slanting, elegant. There was a
photograph inside of a child aged about two or
three, in the arms of a man, in his fifties perhaps?
Next to him is a woman of the same age. I turn
the photo around. *Zoe with Gran and Gramps*.
I'd never seen any photographs of myself before

the age of five. Catherine had said my pictures had been lost during our move to England when I was seven; one of the many lies she told me.

'It's beyond bizarre.' I turn to check Jamie's still wearing his headphones. 'Have you visited her yet?'

It's the first time I've had the strength to ask this question, the first time I've thought about Catherine without wanting to throttle her.

'Not yet,' says Emma. 'I wouldn't visit her without telling you first.'

'I thought you already had.'

Her mouth drops open.

'I couldn't do that to you, Steph.' As we stop at a red light, she turns to face me. 'If I were to visit her, would you be angry with me?'

'I couldn't be angry at you for that. It was her who created this mess, not you. You were the innocent in all of this.'

The light changes to green and Emma turns to face the front.

'So were you, Steph. None of this is your fault.'

'But why did I forget? How could I have forgotten my own mother?'

'You were only little.'

Fifteen minutes and we'll be there. I feel so sick with nerves. Jamie takes off his headphones.

'Are we nearly there?'

'Yes,' says Emma. 'Are you okay? Nervous?'

He shrugs. 'A little bit.'

He's been so hard to read over the past couple of weeks. I've tried to talk to him about everything, but he says he's okay. I suppose it'll take a long time for it all to sink in. He was close to Catherine, but I think he's scared to talk about her in case it upsets me.

'Are you okay, Mum?'

His question takes me by surprise.

'I'm fine.' I smile at him.

'No you're not. You're bricking it.' He laughs.

'What a lovely expression that is,' says Emma, smiling.

We finally pull up outside a terraced house opposite a primary school. How awful must it have been to have lost your grandchild and to have to hear other people's children all day? Maggie must be a strong woman.

'Number seventy-three,' I say, reading from the card I still carry.

The net curtains twitch in the window. My father and my grandmother are in that house. It feels so strange, yet when I look along the street, I feel a sense of peace that I have longed for for most of my life. I hadn't even realised it.

Emma puts her hand on mine.

She takes a deep breath and says, 'Are you ready?'

'Yes. I think I am.'

Acknowledgements

Thank you to my agent, Caroline Hardman, for seeing my potential and for placing this book with the fantastic team at Avon. Huge thanks to my editor, Phoebe Morgan, for championing this — your insightful and razor-sharp editorial skills have made this a better book.

To my friends, Sam Carrington and Lydia Devadason, who have encouraged me from the beginning. You have been a constant support over the years — I couldn't do it without you.

To my writing group, WU, your friendship, critiques, and drinking sessions have been brilliant (onwards and upwards!).

Big thanks to my mum, Carmel, for reading everything I have ever written. A shout-out to my friends Claire, Lou, and the gang at Random Makes. Thank you for cheering me on, you guys rock!

To Nan, who has been a huge inspiration to me.

Finally, to Dom, Dan and Joe. (Dan, you're going to have to read this one now.)

We do hope that you have enjoyed reading this large print book.

Did you know that all of our titles are available for purchase?

We publish a wide range of high quality large print books including:
Romances, Mysteries, Classics
General Fiction
Non Fiction and Westerns

Special interest titles available in large print are:
The Little Oxford Dictionary
Music Book
Song Book
Hymn Book
Service Book

Also available from us courtesy of Oxford University Press:
Young Readers' Dictionary
(large print edition)
Young Readers' Thesaurus
(large print edition)

For further information or a free brochure, please contact us at:
Ulverscroft Large Print Books Ltd.,
The Green, Bradgate Road, Anstey,
Leicester, LE7 7FU, England.
Tel: (00 44) 0116 236 4325
Fax: (00 44) 0116 234 0205

Other titles published by Ulverscroft:

THE CHILD

Fiona Barton

When a paragraph in an evening newspaper reveals a decades-old tragedy, most readers barely give it a glance. But for three strangers, it's impossible to ignore.

For one woman, it's a reminder of the worst thing that ever happened to her.

For another, it reveals the dangerous possibility that her darkest secret is about to be discovered.

And for the third, a journalist, it's the first clue in a hunt to uncover the truth.

The child's story will be told.

I KNOW MY NAME

C. J. Cooke

Komméno Island, Greece: A woman wakes up without any recollection as to why or how she got there. She has no way of leaving — and soon discovers that the island's handful of inhabitants, who nurse her back to health, each appear to be hiding something . . . Potter's Lane, London: Eloïse, the mother of a newborn and a toddler, vanishes into thin air. Her husband, Lochlan, is desperate to find her — but as the police look into the disappearance, it becomes clear that the marriage was not the perfect union it appeared. As Lochlan races to discover his wife's whereabouts, Eloïse enacts an investigation of her own. What both discover will place lives at risk and upend everything they thought they knew about their marriage, their past, and what lies in store for the future.

DETONATOR

Andy McNab

Betrayed and left for dead high in the Alps, Nick Stone is in trouble. The blood on his hands tells of a head wound he can't see, and his foggy memory confirms it. He knows only one thing for certain — someone, somewhere wants to kill him. And they think they've succeeded. Stone wants revenge, but the only person who can help him is a seven-year-old boy. Not much protection in the pursuit of a gang of faceless men who trade in human misery. This is about to become Stone's most personal mission yet. Payback is top of Stone's agenda. The fuse has been ignited — but who really holds the detonator?

THE DEATH OF HER

Debbie Howells

A woman's body is discovered on a Cornish farm, battered and left for dead in a maize field. As she's airlifted to hospital, her life hanging in the balance, no one's sure who she is. Three days later she comes round. She knows her name — Evie — but no more, until she remembers another name: Angel — her three-year-old daughter. As the police circulate Evie's photo, someone recognizes her. Charlotte knew her years ago, at school, when another child went missing. When the police search Evie's home, there's no sign of Angel. More disturbingly, there's no evidence that she ever lived there. Evie believes her daughter is alive, but the police remain unconvinced — unaware that there's someone watching her every move, with their own agenda and their own twisted version of reality . . .